OUTSHINE

What death takes, it will not restore

HOLLIS THOMPSON

CONTENTS

'Cursed is the man who dies, but
the evil done by him survives.'

Abu Bakr

PART ONE: LIFE
1.REST|ORATION

Isabel Harding lunged for the door, trying to claw back the handle before it slammed shut. A howling wind prised the bag from her shoulder, needing her best efforts to keep from dropping it on the ground.

Muted blonde, shoulder-length hair whipped across her face. She turned up the collar of her long coat and battled her way onto a crowded pavement. Two hours before, the day had been still and temperate, the summer persisting deep into the autumn. Now, the air felt charged and sinister. Clouds loomed on the horizon. Dying leaves were plucked from low-hanging branches and driven sideways through the air, like auburn missiles firing clear across the village green. It was like a different season altogether.

The daily commute had become a daunting prospect, rather than a pleasant stroll. She hunched her shoulders and hopped off the kerb, weaving through a queue of idle traffic. Motorists watched her through every windscreen, people she would gladly have traded places with. After years without a car, she craved both independence and a door she could lock from the outside world.

Much had changed since the nightmares of her summer. She spent every minute of the day daunted by knowledge she couldn't share because no one would have believed her. *Two years after his untimely death, Wren Lawton had appeared at the house they had once owned together. He was alive, but ...*

Here was where the real problems started. He had been a different person altogether, someone who claimed to be Wren, trapped inside the body of a stranger. He had a different face, a different body, a different voice ... different everything. No wonder she hadn't believed him. No wonder she had pushed him away.

That rejection had sent him over the edge. Wren had strangled her partner, Scott, to the point of collapse, then dumped him in the wilderness, exposed and comatose. The mere thought of it made her shudder. A miracle had spared Scott's life, but their problems had only begun. His suffering worsened almost daily. He was a broken man, faced with his own mortality.

And who could blame him?

Wren, meanwhile, had vanished. But what might have seemed like the best outcome for everyone at the time brought a crippling uncertainty along with it. Isabel had no way of knowing where he had gone to, whether he was at peace or vying for control of a new host. He could have been watching her at that very moment, from inside anyone she passed, wearing a perfect disguise. He could have been anywhere.

The wind continued to snatch at her bag, sucking and gusting. She reached the far pavement and abandoned the roadside altogether. That area had many shortcuts. A narrow footpath led her between the rear gardens of a row of terraced houses. Six-foot fence panels closed in, stifling what remained of the afternoon sunlight. Dead leaves had settled in patches against the concrete kickboards, dormant, as though lying in wait. It was a corner of the world that hadn't changed in all the years she had known it, despite the horrible things she had learned. It was a place where she could ruminate on a simpler time.

The path continued between the borders of grassy fields, bringing her back into the open. Through the tangled branches of a spiny hedgerow, she could see a distant playground. It looked abandoned with winter approaching, but she didn't trust her eyes. Wren could be anywhere, and worse – *if he could return then who else could be lurking out there, bubbling away beneath the surface of a stranger?*

How many posed a threat?

Slanted paving slabs drew her attention back to her feet. The only way to keep from losing her mind was to plan her escape. She needed to sell the bungalow and move somewhere isolated, where Wren could never find her. Other than a new job, little else would change. She and Scott were otherwise alone in the world.

The wind rose with a sudden bawl, bringing every branch and limb to frenzied activity. The fence panels behind her rattled and shook, while a pressure on her back goaded her along like a hand against her coat. She tightened her grip on the shoulder bag. Were it not for two-inch heels, she would have attempted to jog. The passageway narrowed and she tried to control her speed, one hand raised for balance.

The skeleton of an oak tree stood proud ahead of her, reaching forty feet and more into the greying sky. It towered above its neighbours of reddened ash and yellowed elder. Shed leaves formed a multicoloured carpet that must have lain undisturbed for days, and the wind chose its moment. Thick clumps lifted from the ground and formed a dense cloud. Some leaves were dried out, brittle, and sharp, scratching her exposed skin. Others clung to her clothes as they glanced the fabric.

She raised her hands to shield her face. The attack was so ferocious that it sent her stumbling in the wrong direction, giving her no choice but to turn around and abandon her detour or risk falling. With her heart in her mouth, she hurried back towards the main road, but her eyes were opened to new possibilities. A beaten track of flattened earth guided her to a break in the hedgerow, hidden from an idle glance by brambles that had grown across the opening.

She had never noticed it before. It was an alleyway between hedges, just wide enough to fit through. The wind wouldn't be able to follow. Needing to take back control of her situation, she bunched her hand up into her sleeve and pushed her way through, instantly freed from the weather's assault.

She paused for a moment to catch her breath. Intrigue had no place in her life. The far end of the path could have remained a mystery forever, were it not for a lack of alternatives. She resolved to press forwards and discover where it led. After two hundred yards, she emerged unchallenged onto a stretch of abandoned road. Pale asphalt was littered with potholes. White lines on the tarmac had long since faded. Hedges grew wild and thick, tall enough to cut her off from the surrounding world. It was a hidden place, one that few could have visited in years.

A robin sang its melancholy tune. Distant traffic rumbled. Isabel advanced cautiously as the road dipped, embankments rising on either side. Ahead of her lay the shaded underbelly of a stonework bridge. Modern vehicles would have struggled to fit beneath its shallow arch, even at the apex, explaining why the road had been abandoned. Grass had sprouted from cracked mortar and draped from its edges.

As she descended towards the weathered stone, a cold breeze snaked around her ankles. Before she could react, the wind was once more in her face, as though it had followed her after all. Isabel's progress slowed to almost nothing as she was blasted sideways one second then thrust forwards the next. Her coat flew open and she struggled to close it again.

Panicking, she sought shelter beneath the bridge. The air calmed once more in seclusion. It was surprisingly dark under there. Mosses on the brickwork mixed with creepers on the walls, making it clear that nature had taken full ownership. The arch rose barely three feet higher than her eye line. Long grasses brushed against her shoulders. All the greenery was static.

She looked back out at the erratic weather, just beyond her reach. She struggled to understand what was happening. The wind was right there – she could see leaves swirling in endless unrest – but from her shelter, she felt almost nothing. And it got stranger. Further up the slope, the towering oak was visible over the unkempt hedges, its branches peering skyward. Despite complete exposure to the elements, not a single branch was moving.

Not even in the slightest.

In fact, as she surveyed the scene, no object more than twenty feet away from her displayed the faintest trace of activity, as though the wind only existed in close quarters. She watched a leaf drift from a distant branch to the cracked tarmac, falling vertically and unopposed. A jolt ran down her spine as she questioned the impossible. *Is the wind lurking beside me, waiting for me to exit? Is it somehow aware of my presence?*

She tried to steady her breath in the momentary silence, to calm down and think rationally. In recent times, she had developed a habit of questioning everything she saw. Nothing she could recall related to her current situation, and she needed to keep a level head if she was going to get home. But before she accepted reason, her heightened senses picked out something else. There appeared to be a figure with her under the bridge – a person, peering out from amongst the creeper.

She yelped, then raised a façade. 'I'm sorry. I didn't see you there.'

The image stood against the far wall, embedded in the overgrowth. She could make out the broad, hunched shoulders of a man. He stood silently in the dimness, never once moving a muscle. She felt exposed and vulnerable, tightening the grip on her shoulder bag.

'Hello?'

There was no reply, but her eyes didn't deceive her. There was definitely someone there. Isabel sidestepped while watching the figure. It had depth and dimension, but it made no movement in the slightest, as still as a statue.

'Who are you?' she asked, dreading a response. But again, the person didn't acknowledge her. She swallowed her reserve and took a bold step forward, resolving to confront rather than withdraw. She didn't see the pothole until it was too late. Her foot plunged four inches into murky, stagnant water. She baulked and leapt away, struggling to maintain her guard. When she looked back, the figure was gone.

The sun emerged through a gap in the clouds and added clarity to her surroundings. There was no one lurking by the moss-covered brickwork after all, nor behind the thick ivy. She swore under her breath and shook her sodden leg, turning her attention to the incline towards home. Whatever was happening, she needed to get behind closed doors as soon as possible, somewhere she felt safe.

There was only one way to get there. She broke out from cover with determined strides up the slope. Isabel kept her weight on her heels, expecting to be challenged, and no sooner was she in the open than the wind pounced on top of her. It snapped and gnawed and nipped, growing stronger with each breath, but she ploughed through, managing almost to outrun it, carving a path through sheer willpower.

The gradient slowly levelled out. Flanking hedgerows were replaced with long wooden fencing. Isabel could hear children playing and latched on to the sound, drawing strength for once from human proximity. Before long, she came within sight of the main road, and for the first time in weeks, felt relieved to see other pedestrians – not beside her, nor even at arm's length, but close enough that someone would come running if she screamed.

The wind seemed to lose much of its ferocity, holding back in the more crowded space. For the rest of her journey, Isabel stuck to the busy roads and hurried down the pavement, her sodden foot squelching in one shoe. Her legs were tired, but she refused to slow until she came within sight of her little bungalow, counting down the seconds to the front gate.

Stepping off the footpath was like triggering a landmine. An unexpected gust shattered her new-found complacency. It pushed her away from the front door and back through the gate, a relentless blast forcing her windpipe closed, as though trying to choke her. She was almost thrown into the road. Her bag was wrenched off her shoulder and she clung to the strap to keep from losing it completely.

She was terrified, but determined. Isabel fumbled her keys into her hand and fought back. She gripped the fence for support and used everything she had to traverse the short distance to her yellow front door. The wind seemed to take on a voice as it thundered past her ears, hissing and howling. Her hair coiled around her head until she was half-blinded. She had to use both hands to feel her way to the lock and pull herself into the hallway.

The door closed behind her with a slam that shook the walls. The latch clicked, and after that, nothing could have followed her inside. But she could hear the wind testing the hinges. Without missing a beat, she pulled her bag open and rooted inside for her asthma inhaler. Her lungs felt restricted, like she could collapse at any moment. She wheezed, then hyperventilated through pursed lips until she found the blue device and took a deep puff of liquid mist.

It worked right away. The relief was immeasurable, a new sense of calm. Isabel leaned against the wall, filled with uncertainty, aware that she was trembling. Her instincts told her she was safe now. She must have been. *But from what exactly?*

2.WITH|DRAWAL

Isabel lived in a bungalow she both loved and hated, one that had seen her greatest pleasures and her deepest traumas. Coming through the front door often stirred up strong emotions. That day, she felt dread.

Thin-striped wallpaper created false shadows in the late afternoon. Her hallway was inexplicably cooler than the outdoors, its colours drained by a foreboding low light. She could still hear the wind outside, with anger in its howl. It drove her towards the centre of the house in case – against all likelihood – it managed to find a way in through the letter box.

Her chest rattled as she steadied her breathing. Keeping the inhaler in hand, she set her bag down beside the black skirting board and crept towards the living room. The gloom increased with every step, as if she were heading into a cave. Some of that was perception, as brutal clashes over the summer still resonated. She could picture her bare toes scrabbling for a grip of the threadbare carpet as Wren had dragged her across the floor. She recalled having to rearrange several pieces of furniture after he had used them to barricade her into the master bedroom.

The bars of the hallway radiator were cold to the touch. The house had a dreary, maudlin atmosphere. It was also devoid of any charm. She kept it clean as best she could so as not to lose her grip completely, but something about the bungalow had forever changed in her mind. The décor had been chosen by the previous occupant and would have been dated even then. Every square inch begged to be stripped bare, the interior reset, just not by her. Isabel longed to move away, prevented by a complete lack of finances and, at least for the moment, limited out-of-town prospects. In a sense, she was trapped.

She couldn't bring herself to turn any lights on, unclear who or what could be watching from outside. She scouted around the little house in the dimness, making sure every window was closed. The muffled gale seemed to remain localised behind the front door, and beneath its noise, she thought she could hear the rhythm of her phone vibrating in her bag. Isabel refused to talk to strangers. She rarely even answered to her friends, wishing everyone would just leave her alone. There were already over a dozen voicemail messages to be listened to, some of which were days old.

Her entire world felt restricted to the bungalow and its dilapidated contents. She paused in the bedroom doorway and remembered the dressing-table mirror she had once balanced above it as a trap. The room itself was dark enough to make her think twice about entering, closed curtains making it too easy to visualise her ordeal from a few short months before, which she had yet to fully process.

Instead, she turned to leave. But in doing so, her windswept hair rustled over the shoulders of her coat. The unexpected sound – so close to her ears – shattered any illusion of calm. She let out a gasp that had built up inside her for some time. Something came to life in apparent response. A tiny object appeared in the bedroom, moving so fast that she almost missed it – a fleck of light rising from between the carpet fibres.

It was little more than a pale dot against the darkness. In brighter weather, she never would have noticed. Isabel froze as it streaked across her view with clear purpose. It was a tiny, glowing spark, like an ember from a dying fire. It made a beeline for the window and disappeared behind the curtains, leaving a yellow stripe seared onto her retina.

Isabel wasn't sure how to react. Determined to remain calm, she tiptoed into the room and approached the window to see where the thing had gone. There were more of them in the garden – bright pinpoints, moving differently outdoors. Lingering, weaving.

Around a person on her lawn.

She closed the curtain again. Someone was standing in the middle of the garden with their back to the house. It was a man, surrounded by light, dressed from head to toe in dark colours. Her instincts took control. Nowadays, she had weapons hidden all around the house, never too far from a knife, a bat, a screwdriver, or a chisel. Reaching under the mattress, Isabel's fingers found the handle of a rolling pin and she took a strong grip, feeding off the courage it gave her.

She took another look outside. There were cardboard boxes on the lawn – boxes she recognised. The man stood amongst them, flicking his hands back and forth as though conjuring. Whatever he was doing, she had to stop it. Isabel hurried out of the bedroom and across the lounge, trying not to make a sound. In her utility room at the far corner of the house she found the rear door hanging ajar, letting cold air stream in.

From this different viewpoint, she peered through the narrow gap. The man was standing beside a metal dustbin with a thick wad of papers in his arms, feeding flames. His face was lit from underneath in flickering orange, but she recognised him right away. This wasn't a dark and sinister stranger, nor her long-dead former lover, but Scott, disguised from most angles by the fading sunlight.

Her partner.

Not that she recognised a single item of clothing he wore, nor understood his behaviour. She lacked tolerance for anything she couldn't predict, and he was no exception. Scott should have been at work, and he wouldn't have expected her back because she had left early.

She put a foot through the doorway. 'What's going on?'

Scott leapt out of his skin, betraying new-found vulnerability. He dropped the papers in the nearest box. 'You startled me,' he said. 'Is it five o'clock already?'

'My question came first,' she said, then wheezed. 'You should still be in the office. What is this?'

'They let me out early. I think they're scared of overloading me in the first couple of weeks back. Why are you holding a rolling pin?'

She ignored the question. Dry heat poured from the dustbin, making the air between them shimmer. The outdoors was altogether too bright after her time in the house. She squinted at the treetops, wondering why the air was so still.

'Come inside,' she said. 'It's not safe.'

'I'm fine,' Scott countered. 'I've been out here for a while, sorting through things we can live without. Is there something wrong?'

'I was …' Her mouth quivered while she formed the right words. 'I was followed home.'

'What do you mean?'

'I don't know. You can look at something for me. Come on, hurry up.' She took another step outside – now fully exposed – and went to seize him by the hand. But instead, she caught a glimpse of what was in the cardboard boxes. 'What exactly are you burning?'

He closed his eyes, as though accepting he had been caught red-handed. 'Just things we don't need,' he said.

'They look like certificates.'

'Nothing I've used in years.'

'Did you at least scan them?'

He raised his palms. 'I knew you'd react like that. Look, there's nothing I need to survive and it's weighing me down. Anything … in fact *everything* in the loft … if neither of us are using this stuff, what's the point of keeping it?'

She folded her arms, peering at a thick pile of ashes inside the metal drum. Scott had clearly been out there for some time and she recoiled on sight of blackened, curling images amongst the soot.

'Tell me you're not burning photographs.'

'Some.' Scott tapped his forehead. 'Memories I don't care to hang on to.'

Isabel shook her head. They had been there more than once before. Three days in a coma had given Scott a warped outlook. Some of the decisions he made followed an unclear path of logic, as though conventional routes had been forever blocked by his harrowing experience.

'I understand how you must be feeling—'

'You really don't. You couldn't possibly know how it feels, because how could you?' His voice wavered between resolute and choked with uncertainty. 'No one is supposed to go through what I did and survive to talk about it. I came back from the dead, just like him.'

Reflections of the crackling fire flickered off his glassy eyes.

'That's not what I meant,' she said. 'It destroys me to think of what happened to you, but it's worse to see what you've become since then. Don't sabotage your life because you think you'll lose what little we have if you lower your guard.'

'But I definitely will lose it,' he said. 'Everything, it's inevitable. If not from Wren, then some other way. You and I, all we can do is wish for more time, and every minute we waste living here is asking – no, begging for trouble. We need to leave, and we won't get far if we're weighed down.'

Isabel glanced nervously at the bushes, expecting them to start moving any second, and perplexed when they still didn't. 'We are going to leave,' she agreed, 'but there's a difference between planning an escape and fleeing in blind panic. You easily could have died for good, but you didn't, and I'm eternally grateful for that. Don't waste our second chance by obsessing over something that might not happen for years.'

'It could happen tomorrow. The thing I saw … the darkness … it hasn't gone far. I can feel it lurking in a way I can't even describe, so close I can sense it. There might be no escape. You'd understand if you'd been with me. You'd realise worthless possessions hold us back from what matters.'

'Tell me, Scott.' Isabel dropped her rolling pin into one of the boxes and tried to reassure him. 'Tell me what you have to live for.'

There was something in the way he spoke that blurred her judgement, something quite disturbing. She couldn't decide whether Scott was scared of the emptiness he had seen or scared of having to wait for it to return. *Was he afraid of death, or pining for it?*

He took time to consider his reply. 'I want a fresh start, with you. That's all I want. But we won't get very far if we try to salvage the life we had before the summer. Burning what we don't need feels like …'

'Moving forwards?' Isabel nodded. Deep down, she had similar urges, though less severe. 'Please trust me,' she said. 'Leave the fire and come inside. Sleep on your thoughts before you destroy something you can't replace.'

He closed his eyes, and although he didn't acknowledge her proposal, he didn't protest when she placed a lid on the metal drum to quell the flames. Two of the cardboard boxes had been emptied before she arrived, their contents doubtless reduced to smoulder. It was enough damage for one day.

She led him indoors, hoping he hadn't disposed of her passport or her driving licence. Ever since his ordeal, Scott had become impulsive, and it was dangerous in such an uncertain time. They found it difficult enough to make ends meet, yet he didn't seem to care how much he spent, as though debt was meaningless to him. She paid close attention to his movements as he went through to the kitchen and washed ash from his face and hands. He worried her. Weeks after his near-death experience, he showed few signs of improvement. Not enough, at any rate.

Her thoughts were interrupted by a sound at the rear window. It was imperceptible at first, were it not for her heightened senses. It sounded like gravel, an invisible fleck of grit against the glass. She looked out at the ageing afternoon to see short blades of grass begin to shiver.

'Scott?' she called him to attention as the hedgerow shuddered. In moments, the garden was teeming with life. Low-lying branches bobbed up and down, tossing their heads like a bull before charging.

'That's strange,' he responded as he came up beside her. 'What's causing it?'

'I don't know,' she said, 'but tell me it was there before I came home. Tell me you saw it.'

'Definitely not,' he said. 'I never would have been able to start a fire in that.'

Isabel edged away from the window without taking her eyes off it. She could almost see the wind moving, gaining volume and intensity. It took on a voice, deep and unearthly. She tightened her grip on the asthma inhaler. Her own voice was shaking.

'Then it really did follow me home.'

3.DISE|ASE

Isabel studied the wind from the supposed safety of her living room. Bushes and low branches jerked back and forth with rhythmic frenzy, but the treetops barely moved at all, and the neighbours' trees were motionless altogether.

The phenomenon had her spellbound. Swirls were etched in the short, square lawn. Shrivelling plants were pressed flat against the flower beds. Grit and small twigs glanced off the window pane with a *tink*, *tink*.

'What's happening out front?' she called over her shoulder.

The reply came back through the kitchen door. 'Nothing like you're seeing back there. A little windy, I guess. Mostly quiet.'

'Do you think it's him?' Isabel felt no need to say who she meant. Wren Lawton was all she ever talked about.

'Why would you conclude that?' said Scott. 'He was sharing someone else's body, not controlling the weather.'

'Who knows what he's capable of.' She leaned forward as far as she dared and looked for figures in the garden, then glanced back and forth between the front and back windows of their property. Eventually, Scott came into the lounge and closed the door behind him. Her upset must have been showing because his behaviour had changed, pivoting from rattled to something more composed and considerate.

'Do you want to leave?' he said. 'As in, pack tonight?'

She shook her head. 'I'm not going back out there. The fact you're seeing it too convinces me this is real, so we need to stay beyond its reach.'

'Are we safe or are we trapped? What if it finds a way in?'

'I'm still not going,' she affirmed.

He approached the window, going closer than she dared to follow. The wind filled every inch of their garden, blowing so hard that some airborne leaves never touched the ground. Even the metal drum shook, its lid rattling loudly.

'There are clouds gathering,' he said. 'Must be a storm coming. Maybe it's to do with that.'

'It followed me home.'

'I believe you,' he said. 'I'm just trying to be thorough. If we never ask questions, we'll end up running from everything.'

She stared through the glass without daring to blink. She was coiled up tighter than a spring, unable to keep still, yet stuck inside the bungalow. Scott put a hand on the curtain, closing it no more than an inch before she stopped him.

'Don't,' she said. 'What are you doing?'

'You need to calm down,' he said. 'It's only wind, and it's not coming indoors. We're better putting it out of mind.'

'I need to be able to see it, even though it scares me.'

A bundle of papers fluttered out of one of the cardboard boxes and flew at the window, as though it had been thrown. He backed away. Despite his denial, she could see doubts forming. 'I hate living here as much as you do,' he said. 'If you're insisting on a plan before we leave, let's make one tonight.'

'Okay then.' She summoned all her courage and nodded. He was right. They had a lot to talk about. He made another attempt to draw the curtains, and this time she didn't stop him. She caught a final glimpse of black stones and brown leaves, as unremarkable as they were menacing, and then the two of them were alone in the gloom.

'We'll keep our shoes on in case something happens,' said Scott. 'I'll keep my car keys in my pocket, but I guess the most important thing to do is show we're unafraid.'

Isabel heard more words than he spoke. *Show we're unafraid ... in case someone really is watching us, after all.* Nevertheless, she went along with his agenda, glad for him to take some responsibility away from her for the first time in a while. She cupped his hand in hers, feeling rough, dry skin.

'I can still hear it,' she said. 'If we're going to talk openly, I don't think I can stay in this room.'

'Then let's cook.'

***

Isabel had first met Scott in questionable circumstances. She was Wren's partner at the time, and had been for a few years. Scott knew Wren from work. Their closeness had felt like a betrayal, something she struggled with even now, when those events were so distant.

The part they had played in his downward spiral.

She had almost forgotten a time when the guilt wasn't festering away at the back of her mind. In the house she and Wren had bought together – a house she had inherited his contributions towards – it often required great effort to think about anything else, and this was one of many reasons why she needed to leave.

As she rolled up her sleeves in the kitchen that evening, she reminded herself to focus on the three tasks at hand – planning a new life, keeping Scott from doing anything reckless, and making soup.

'I opened a joint account this morning.' The blind had been drawn over the front window to keep her from looking out, but she could hear no signs of activity. She had retrieved her shoulder bag from the front door and emptied a selection of vegetables onto the counter. 'I got a good interest rate through work, better than anything else on the market. You should put as much money into it as you can.'

He nodded idly. 'I'll make a transfer once the bank replaces my lost card. I don't need much, day to day.'

'Thank you.' Her mood improved, if only slightly. Having visibility of Scott's money was a step towards controlling it, meaning she could intervene if he did anything careless, something they both seemed to acknowledge was a possibility.

'Once you've found a new job, we should rent somewhere close to it for the first six months, get to know the area.'

'Are we still going south?' he asked.

'I think so, don't you? All that's really important is to choose a place we have no links to, somewhere no one would look for us. I'm thinking of changing my name. You should start calling me Charlotte.'

'Your middle name?'

'I've never thought of this before, so it won't occur to him, either. It's worth it.'

'You really think he's coming for us, don't you?'

'If we don't manage to stay hidden, it won't be from a lack of trying.'

Isabel took a long, sharp knife from one of the drawers and chopped into her ingredients. Against the knife's steady percussion, Scott folded his arms and leaned back against the kitchen counter. The naked bulb on the ceiling highlighted the lines on his weary face.

'I'm more difficult to hide,' he said, morosely. 'Unless I abandon my career, he'll have an easy way to trace me. We worked closely together, in a closed industry. He'll know all the companies I could work for.'

'Then you need to find an obscure business, new enough or small enough that he won't have heard of it, and make sure your profile stays off their website.'

She was glad Scott wasn't rejecting her conditions outright. It would have wasted more time if they argued. She knew there was no logical way to disappear without a completely new identity, and if they couldn't manage that, then they could at least keep their faces out of the public domain.

'I guess my main issue is whether I'm employable at all,' he said after a pause. 'I'll need to declare my medical status, or at least the time I've been signed off. Would you hire me if you knew how recently that had happened?'

'You don't need to disclose anything you don't want to.'

'Then it's worse if they run a check and find out. And what if I have a turn and can't hold myself together? I'll be on probation. They won't need to give a reason to fire me. I do want to go. This house can burn down for all I care. Let it rot. But what if no one wants me?'

Isabel applied too much force to her knife and cut through a carrot with a punctuating clap. A round slice rolled off the counter and he caught it on the way to the floor. The move showed unexpected dexterity, suggesting that some of his faculties were working just fine.

'You'll feel better once you commit,' she said. 'It won't be as hard as you think. Don't worry about your career. Any job is good enough for now, so long as it's a steady income. Accept something low pressure and re-evaluate after a year or so. We only need to get by.'

He seemed lost in thought for a moment, then to her surprise, he brightened up. 'You raise a fair point. I always said I could do a better job than a lot of the people I worked with, so maybe this is my chance to prove it.'

Scott dusted down the vegetable with his wrist and popped it in his mouth, biting down with a crunch. Isabel lowered the knife.

'What on earth are you doing?'

He shrugged. 'Didn't want to waste it.'

'I mean why are you eating carrot at all? You hate carrot.'

He paused mid-chew, as though unsure if he should swallow. Isabel watched him think about the taste for a moment – really think hard about it – then he covered his mouth and pushed the mush out with his tongue. 'Just so long as I'm not allergic.'

He tried to shrug off his words, leaning back against the counter, but Isabel could see it had rattled him. 'Did you forget?' she asked.

'Maybe it's been so long since I tried, that …' He folded his arms and looked down at the floor. 'Why are you cooking it if you know I don't like it?'

'The carrots are for me,' she said. 'I cook them separately. This is the Good Friday soup, remember? The one we ate for three days straight.'

Scott's eyes moved back and forth like he was searching inside himself. 'Good Friday soup?'

'You really don't remember, do you?'

Easter had been a long time ago and so much had happened in the interim. Parts of his life had been erased. Isabel put down the knife and threw her arms around him, holding on for dear life.

'It seems to strike at random.' His lip was trembling. 'I know what happened on your birthday, but Good Friday's gone completely. I remember coming home from hospital, but not starting back at work. And you think I'm going to like what you've started to make, but will I really?'

'It's okay,' she said. 'You have to allow time for these things to stabilise. They said your recovery would be gradual. We just need to be patient.'

'You don't know what it feels like when you can't trust your own mind. I feel defective.'

'Well, you look about the same to me. So long as we have each other, nothing else should matter. We've faced worse than some memory loss, haven't we?'

'I can't argue with that.' He laughed – a nervous, vulnerable laugh. But even a forced laugh had value in those uncertain times. She clung to his neck as she clung to the hope that everything would improve with distance. Their situation seemed impossible, but in a few short months, maybe they could build a new life in an unfamiliar part of the country, and all this would seem like a distant memory.

One he might forget.

A noise came through from the living room, loud enough to interrupt their discussion. Scott broke their embrace and opened the door to the lounge, creeping into the dimness.

'Did something just fall over?' he said.

Isabel followed. A cold draught glanced her arm, drawing her eyes towards the curtains. She recognised the sound of tiny stones striking glass. 'Can you hear that?' she said. 'Over an hour, and it's still out there.'

Scott beat her to the punch. Before she could part the fabric to look out through the window, he marched towards the back door.

'Where are you going?' she asked, shocked by his determination.

'I've had enough. I'm going to see it for myself.'

'Don't go out there.'

'I need to know,' said Scott. 'If it hassled you all the way home, I want to show we're unafraid.'

'It's too dangerous.'

She tried to intervene, but he moved quickly, turning the door handle before she could stop him. Immediately, something tore it from his grasp. She watched in horror as he was dragged onto the lawn, as though wrenched by the arm. The sun had long set, and in the twilight, there was turmoil. The air was filled with grit and clods of earth, chopping and twisting. The metal dustbin had tipped on its side, the flames snuffed out.

Scott's clothes ruffled. His hair flattened down against his scalp. But Isabel realised the wind wasn't pushing him about. It wasn't pouring down his throat. He was able to walk across the garden – nudged perhaps, but barely opposed, almost as though there was no wind at all.

Confusion brought her to a standstill in the doorway. A branch as long as her forearm broke off one of the trees and tumbled end on end through the air, passing between him and the window, but striking neither. It looked like a demonstration of power, but was surprisingly non-violent. It was as if he was safe inside the eye of a vortex.

'Are you alright?' she called from the doorway. The hairs on her neck stood to attention. She gripped the door to hold it steady, receiving none of the leniency given to Scott.

'I'm fine,' he replied in apparent disbelief. The air between them shimmered.

'What do you think it is?'

He shook his head. A bitter cold turned his breath into steam which existed for an inch before the wind swept it away. He raised his hand from his side, breaking the path of the circling debris, and in the blink of an eye, the whole thing stopped dead. The wind departed, as though exorcised. Debris scattered in all directions, colliding with the wall, the hedge, the flower bed, and the window.

Scott was left standing alone in the middle of the garden as chaos turned to a disturbing quiet.

'What did you do?' asked Isabel. The door became loose in her grasp and she let it swing wide.

'I don't know.'

'Come inside,' she said. 'There's only one explanation, the same one I gave you an hour ago. Maybe now you believe me.'

Scott stood for a moment, as though mesmerised. When he moved, it appeared thoughtless, his mind elsewhere. His gaze passed from one feature to the next, as though searching for answers. She needed answers, too. As much as she hated the thought, she stood by her words – only one explanation seemed remotely plausible. Nothing else fit.

Something alive had been out there, in whatever form. Something conscious, with a spark of intelligence. And it knew who they were.

4.DISD|AIN

Dramatic skies followed a night of stormy weather. A clean atmosphere was obscured in many places by thick clouds. Columns of sunlight connected with the ground, making rain-soaked branches glisten, and creating the impression of movement.

Isabel kept watch through a gap in the bedroom curtains. Her cheek was pressed into her pillow, forcing one eye closed. She refused to accept the calm was anything other than temporary, a trick, that the wind wasn't going to choose its moment to return. She had watched the sunrise from that position without moving an inch, all the while listening to Scott sleeping uneasily in the bed beside her.

'What time is it?'

His voice brought her out of her trance, back into the room. He sounded barely awake, and she looked over her shoulder to find him sitting up beside her with his head in his hands. The covers were down around his waist where he had kicked them off while unconscious.

'Probably eight o'clock,' she responded. 'I don't know, I've lost track of time. You were screaming in the night.'

'Why didn't you try to wake me?'

'Because you need rest. And besides, when you drop off, it's almost impossible to bring you back around.'

He scratched his chin, his fingers scraping over stubble. 'I'm sorry. I don't know what I was dreaming about, but if it's any consolation, something must be working because I feel more like my former self.'

She flexed her toes before rolling out of bed, trying to maintain a state of readiness. Scott, by contrast, hauled himself to the edge and used the headboard to pull himself to standing. The mattress sighed with apparent relief.

'We should make another appointment with the doctor,' she said. 'Your nightmares seem to be getting worse.'

'I already know what they'll say,' he responded. 'It'll be "keep going and hope things start to improve". Or maybe they'll prescribe drugs to calm me down, which would lower my guard and make me useless in a crisis. Nobody wants that.'

She nodded gently. Isabel understood why Scott's nightmares made him cry out in the darkness. He had given such a detailed account that she sometimes had them, too. He had drowned, cold water pouring over his face and into her mouth, with a feeling of being conscious but paralysed. Often, for brief moments when she first awoke, Isabel felt like the one that Wren had strangled and submerged, such was the intensity of the illusion.

That night, however, she had neither dreamt nor slept at all. She put her head between the curtains and looked out of the window. Flower beds had been overturned by the evening's wind. Many of the smaller plants had been uprooted. The metal drum had been rolled into the bushes, despite weighing several kilograms. It reminded her of the aftermath of a hurricane, and the worry must have been written on her face.

'Let me drive you to the bank today.' Scott spoke with a congested throat, which he then cleared loudly.

'Okay,' she replied. 'But not home tonight. You need to knuckle down and start looking for a new job, as early as you can.'

'I can do both.'

'No, Scott.'

He joined her at the window, avoiding eye contact, as he often did when under her scrutiny. 'I take you're point. They're watching me too closely at work to job hunt during the day. How will you get home? I assume you have that covered off already?'

His question was a subtle jab. She had one other person in her life, one who came to her aid whenever asked. Scott didn't approve, for obvious reasons. 'I was seeing him anyway,' she said. 'It won't be a problem.'

Andrew Goodwin had been Wren's unwilling host throughout their dealings over the summer. It had been Andrew's eyes through which Wren had spied on them from afar, Andrew's mouth through which he had lied and begged and threatened, Andrew's hands that had wrapped themselves around Scott's throat.

It was difficult not to judge one man for the crimes of the other, an altogether unnatural challenge to view them as two distinct individuals. 'I don't trust him,' said Scott. 'I can't. He left me for dead.'

'He saved you. He brought me to you. I get why you're hesitant, but I promise he's not a threat. Andrew says he's alone now and there's no reason to doubt him.'

Scott began to fidget. He paced across the room. 'How could you ever be certain? You've told me before – he was normal one moment, then psychotic the next.'

'No, I didn't,' she snapped. 'He was someone different entirely, which wasn't his fault. We can't judge him because we don't know what it felt like, and he was there when I needed him.'

'Well, he wasn't there for me, and I don't like you spending time with him. It smells like another trick.'

Isabel tensed her jaw, sending a clear signal that she wasn't going to listen. 'Well, I don't need your approval. Andrew's grateful to you for not pressing charges, but that doesn't even begin to repay him.'

Scott ran his fingers through his short, brown hair. There seemed to be a lot more greys than three months before. 'I only let him go because of you. As far as I'm concerned, he's guilty as sin.'

'He didn't have a choice.'

'Of course he did.' Scott lost control of his voice. 'He could have gone to the police at any time, but the fact is he didn't, and I nearly died.'

Isabel was shocked by his intensity. It was clear just how far he was from forgiveness. She moved towards the doorway, putting distance between them. 'I'm not defending his actions,' she said, 'but nor do I think he's a bad person. We're going for a late lunch. If you're so concerned, why don't you come with us?'

'Even if I could, you know I wouldn't.'

A vibration from the lounge interrupted them both. She recognised the sound of her mobile phone against a wooden surface. She tensed, unable to speak until Scott was almost through the door.

'Don't answer it,' she cried. 'Send it to voicemail.'

He froze mid-stride. 'What's the matter?'

'Please.' Isabel locked eyes with him, rooting him to the spot until the vibration ran its course. The mood of their interaction changed completely.

'Who was it?' he asked.

'I don't know. I haven't given my number to anyone in years, not since … not since he died. Anyone who knows me sends a text instead of calling. Just leave it, Scott. Act like it never happened.'

He didn't move a muscle, evidently startled by the change in her. 'I can't always be there to protect you,' he said through gritted teeth. 'Be careful today. Always sit near the door. Take no chances, especially with Andrew Goodwin.'

Isabel nodded. Shaken to the core, she didn't dare argue.

***

Something seemed to lurk behind the eyes of every stranger, something like repressed aggression, a veiled sense of malice. Even with thick safety glass shielding her from her customers at the bank, Isabel felt exposed, intimidated, afraid someone in the queue would lose control and turn against her.

It had been a long day. From the minute the bank had opened, a steady stream of patrons had trickled in, never once relenting. By the early afternoon, she had been worn down to the point of exhaustion, wishing she was back at home. With her guard depleted, she didn't recognise a tall man approaching the counter until his nose was against the partition.

'You look like you need a rescue.'

The glass muffled his voice, but it came through a pair of speakers. She leapt in shock and put a hand to her chest. His thin smile waned and she realised she was looking at Andrew Goodwin, perhaps the only person she felt inclined to trust. She hadn't seen him for a while. He wore thick-rimmed glasses where once he had always worn contact lenses. It drastically changed his appearance, erecting a barrier between his eyes and the outside world. Dark hair had grown long enough to sag under its own weight, but she could still picture him with a shaven head and bruises on his face, staring like a man possessed.

'Did I startle you?' he said. 'I tried waving from the door, but your mind must have been elsewhere.'

'You frightened the life out of me,' she said. 'Weren't you going to wait for me outside?'

'I didn't like it.' He shook his head. 'It stirred up memories that I didn't know I had.'

'Of course. Give me a moment to hand over and I'll be with you.'

Andrew stepped out of the queue and waited by the wall. While she finished up her last few pieces of work, she kept glancing in his direction. He looked withered by the unwanted attention of those around him. She wondered how many recognised him from the media reports and how many just wanted to look at the scars. All would think he was lucky to be alive without realising how unlucky he had been to be afflicted in the first place.

She gathered her belongings and retreated from the window. Scott was one of those people. He only saw the worst in Goodwin, unable to get over his merging with Wren. Isabel felt differently. She had endless sympathy for the way Andrew had suffered. Wren had sent him plummeting off a railway bridge in a desperate attempt to kill them both. Surgeons had taken days to stitch him back together, leaving his body crisscrossed with scars that would never heal. Metal rods had replaced shattered bones.

Where one side of his face was smooth and clean-shaven, the other told a tortured tale, with raised lumps of tissue running along his jawline from chin to ear, crossed with deep pits that resembled the railway tracks that had broken his fall. She met up with him occasionally and kept in regular contact, sharing a bond that was growing stronger. As she let herself out and approached, he picked himself off the wall, as though trying not to show any outward sign of weakness.

'I'm glad you could come.' She leaned up to kiss his unblemished cheek.

'I couldn't resist the invite. It's good to see you're still in one piece.'

She took his arm and led him out of the bank, heading onto the pavement by the village green. There wasn't a flicker of movement in the air, not so far as the eye could see. The bustle of the area helped to calm her nerves, though she kept a steady pace.

'How have you been coping?' Andrew asked.

'I take things one day at a time,' she said. 'We both do. Scott's less inclined to admit it, but he's feeling the strain as well. Nothing's right anymore. We need to go.'

'What's holding you back?'

'His job.' She sighed. 'I'd leave tomorrow. That feels like the safe thing to do. But we couldn't make a go of it without Scott's salary and he doesn't seem up to the search.'

'He's stalling?'

'Not exactly,' she said, aware she sounded unconvinced. 'He's worried no one would take him on, and he may have a point. It's everything from the mood swings to the way he forgets what you're saying midway through the conversation.'

Andrew walked with an uneven gait. His scars faced away from her, and she noticed how rarely he turned his head. 'So has nothing improved?' he asked.

'Some things have,' she said. 'One of us normally gets a full night's sleep, though we seem to take turns. We'll be alright. We have to be. Let's talk about you instead. You're walking better than the last time you came over.'

They arrived at a small café at the end of the park. He held the door open as she went inside. Andrew continued to speak freely, as though he didn't care about anyone overhearing. 'I'm not much different, either. I didn't have much to lose, so I came out the same way I went in. The headaches come and go. The doctors poke and prod. I swear the police are keeping an eye on me, despite Scott calling them off.'

'Have you seen anything of Wren?' She couldn't help herself.

'Not that I'm aware of. I don't hear voices, but I still get headaches. The doctors tell me it's nothing, then scan me anyway.'

Heeding Scott's words, she chose a table close to the door, sitting where she could keep an eye on the unpredictable weather. She pretended to look through the menu on the placemat. 'Do you think it's possible he might not even be in a body at all?' she said. 'That he could be somewhere out there, just … you know … on his own?'

'You mean like a ghost?'

Isabel lowered her voice to a whisper, hoping he would follow suit. 'I've been seeing things I can't explain, and I'm worried.'

'What kind of things? After what we went through, take it seriously.'

'Something was in my garden last night,' she said. 'A wind, but like nothing I've seen before. Honestly, Andrew, it had a real presence. It followed me home. Me, specifically.'

'What did Scott make of it?'

She glanced out across the village green. 'He didn't have the same experiences we did over the summer.'

'Which means what, exactly?'

'He's sceptical,' she said.

'Or in other words, he thinks you're making it up.'

'This might sound bad, but I can't actually tell.'

A figure wearing white stirred in Isabel's peripheral vision. She turned to see a teenage waitress working her way up the tables, checking on her customers. The mere prospect of direct attention caused Isabel to raise her guard. She fell quiet, which doubled the impact of her mobile phone as it burst to life in the palm of her hand. She shuddered.

'Something wrong?' said Andrew.

She placed the handset down in front of him and they read the screen at the same time. It was an unsaved number, but she recognised the pattern of digits. 'They've been ringing me all morning,' she said. 'Just ignore it.'

'Did they leave any messages?'

She raised her fingertips, bringing him to silence. Her heart was in her throat as she counted down the seconds until the caller stopped trying. 'If there are any messages on there, you can delete them. I don't care what people want.'

'The area code is local. It could be important.'

'I don't care,' she repeated.

Andrew acted on her instruction and navigated through the call log. There were more messages than could fit on the screen. His finger paused over the first.

'Let's listen to a few. Come on, let's do this together.'

'I don't want—'

Before she could stop him, he turned on the loudspeaker and pressed play. The first message came through at full volume, and it made them both jump – static, four seconds of hissing and white noise until it ended with a click.

Isabel stared into Andrew's eyes, needing to see his reaction before she could decide what to think herself. He did nothing, but she could tell he was unsure.

'Most of these are a similar length,' he said, turning down the volume before he tried another. Once again, four seconds of static poured out of the speakers, with not a word spoken. 'Should we call back?'

A chill ran down her spine. 'Not a chance. They'll give up eventually if we just ignore them.'

'I can do it from my phone. They won't know we're together.' He reached into his pocket and produced his own handset, glancing back and forth as he copied the number onto his screen.

'Don't tell them who you are.'

Andrew raised the phone to his ear and made the call. Someone answered almost immediately. Isabel sat listening to one side of the conversation, torn between being desperate for answers and afraid of what they could be.

'Who is this?' he said, his eyes to the floor. 'No, who are you? … You've been calling my other number for days … From what I can tell, at least seven times.' There was an agonisingly long pause, then his face sank. 'She does, as it happens … I see.'

He lowered the handset and contemplated it for a moment, before – to Isabel's horror – offering it to her.

'You should take this,' he said.

She felt the colour drain from her face. 'What is it?'

'Just trust me,' he said. 'You need to hear what this man has to say.'

5.ETHE|R

Isabel had made a conscious effort to build a close friendship with Andrew Goodwin. She had seen him as key to processing her suffering at the hands of Wren Lawton. She had shared her innermost thoughts with him, things Scott wouldn't have been able to handle.

Her guilt and despair.

As they bonded, it had become apparent that his own issues were unique to his experience. Andrew seemed averse to his own company, to the point where the mere prospect of isolation made him visibly nervous. To him, crowds were safe spaces, and windows gazing down offered a sense of security, as though they could reduce the chances of his being reimprisoned.

She sensed his agitation as he marched beside her. The shopping precinct would have promised him so much, only to deliver disappointment. There were no crowds at all. Many of the shops were closed, their shutters locked and riddled with graffiti. The walls and pavements were dull grey concrete, mirroring the leaden sky.

Her own nerves didn't help. Though she was relieved by how few people were around, every shift in the breeze had her on a knife edge. 'Scott would go crazy if he knew we were out here together,' she said.

'Invite him over if you want,' said Andrew. 'I'd be more than happy to let him take my place.'

'That's not what I meant.' She couldn't speak her true reasons aloud. If Scott struggled with the thought of her and Andrew meeting at the bank, then he definitely wouldn't approve of them driving across the city.

Andrew's pronounced limp resulted in an irregular stride. He kept his eyes on his surroundings instead of making eye contact. 'You want to know something? Every night, the last thing I do is hide my glasses in a different place to the night before. I can't see more than three feet without them. My body would be a hard thing to pilot if someone took over while I was unconscious.'

'Does that help you to sleep?'

'It shouldn't, but it does. We may feel trapped in our lives at the minute, but there's always something we could do to help ourselves. Don't let Scott control you.'

'I don't think he's controlling me.'

'And I don't think you should feel bad for being here.'

She nodded. It wasn't nice to cast a negative light on her partner, not after all he had endured. But he definitely would have opposed her decision to come there. Litter tumbled as it blew along the gutter and an empty wine bottle rolled under her feet. She grabbed Andrew's arm for support.

'Are you alright?' he asked.

'Fine,' she said. 'That's the second time that's happened lately.'

She felt a subtle pressure against her back as she followed him down a narrow side alley off the main square. The path was so narrow that scarcely any light made it through a row of full-height windows. Faded gold lettering adorned a black door, which he held open while she rushed inside.

'Hello?' she called.

It was a solicitor's office – a cramped space, sparsely furnished, decorated in sombre tones. A grandfather clock tick-tocked in the corner, showing disregard for the pensive silence. A man in his sixties looked up from behind a mahogany desk. Bushy eyebrows hung low on his face, the whites and greys matching his shirt and tie.

'Can I help you both?'

'Yes,' said Isabel. 'You sound like the man I spoke to an hour ago.'

'Miss Harding?'

'That's right.'

He beckoned them over to a pair of leather armchairs in front of his desk. Andrew sat with his back to the window. The reflections on his glasses dulled. Isabel's paranoia got the better of her and she turned to face sideways, where she could keep an eye on the weather.

'Thank you for coming,' said the man. 'I appreciate this must be a difficult time.'

'In many ways,' said Andrew.

'I can only apologise for my persistence. News like this shouldn't travel by voicemail.'

Isabel straightened her skirt, nervous in unfamiliar surroundings. She took her inhaler from her pocket and clutched it for comfort. 'Just so you're aware, I'm not here to make a profit. This is just to see how the land lies, and then I'll decide what I'm comfortable with.'

'I appreciate your honesty.' The solicitor pulled a paper file from a stack of plastic trays on the corner of his desk. Inside were sheets of faded paperwork, some of which were typewritten. Isabel caught a glimpse of the header on the first page – Jon Lawton, Last Will and Testament.

Wren's father had passed away.

She pursed her lips and exhaled slowly. 'So it's true.'

'I'm afraid so,' said the man. 'From everything you told me over the phone, do I infer that the two of you had drifted out of contact?'

'I hadn't seen him for a few months,' she said. 'He didn't look well, but I never thought to question why. What happened?'

'He collapsed at home.' The man's tone was soft, but factual. 'Someone found him after a few days.'

'So no one was with him when he died?' she asked.

'I don't think so, no.'

Andrew's chair squeaked as he adjusted himself, adding to an uneasy atmosphere in the room. 'Neither of us could say we were his friends. I only met him once, myself. Why do you need Isabel in particular?'

The solicitor came across a photograph in the binder and glanced between it and Isabel's face, as if trying to verify her identity. 'Mr Lawton made his will a number of years ago, through an associate of ours who has since ceased to practise. Only two beneficiaries are listed – Mr Lawton's son, and his son's partner.'

Isabel closed her eyes. 'You mean it assumes we're still together.'

'That seems accurate,' said the man. 'There isn't enough detail to create ambiguity. This was never meant to be a division of his possessions. Everything he owned was left to the two of you as a combined entity.'

Andrew shifted in his chair again. Isabel caught him glancing towards the door. He seemed more uneasy by the second. 'I doubt a man like Jon Lawton had much to his name,' he said. 'How much of an estate are we talking about?'

'The list is short, you're correct. Primarily, it's just the houses.'

Isabel frowned. 'Excuse me … you're saying houses, plural?'

'Indeed,' said the solicitor. 'Mr Lawton owned one property locally and another in South Wales.'

She glanced at Andrew, feeling an irrational urge to apologise. 'I knew nothing about this,' she said. 'It must be Wren's childhood home, but he told me Jon sold it when he moved up here.'

The solicitor produced a brown paper envelope and slid it across the desk. 'Mr Lawton has no next of kin, either named or within my power to identify. As the only surviving recipient, both houses are legally yours.'

'And if I don't want them?'

'Sold off,' said Andrew. 'Proceeds to the state. Seems a waste.'

Isabel took the envelope, finding two sets of keys inside and a bundle of documents, which she thumbed through. 'Some of these are dated forty years ago. I'm right. I must be. It's where Wren grew up.'

'So which one of them lied about it?' said Andrew. 'And why?'

She didn't even want to guess. It felt deceitful even to contemplate accepting both properties. Even when Wren had been alive, she would have felt no entitlement to his family's possessions. She went deep inside herself, burdened by the opportunity presented to her. Once again, her past had been dredged up in an unpleasant way. Once again, a supposed miracle seemed like a curse.

'I need to think about it,' she said, matter-of-factly. 'I took my current house from Wren, and in horrible circumstances. I'm not sure I can accept another. It was naïve to put me on the will in the first place. Jon never should have bothered.'

'This could be a gift horse,' said Andrew. 'You can sell them both. I wouldn't hesitate.'

She flashed him a look. 'Most gifts don't come at a cost.'

Something struck the window, commanding the room to silence. She turned to see an object the length of her forearm lying on the pavement. It was blacker than night. An oily mark on the glass showed where it had impacted, and she took a moment to establish what must have happened.

It was a bird, a carrion crow, which appeared to have flown beak-first into the central windowpane. The collision was so violent that a hairline crack had formed, a little more than an inch long.

'That's strange.' The solicitor froze with his elbows on the desk. 'The wind must have disorientated it.'

The creature writhed on the spot, its neck twisted back and its feathers ruffled. A wing extended before her eyes, reaching almost half a metre into the air like a black sail before a rising gust forced it back down at a crooked angle. Andrew pulled himself out of the leather chair and stepped forwards. 'Do you normally see birds down an alley this dark and narrow?'

'Never one,' was the reply.

'We can't just leave it out there,' said Isabel. 'It's suffering.'

'What would you suggest?' said Andrew.

She leaned over the arm of her chair and glanced towards the clouds. There were a handful of other crows above them – a murder, struggling to fly against unexpected turbulence. The pages of a newspaper were tossed into the air and scattered ten metres up. The window creaked in its frame and she could have sworn the crack grew by half an inch.

She stood and moved further into the room. 'This is the thing I was talking about.'

'The thing in your garden?'

'It's coming back.'

As she looked on, the intensity of the wind increased until the crow began to slide away down the pavement, leaving a trail of fluid in its wake. Her throat tightened at the thought of having to go out there, and when he spoke, Andrew's voice was filled with disbelief.

'That can't be natural,' he said. 'It's too strong, even funnelled between the buildings.'

'It was even stronger last night,' she said. 'We can't stay here. It'll be through that window in no time and the glass could kill us all.'

He appeared to take her seriously, turning to the solicitor. 'Is there a rear exit?'

'No,' came the reply.

'I'm the one it followed,' she said. 'You might be safe if you both stay here and I leave.'

'I'll come with you,' Andrew insisted.

A plastic dustbin rolled past, followed by its contents. She heard a howl, a deep moan like a wailing voice. She took the envelope of documents and folded it twice before stuffing it into one of her pockets. 'Are we finished?'

The solicitor shook his head. 'Not at all. I need signatures, and we've arrangements to discuss. This wasn't intended to be a short meeting.'

'I'll have to call you.'

She clasped her asthma inhaler in one hand, as tightly as she could. The day before, she had walked a mile through the wind's barrage. Here, there were only a few hundred yards to the car park. Once she was inside a heavy vehicle then surely – *surely* – she would be safe.

The wind seemed to know when she stepped outside. Its intensity grew to a new level, sucking the air out of her lungs. She covered her mouth with the crook of her elbow as it wrenched the door handle from her grip and drew her into the alleyway. Her shoulder bounced off the wall not once, but three times, pulled away then thrust back in.

She turned her back and doubled over, giving her throat a moment's respite. She saw Andrew exit behind her and wrestle the door closed, standing flat against the brickwork. Anyone could have seen how much less he suffered. Isabel was undeniably the target.

Her shoes slipped on the concrete. She stumbled, and the wind didn't give her the chance to recover. It changed direction, back and forth, sending her staggering out of control. Her hands scraped along coarse bricks, tearing through the skin on her knuckles. A relentless, freezing blast of air forced itself into her face, sealing her windpipe.

A sheet of dampened card slid out from under her foot at precisely the wrong moment. Isabel fell to the ground. Howling filled her ears, like an endless rage, but she could make out Andrew's voice beneath it saying 'Don't try to stand. See if you can crawl your way back to me.'

'It's holding me down,' she cried. Dense knots formed in her shoulder-length hair, then invisible, icy fingers seemed to take hold of them. With excruciating force, she was dragged across the paving stones, just as the dead crow had been. Panic swept across her as she fought for breath.

'Wren?' She choked, unable to speak louder than a whisper. 'Jon? Whoever you are, please. Please talk to me. Stop this now.'

It didn't seem to listen. Pieces of grit battered her bare skin, stinging like shotgun pellets. The feel of the pavement changed as the wind gathered pace and she slipped off the kerbside onto coarse tarmac. A road. Passing vehicles swerved to avoid her. Every time she tried to climb to her feet, she was thrown flat, all the while unable to see straight. She desperately needed the inhaler, but couldn't raise it to her lips. Then something broke through the torrent and dispelled it. She heard screeching tyres and looked up to see a red Honda Civic skid to a halt right beside her. 'Get inside,' a voice shouted. 'Quickly.'

It was Andrew. As the wind had drawn her away from the tiny office, he must have run for the car. It disturbed the twirling cyclone, too heavy to shift, breaking Isabel's entrapment long enough for her to pull herself together.

She opened the door and crawled inside, immediately taking a puff of gas. 'Get us out of here.'

Before the wind could reform, he put his foot down and tore away, moving faster than it could possibly keep up. They shot along the road through the flowing traffic, away into town. She watched through the mirror, her face red, her hair twisted and tangled. She couldn't bring herself to say anything. The wind was getting stronger by the minute, and it knew exactly where she would be heading.

She had no doubt it was coming after her.

6.DEPA|RTURE

The rush home was frantic. Isabel wrenched open the bungalow door and piled in off the street. Strands of windswept hair snagged on the woodwork, but she forced her way through, tearing them out at the roots.

Numb to the pain.

She was too wound up to focus. Every second of the journey had felt like a desperate bid for survival, racing back before the wind caught up and engulfed her. There could be no denial. Some kind of creature was after her, one without physical form, but with clear intent to harm.

She put a hand on the wall for support, a rasping in every breath from her second asthma attack in as many days. That thing had followed her miles out of the city and chosen its moment to strike, and followed her specifically, just as it had followed her home the day before. Fading autumn daylight crept through open curtains, filling the house with shadows. She wanted to keep running – to go with Andrew where the wind wouldn't find her – but she couldn't leave without her partner.

'Scott?' she called out. 'Scott, are you in here?'

His phone had been switched off for some time. Isabel marched down the hallway and across the lounge, hoping to find him in the garden burning more boxes. Instead, all she found was the metal drum on its side, untouched from the night before, surrounded by still air and deceptive silence.

The front door slammed. Isabel felt the floor shudder. She ducked behind the settee as a draught entered the room, followed swiftly by a familiar cough. 'Scott.' She stood up sharply. 'Come on, we need to leave right now.'

Scott froze mid-stride, appearing shocked by her tone. 'What's wrong?'

'The wind attacked me again.' Her arms were tense, her fingers taut. 'Properly this time. It pushed me into the road.'

He approached with apparent caution, raising his hands to the knots in her hair. 'Are you hurt?'

'I'm alright,' she said. 'A few scrapes, but it was close.'

He wore a look of reluctance above his collar and tie. 'It's no surprise you were caught out. We've had blustery weather all day so far.'

'That's not true. When I went out for lunch, it was utterly calm. Look outside, there's not a whiff of movement.'

She gestured towards the window. Scott hesitated. 'It was blowing a gale outside the office this morning, right up until I left, maybe half an hour ago.'

'Which is when it came to me.' Her stomach lurched. 'We have to assume it's watching both of us, then. We need to leave.'

'And go where? Remember, we were safe here last night, and we agreed to form a plan before we left ...'

'That was before I thought it could lift a brick off the pavement and smash its way inside. It could blast down the walls for all we know.' She paused to catch her breath again, swallowing hard with a dry throat. 'My point is we have to assume the worst. Let's go where it can't follow, somewhere it can't reach us.'

'We will. We've agreed to this already. We want the same thing.'

'But now, Scott. Not tomorrow or in a month. Throw some things in a bag and off we go.'

He increased the distance between them, raising his hands in surrender. 'I've stood inside that wind, myself. I was right in the middle and never once felt threatened. I agree it's more than freak weather, but that's all we know for certain. Please come and sit down.'

He tried to usher her away from the window, but she stood her ground. In the corner of her eye, she kept imagining movement, keeping her from being able to sit still. 'This isn't a case of finding out what we think it is,' she said. 'It's about confirming who we both know it has to be.'

Scott appeared to grow more agitated. 'Let's suppose you're right, and that's Wren. Why would he attack you? He thought the world of you.'

'I don't know,' she said, rubbing her temples. 'Maybe because of the last time I saw him? We argued in the hospital, while you were in your coma. He was deranged, nothing like the man I knew. He changed so much. His feelings towards me could have changed, too.'

'And me? I'm the one he tried to kill, yet the wind barely touched me.'

'Then it's either someone who likes you, or someone who doesn't know you at all. But they definitely hate me because of the way they attacked. And don't tell me that's all in my head, because Andrew saw it, too.'

Scott turned to face her. He was darkened by her shadow. 'You were with Andrew?'

'He came to see me after work, which you agreed to this morning. Then I asked him to take me somewhere.'

'You got in a car with him?'

'I had to,' she said. 'Something came up that couldn't wait.'

Scott seemed lost in thought for a moment. 'How many times do we have to go through this? You're asking for trouble whenever you two meet.'

'I know, I know. All we do is go in circles. He saved me today. He kept me safe.'

Scott held her stare and they locked in a stalemate, neither one relenting. 'What did the wind make of him? You know what Wren would have done.'

'There was a lot going on. I can't say for certain.'

'Is he in the same state you are?'

'Well, no …' Isabel sighed, resolving to come clean. 'We had an appointment with a solicitor.'

Scott blinked more than once. 'For what?'

'Wren's father, Jon. He's dead.'

The news stopped him in his tracks. He hesitated, as though revisiting some of his distress. Jon Lawton was father to the man who had almost killed him, father to a man who had defied death, now taken by it.

Scott's voice grew faint. 'What happened?'

'I've been left all of his belongings,' she said. 'Basically, by mistake. I was the only surviving person named in the will.'

'I mean how did he die?'

'I didn't get specifics. I didn't even think to ask. I just know he was home, so I assumed bad health.'

Scott teetered on the balls of his feet, then lowered himself onto the sofa.

'Are you alright?' she asked.

'I can't believe—' He cut himself short, raising a hand to his face. 'Are you saying the wind got him?'

'Perhaps,' she said. 'And if it didn't, there's every chance it's because the wind *is* him.'

Behind glassy eyes, it seemed Scott wasn't really listening. Despite her restless desire to escape from the house, she sat down beside him. 'Why are you so upset?' she asked. 'You hardly even knew him.'

'That's not the point, don't you see? If Jon Lawton is gone, then maybe you're right and it's starting again. If he had no one else in his life, then who else would he haunt?'

Isabel looked up and checked through the window. 'We should leave, as I've been saying. Throw some things in a bag and let's go before it finds us. Forget about your job and everything else. Let's just leave.'

He shook his head, shivering. 'I want to talk to it.'

'Are you serious?' said Isabel. 'Don't say that. It could hurt us both.'

'Maybe we could reason with it, maybe stop this before it starts.'

Isabel took his hand and gripped it firmly. 'Jon left me everything he owned, which I'm sure he didn't mean to. I can refuse, but the damage is done. What more reason would he need to come after me?'

'He is – he was – an old man,' said Scott. 'Are you sure he's capable of what you're suggesting?'

'Wren got his violent streak from somewhere.'

She leaned against her partner, offering the comfort of her body weight, but Scott shook her off. 'I can't handle this.' He was on his feet before he knew it. 'I'm sorry, I just need to—'

***

He stumbled to the bathroom and shut himself inside, desperate for privacy. Alone, he ran the taps and put his face under cold water. It was near impossible to calm down, to reduce his level of distress.

Jon Lawton was gone, perhaps forever, or perhaps waiting outside at that very moment. The mere thought of it shattered any hope for future happiness. He creased over with his head in his hands and let the tears fall, shedding his façade for long enough to let the emotions out.

He drew a deep breath and held it for five whole seconds, piecing himself back into an ostensibly complete human being.

Isabel couldn't be allowed to see how strongly he was affected. She needed his support, not the other way around. While she sat quietly in the lounge, naïve and oblivious, he straightened up and tried to recompose himself in the mirror, to force his true self back down beneath the surface.

He took a towel off the rail and dried his cheeks, trying to pretend his episode had never happened. The man in the reflection held his gaze, helping him to reset. He could handle this. He had survived worse, and against impossible odds. He had grown since then. He had learned a great deal. He wasn't Scott as everyone had known him, and thank goodness. He was a different man altogether, a better man, a more decent man.

A man twice reborn.

7.PRED|ACITY

Death had a duality, like any permanent change of state. On the one hand, it was cruel. It vanquished, it dominated, it rarely gave warnings, and it never sought permission. That was the death most people dreaded, a fear born of misunderstanding and a lifetime in its shadow. But death had another side. It lacked prejudice. It released. It promised and rewarded.

No one understood that quite like Wren Lawton. Twice now, he had seen what death had to offer. He had drifted in the endless, silent darkness, the almost incomprehensible sense of nothing at all. Without being there, he never would have appreciated the lure of such inertia. There was no anger on the other side, no pain or despair. Negative thoughts lost their influence. Wren's taste of it had been like wiping his conscience clean, and ever since, he would have welcomed his demise with open arms. But the choice didn't seem to be his. Unseen forces had twice dragged him back from the brink, cursing him with life renewed. He was trapped in a world that had long forgotten the goodness in him, forcing him to fill every waking breath with necessary lies.

Two and a half years had passed since a heart attack had levelled him on a beach promenade in broad daylight. His physical form was long gone, reduced to a pile of ash in a wooden box. Only his consciousness had survived, the essence of him, stuffed into a stranger's body. Andrew Goodwin had been his first. Within Andrew, he had made a great many mistakes. He had laboured to reinstate his past life. If anything, he had been too honest, assuming those who cared about him would accept the strange miracle of his return. The result had been a disaster, leading to such harsh rejection that Wren had thrown himself from a railway bridge in a desperate bid to escape.

He had wanted – and expected – the soothing darkness, but after a brief taste of it, he had simply woken up in someone else, thrust behind the gossamer shell of another recent corpse. This one was steeped in irony.

Isabel's partner, Scott.

The man he had murdered.

Wren hadn't been given a say in the matter. It seemed as though Scott had been selected, even resurrected by his well-meaning captor. On that fateful day by the lakeside in the summertime, that same unseen force had heaved Scott's drowning body back to shore and kept it breathing. His captor – his own mother – hadn't tried to save the man inside. Perhaps she hadn't cared. All she had needed was an empty vessel for her son.

Scott had been a twisted love rival. His blunt words still resonated in their shared memories, as fresh as the day they were spoken in anger. *'Be a distant friend or be nothing at all. You can get out of the car right now and kiss goodbye to ever seeing her again.'*

Scott had died in the car he referred to. Wren had since taken over every aspect of his existence without misgivings, taking pleasure in the deposition. It hadn't even been that hard. Scott was the opposite of Andrew Goodwin – a man of strong heart, but of weak mind. Wren had found it almost too easy to assume control, as though Scott had never pulled out of his coma and wasn't there to resist. No stray thoughts echoed inside that head. He felt like a complete person for the first time in years, no longer afraid of losing control when he fell asleep, his host reclaiming what was rightfully theirs.

Wren was familiar enough with Scott's behaviour to fool most people, even those at work. Any missteps, he could blame on the coma. Isabel had no idea who she was living with. She showed him tenderness. She didn't resist when he took her by the hand. But as he stood in the bathroom of the little bungalow, he once again faced a duality. Their relationship was under pressure from external forces. They were being plagued by a mysterious wind, something he didn't yet understand. And now, Jon Lawton was gone. His father, dead. Wren buried his face in the towel for a second time, trying to dry his tears. Jon could have been sick for months. Maybe someone could have helped. He had been too caught up in himself to find an excuse to visit, and the sudden guilt almost knocked him off his feet.

With great difficulty, Wren reassembled his façade. Hearing Isabel share the news with such disinterest was devastating in itself. She didn't even seem to care how it happened. He needed to find out more, not grant her wish to flee. He needed her to do what he wanted.

He straightened his appearance and let himself back into the lounge. 'Sorry I ran off,' he said, clearing his throat. 'I don't know what came over me, but I'm alright now.'

Winter's afternoon filled the space with dark corners. Isabel stood by the window, staring out into the garden. She still seemed agitated. 'Hurry up and pack a bag so we can leave.'

He tried to mimic Scott's body language as he closed the gap between them, reliant upon muscle memory. It had taken some adjustment to get used to his new physique. Scott was short and stocky, with a natural strength Wren hadn't experienced before. 'I still don't think we should act in haste. Stay here with me tonight, then leave prepared in the morning. I'll fortify the windows if you think it will help.'

'Don't waste your time,' she said, stubbornly, though a feeble wheeze undermined her apparent fortitude. 'Nothing's keeping me here for another minute longer.'

'I understand.'

He couldn't argue too hard or risk her shutting down, refusing to hear his carefully selected logic. And broadly, he agreed with her. The bungalow had become Scott's domain, full of irritating little changes made in the years since Wren had lived there. Moreover, the place they had both worked together seemed to have forgotten his contributions, perhaps because Scott had managed to steal most of the credit.

The world punished Wren daily by making him answer to Scott's name, a more painful experience in times of love than of anger. His revenge was to slowly remove all physical trace of Scott's past. The sooner he could move away and start a new life, the better. The sooner he could burn every photograph, the better. The only reason it hadn't happened already was the challenge of doing it in character, without accidentally revealing his true motivations.

'At least come away from the window,' he said. 'Stay or go, it'll do no good to keep staring out there.'

He went to the corner of the room and flicked on a table lamp. The mood changed. Instead of looking out at fading daylight, the glass became a mirror. He couldn't see through it, whereas anything outside would have seen right in.

'Turn that off,' she said.

'Close the curtains,' he countered.

'How can you be so calm? I've seen it almost smash through a window thicker than that, and will you look at the state of me?'

Her hair was a tangled mess after being attacked on her way to see the solicitor. Her knuckles looked red raw from being dragged across rough concrete. She had bruises down her forearms.

'I'm not saying you're wrong to be worried,' said Wren, 'but it couldn't get in here last night, could it?'

'It's stronger now,' she said. 'Once it gets here, we'll be trapped, not protected. How do we defend ourselves if it finds a way in?'

Wren sighed with frustration. The wind had been outside his office for much of the day. He would have tried communicating with it, but the management had him under close scrutiny since his extended leave of absence, as though they expected him to break something. He couldn't exactly start talking to the weather.

Despite believing every word she said, he couldn't let her pull him away until he knew more. He made a conscious choice to riddle her with doubt. 'There was nothing out there when I came home, and there still isn't now. What makes you so sure we're in danger?'

'It followed me—'

'You clearly left it far behind. If it follows, that means it knows the way, and can be bothered making the effort. That's a lot to assume will happen.'

He could see Isabel chewing the inside of her mouth, his words chipping away at her resolve. 'We should prepare for the worst,' she said.

'Then we'll pretend we're not here. How would it know any different? Close the curtains, take a seat, and catch your breath. We don't need to do anything drastic.'

The assurance drained from her body language. Isabel looked deep into his eyes, and just for a second, he thought she saw through skin and bone to the man inside, that he had spoken too far out of character. Thankfully, she seemed too caught up in herself to see the inconsistencies in his behaviour.

Blinded by paranoia.

'I'm scared,' she said, then sat down on the sofa.

He seized the chance to pull one of the curtains closed. 'Nothing you've said is implausible. I believe you. But we need to think very carefully before we make our next move. Give me all the detail about Wren's father. What happened when he died?'

'There isn't any detail. Our conversation was cut short when the wind attacked.'

'Why would he leave you everything in his will?'

'I assume it was a mistake.'

She reached for her bag and produced a brown envelope. Wren snatched it out of her hand. Inside were reams of paperwork, and several sets of keys. 'You're absolutely sure you don't know what happened to him? What exact words did the solicitor use?'

'He said that someone found him after a few days, which implies he died alone. That was last week.'

Wren wanted a death certificate to prove what she was saying, but all the envelope contained were blank forms and guidance notes. 'Who raised the alarm?' he asked. 'Which room was the body in?'

'Does it matter?' said Isabel. 'The solicitor could tell we were never close, so he didn't elaborate. Maybe he didn't know. He didn't even mention which house he was in at the time.'

'What do you mean by that?' said Wren.

'Jon has a second home that no one knew about, or rather "had". He kept it secret.'

Wren froze. 'A secret?'

'I had that same reaction,' Isabel continued. 'We think it's where Wren grew up. He told me it was sold off, years ago. He lied, obviously.'

Her casual accusation cut deep. Wren hadn't lied. He knew as little as she did. Scott's image glared back from the reflection in the window. He watched the lips move in sync with his words. 'There must be an explanation.'

'I want no part in it. There's enough uncertainty as things are. I don't even want to set eyes on either property, let alone profit from their sale.'

'We could be talking about hundreds of thousands of pounds—'

'And one more reason for someone to hate us.' She seemed exasperated, almost breathless. 'Forget the wealth. I should have told the solicitor to shove it, there and then.'

'Now, hang on a second.'

'No, Scott,' she said. 'You're not listening. We're talking about the place where Wren grew up, where he was born. He could be there right now, in whatever form he takes these days. Why would I go within a mile of there?'

He couldn't argue. He, too, had no idea why his father still owned the house. He tried to think fast. 'This is our chance, don't you see? Five minutes ago, you wanted to pack a bag and get far away. Here's your opportunity.'

'Not there.' Isabel stood. 'That's worse than staying put. I'm not heading halfway across the country to be somewhere I'd feel even less safe.'

'Think of it as our reward,' said Wren. 'Maybe Jon didn't change his will because he felt guilty for all you went through. You've been pushing for a fresh start all summer so let's at least see what these houses have to offer. The wind won't go all that way looking for you. I promise you that.'

'So now you agree it's following me?'

'Either way, it can't hurt to pay a visit.'

Isabel perched on the edge of one of the cushions, looking vulnerable. 'We wouldn't find any of the answers you'd want down there, Scott. All we'd find is more trouble.'

Wren closed the gap between them. Grief sat heavy in his stomach, unlike anything he had ever felt before. He took Isabel's hands and realised they were cold. 'This could change our lives. You understand that, don't you?'

Her composure faltered. For a moment, he thought she was going to accept his proposition. But then she stiffened. 'I can't do it, Scott. I'm not – *not* – going anywhere I think is unsafe.'

He found himself nodding. He couldn't push the matter, and he had learned to bide his time. 'Alright, you don't have to. Let's sleep on it before we make any decisions. Please do that much. We'll lock the doors, go into the room with the smallest window, and pretend we're not here.'

Isabel calmed in his embrace, reassuring him that they still shared a strong connection. In truth, he was the one that needed the comfort. His own father had kept his childhood home, and been secretive about it, allowing Wren to believe it had been sold. What justification could he possibly give? What was waiting down there?

Even as he held her close, Wren stared down at the keys in the brown envelope. He couldn't let her return them without finding some answers, and if there was any risk she might act on a whim, then time was of the essence.

He had to see it for himself.

8.ENTW|INING

Night passed without incident, none that Wren was aware of. Morning banished the clouds, and in the unforgiving light of a new day, he was relieved to find no danger lurking outside the little bungalow.

He stood in the front doorway with Isabel by his side. Scott's jet-black Range Rover was parked on the pavement, a short dash away. Even the strongest gusts would never shift it. All that rose above the silence was the ever-present hum of distant traffic, but it paid to be cautious. The dormant scene was vital to convince Isabel not to leave the city, which in turn was vital for his own plan. With a little encouragement, she marched quickly down the path to the passenger door, in the open for no more than five seconds before, with a clunk, she was safely in the vehicle. She didn't speak, as she had barely spoken all morning, instead nodding to confirm she was secure.

He hated seeing her so disturbed, but adjusting to their life together was never going to be easy. Isabel loved Scott. She had been with him for years. He couldn't express the way it made him feel, not to any living soul. Though Wren had ultimately conquered his rival, he struggled to accept that, even with its ups and downs, she may have preferred the life she thought she was living to the life they had once shared.

He locked the front door of the bungalow and followed, without her trepidation. He knew little more than she did, but he remained unconvinced that the wind was a serious threat. So long as she stayed indoors, she would be beyond its reach. He had persuaded her to spend another day at the bank, distracted, and surrounded by people who would help if any trouble found its way to her. Andrew Goodwin had agreed to collect her after hours, which he could stomach for one day.

He, himself, had no intention of going to work. His employers would probably be relieved if he called in sick, and he could make good use of nine hours he wouldn't need to account for.

Long enough to hit the road.

***

Autumn's effect became more pronounced, the further Wren drove from the city. Orange-coloured trees stood in orderly rows between patchwork fields of browns and yellows. Mid-morning shadows were long and well-defined.

He headed west down a dual carriageway with the sun at his back. Cool air trickled in through half-open windows. His plan was simple, but he needed to keep moving. He could get to his father's house and back in a day, returning the keys before Isabel realised they were gone. He kept his foot pressing down on the pedal as the car dipped and swerved, taking corners with reckless abandon.

He drove in silence, troubled by his thoughts. It hurt to lose his father, in some ways worse than the pain of his cardiac arrest. And yet the grief came with a burning intrigue. He had been raised in that house. His mother had died within its walls. The fact his father had pretended to sell it didn't make a lick of sense.

Had Jon known what he was doing? Had he been of sound mind?

Across the Welsh border, lanes merged. A flat landscape began to undulate, like the corners of a ruffled blanket. He drove for several minutes in the shadow of steep hills. The route was etched into his mind, even from within a stolen body. He took an unmarked turnoff, where an isolated road led him upwards between towering hedgerows, to emerge high up on the hillside.

The view opened out, and after such a long absence, it stole his breath. He could see for miles, to the glint of distant traffic on the facing slope. It was a valley of forests and greenery, with few traces of human activity. An overhang of stone promised a swift and perilous descent into swaying treetops, and beside a narrow gravel car park, he saw a white sign with rusted lettering.

Welcome to Pontrhyd-y-werddon.

Welcome home.

Even weighed against his troubled afterlife, it was a poignant moment. He never could have pictured himself coming back there, not least under such sobering circumstances. Pontrhyd-y-werddon was a moderate cluster of houses on a high vantage point. There were perhaps a hundred properties in total, a mix of semi-detached and terraced, none of which were a day less than seventy years old.

The village had looked tired before he moved away, but in the years since, the process seemed to have accelerated. Deep potholes rocked the Range Rover back and forth as he descended. The pavement was littered with debris, including a skeletal tree that must have blown down in a storm and had never been cleared. As he came among the first buildings, he saw long grasses draped over the side of every gutter. Moss clung in strips between the cracks in peeling paint. Hedgerows grew thick, obscuring windows.

A sense of sadness hung in the air. He headed for the bottommost row of terraces, with his former home at the far end. It was a huge relief to find it in a favourable state. The paintwork looked fresh and unbroken. The bush beside the front door was trim and neat. He instantly became possessive. His rightful inheritance was there for the taking, if he could prove his entitlement. He couldn't, of course. He knew that. Instead, the property was destined to be auctioned off, doubtless to be stripped down to bare brick and renovated, so ending the Lawton legacy.

He parked beside the short front path and lifted the brown envelope he had stolen from Isabel, digging out the keys. Tears of anger formed in his eyes. This could be the last time he ever saw inside the house, at least without having to feign disgust for the sake of appearances. He climbed out and approached. The front lock was stubborn, but he knew how to work it. Hinges groaned as they opened, and a subtle draught crept past him like a ghostly exhale.

There was something in the smell – indescribably familiar, thick, and everywhere. The scent of nostalgia flooded his nose and triggered countless memories, but also something beneath that, something less palatable. How he was so certain, he couldn't say, but he knew beyond reasonable doubt that his father had died in the hallway. He knew it wholeheartedly, as though able to sense death like so much electricity in the air.

The plain fibres of the carpet looked to have been disturbed, as though brushed or scrubbed clean before being reset. It suggested where Jon Lawton had lain forgotten for days. The hairs rose along his forearms. Both of his parents' lives had ended in that building, the walls saturated with dramatic pivots in his history. The importance of those walls was impossible to overstate.

He made a whistle-stop inspection of the house. Dining room furniture had long since been removed, taken with Jon to the city. Four bright patches on the carpet revealed where a thick oak table had stood for decades in its rightful place. To the rear of the house was the lounge – the largest room, though still less than five meters wide. There was nothing inside except his father's worn settee facing an old television. Even with a low ceiling, the room seemed almost cavernous without any of the furniture he remembered. The two armchairs, the side table … all had been moved closer to Wren when his father had followed.

He lingered in the doorway, reluctant to enter, looking out through the window at the forest and distant hills. Thoughts raced through his mind. His feet moved as though on autopilot, carrying him upstairs to his bedroom. His hand gripped the banister loosely to slide up the smooth wood. He had spent twenty years sleeping in the same single bed and he opened the door to a shock.

It was still there.

His room hadn't been touched since the day he had left. There were posters on the wall from when he was a teenager, and flat-pack furniture he remembered assembling, overtightened joints having split the woodgrain. He remembered being told that everything had gone. His father hadn't minced his words. That was maybe four years ago. He felt a sense of unease. Dust-covered bedsheets lay unwashed, preserved in his memory. It was almost like a tomb, the house a mausoleum, though no one else would see it that way. Left to Isabel, his possessions would be thrown in a skip. She might even relish doing it.

He continued to the master bedroom. It was empty, apart from in one corner. Beneath the window stood a bureau desk with a fold-down lid. A ring binder lay open upon its surface, beside a notepad and a half-full cup of tea. Wren could picture his father in the folding chair, hunched over, embroiled in something he had started but evidently never finished.

Wren approached for a closer look. A thin film of dust had settled over the stagnant drink. The open page in the binder resembled a family tree, with his own name at the bottom. But it was clear from a glance what he was looking at. Jon Lawton had been studying the village – the friendships, marriages, feuds, and rivalries. It was the history of a place, rather than a bloodline. The pile of papers were an inch thick and the handwriting small, a wealth of notes that must have taken an enormous amount of time to assemble.

They were conspicuous by their presence when so much else had been removed. He flicked through them, pausing whenever he encountered a diagram or a sketch. Wren's sheltered upbringing meant that most of the details were new to him. Jon had identified eleven families that made up most of the inhabitants. These were grouped by allegiance, a divide created loosely by geography, with the people high up estranged from the ones down below.

Countless hours had been poured into documenting their lives. Wren sat down, the chair creaking under his weight. He could see right up the hillside from there, almost to the thick stretch of woodland at the top. Most houses were at least partially visible. There were binoculars on the floor by his feet, and he imagined his father sitting there, gathering evidence through observation.

It was all written down. People rose and left for work, then came back in the early evening. Lights went on in bedroom windows, then went off again by midnight. Wren searched for hidden meanings, or that one document that explained it all. But the nature of the observations worked against him. The content seemed entirely mundane. *Why did Jon care enough to write it down? What could have possessed him?*

He felt a tingling beneath his forehead that refused to relent as he rubbed his temples. It was like fatigue, growing stronger as his mind wandered. Wren lowered his guard in a way that he hadn't been able to for months, swathed by privacy and a rare sense of belonging. With each paragraph he scanned, his eyelids grew heavier, until he eventually closed them altogether. For a blissful few seconds, he drifted in darkness, as though revisiting the purgatory where he had once found peace. Then his mobile phone rang in his pocket.

He sat up with a jolt, regaining his sensibilities. As he pulled away from slumber's grasp, he looked down at the research and realised the words had become difficult to make out. Darkness was falling, which meant hours must have gone by. He stood up, backing away from the desk. His first thought was Scott, and whether he had lost control while unconscious. But his body hadn't moved an inch, and the notes were undisturbed.

Still, no other explanation made sense. He checked the time. Wren had missed the chance to slip home before Isabel noticed he was gone. The phone continued to ring in his pocket, and only one person ever called him. He swore, then swore again. Something felt gravely wrong, something he had no time to process.

He cleared his throat and answered, trying to hide his unease. 'Hey there.'

'I'm back from work.' Isabel's voice crackled through the speaker. 'I can see treetops moving in the garden.'

'You mean it's windy again? Did it attack you?'

'No, not yet. It's only very slight, probably not the same thing. But I still don't like it. When are you coming home?'

A handful of street lamps flickered to life up the road through the centre of the village, the first sign of life that he had seen on his visit. He deliberated until the silence was palpable. There were already too many lies in his life to sustain another. 'There's something I need to tell you … I've been at the Lawton house, the secret one.'

He could almost hear her face drop. 'What?'

'I wanted to see it for myself, and I knew how you'd react, so I came here alone.'

'Of course you knew how I'd react,' said Isabel. 'Scott, we discussed this and agreed it was a bad idea. I don't want to know what's down there, and I don't like the thought of you being so far away.'

He swallowed hard. 'I've found something already. There's still furniture down here, and all this research—'

'I don't care,' she said. 'How long until you're back?'

He closed his eyes and grimaced, still able to feel the tingling in his forehead. 'Even if I set off now, it would take most of the evening.'

'So you haven't even left yet?'

'Please, just listen,' he said. 'I got sidetracked. There's too much to absorb in one afternoon. It feels like I just got started.'

'What does that mean? What have you found?'

'I don't know yet. There are notes and … I don't know. Even if I came back tonight, I'd still want to return, first chance I got.'

'Surely you're not suggesting you stay there overnight?'

He thought for a moment. 'Maybe I am.' She gasped, and he knew how unlike Scott he must have sounded, so he chose his next words carefully. 'I need a bit more time to understand what I'm looking at. Now that you're safely indoors, I could sleep here tonight and drive home in the morning.'

'Sleep in that house?' she said. 'Have you gone mad?'

'I'll find a bed and breakfast.'

'But you know we're supposed to be saving.'

'Please, don't.' He tried to control his voice. 'This is important to me. You got to hang around with Andrew Goodwin yesterday and I just had to accept that, so you owe me something in return.'

'How is this even remotely similar?'

'It's about trust and freedom, both of which you're losing sight of. I have a real chance to make everything … logical again, to understand it so I can move on with my life. There are insights here, more that I was hoping for. Are you too absorbed in your own problems to acknowledge that?'

'Something attacked me yesterday.' Her words sounded like they came through gritted teeth. 'You know damn well how much I've been supporting you lately, but you're the one who's abandoned me here.'

Wren took a deep breath and held it momentarily. 'Well, I didn't mean to, and I'm sorry for that. It was only meant to be a quick look around, and that's the honest truth.'

'What am I supposed to do if the wind picks up and you're not here?' she asked. Crackling on the line threatened to cut her off.

'Keep the curtains closed and put it out of your mind,' he said. 'It can't get inside. Call a taxi in the morning, or Goodwin if you must. Don't walk to the bank.'

'You can't expect me to …' He struggled to make her out through the static. '… and say there's another … How am I supposed … don't have a car.'

'Even if I dropped everything,' he started, but thought twice. Wren extended the phone to arm's length, listening to a stuttering hiss.

And ended the call.

He didn't want to discuss things any further. His mind was already made up. He turned the phone off completely and slipped it into his pocket. There were too many unanswered questions. Isabel would have to accept he wasn't coming back, and even if she didn't, the outcome wouldn't change.

He needed to know more about the sensation in his head and what it meant. He couldn't resist the urge to glean insights from those notes. He might even be able to salvage something physical from the ruin of his bygone life. Most tempting of all, he could savour one last evening as his true self before Isabel inevitably got her way, and his memory was lost forever.

He could feel like the real Wren Lawton.

9.BREA|CH

Wren woke with a start, to absolute darkness. He was reminded once again of the endless void he longed for, but this darkness had to be real because he couldn't see his hands.

Instead of floating, weightless, he felt gravity draw him into the worn-out frame of his father's sofa. He tensed his thigh muscle and heard a creak. He was therefore in the living room, with no impression of how far away the walls were, nor the drawn curtains across the windows. He could easily pretend he was back in the bungalow, listening to Isabel asleep beside him. Perhaps it would turn out to be true.

He gazed into the black. It had only been intended as a minute's rest. He had sat down on the sofa, purely for the experience. That must have been hours ago. He hadn't even begun to search for a place to stay overnight, other than to rule out sleeping in his old bedroom. That was a step too far. The room had become a dust-covered shrine worthy of being preserved, not tainted by introducing Scott's reek.

Whether it was one o'clock in the morning or five o'clock, he couldn't say. Wren slipped off his shoes and wrapped himself in a throw blanket. Sharp springs poked through aged cushions and dug into his side. Any shift in his position had unpleasant consequences. His mind did something similar, his conscience taking jabs as it wandered. It had been a rash, impulsive decision to visit the house. Wren hadn't been more than a few miles away from his partner in months and he hated not being there to protect her.

To control her.

Anything could happen in his absence. Lingering doubts could find the freedom to develop. She was already consumed by her obsessions, and Wren's recent behaviour only threatened to make that worse. Unless he could be with her to seed doubts and keep her guessing, he risked losing the fresh start he strived so heavily for – a life unburdened by having to recall Scott's entire life story on demand.

Then there was the headache. Deprived of other senses, the tingling sensation beneath his forehead seemed much stronger. Parts of his brain were stimulated by it, like a sense of being in a familiar presence. He wondered whether it was a connection to his father, or even his mother, like a phantom limb still tingling long after any physical bond had been severed. He wished he had anyone to talk to about it, anyone who could understand.

He had tried to numb the effects with alcohol. There had been no food in the cupboards, further proof that no one lived there. But a bottle of whiskey had improved with age and helped to steady his nerves. It was his first drink since the days of Andrew Goodwin and it had left him dehydrated. The lack of spatial awareness was perhaps the only thing keeping him from the effects of being drunk. With no sense of the walls, they couldn't start spinning.

He knew the sofa from its heyday. He forgot about his borrowed body and imagined he was eighteen again, that his father was asleep upstairs while he watched television. They had never really been close to one another. Jon Lawton might have readily explained to any casual enquirer why he was spying on the other villagers. There could have been a very good reason for it, but Wren had never known to ask, nor would have been inclined to because of the gulf between them.

A sense of movement in the room interrupted his thoughts. An object emerged from the darkness, almost imperceptibly small. All he could see of it was a fleck of light, like the offshoot of a bonfire, buffeted across the room on the motions of a non-existent breeze.

He didn't know what to make of it. Wren had sometimes experienced a similar sensation when he stood up too fast, in the days of his declining health, in the run-up to his heart attack. The thing left a smear across his retina like a wavy line, a dream-like aura. He flexed bare toes to check he was awake, and to his surprise, the spark reacted. It lurched in the direction of the window and vanished, leaving nothing but a ghostly after-image on his eyeball.

He remained in position for a moment, more perplexed than scared, close enough to sleep that he could feel a mild paralysis. But before he could decide what to do, a second speck drifted through the carpet threads. This one was closer than the first, and made the faintest noise as it moved, like the high-pitched buzzing of a mosquito's wings, or the scrape of a fingernail drawn across a blackboard.

This object had no sense of purpose. It danced through the air almost playfully, until it got too close, and an unseen hand seemed to grab hold and fling it towards the window. A third one took its place almost immediately, then a fourth, then three at once, then seven.

The room became awash with tiny lights that made the air shimmer, though Wren felt no heat. The noise grew less subtle as it multiplied – buzzing wings, scraping nails, and scratching, like rats moving behind the walls. Shadows flickered dimly off the wallpaper and made him nervous. He could be overwhelmed if he didn't act fast.

He gripped the armrest to pull himself upright, but the room was against him. Tired springs creaked as his weight transferred and the specks became agitated, darting from side to side, mixing like a disordered swarm. He stood up, and every one of them changed direction, repelled across the room, twisting now like a shoal of fish. Their point of entry into the room shifted to the curtains instead of the floor, pouring through like a cascading waterfall. Each spark itself only lived for a few seconds, but they kept on coming, splashing on the ground.

Two hundred, then three hundred.

Thoroughly awake, he felt cold sweat beading on his forearms. The room glowed with unnatural brightness, which he used to retreat across the room until his hands met with cool, rough wallpaper. Some sparks tried to break loose and come after him, but snapped back into line, as though tethered to the rest. Then, when Wren was as far away as he could get, everything changed again. The sparks vanished altogether, as though turned off at the source. Wren was plunged into darkness, his eyes stained with countless light trails, and stayed frozen that way until a new sound emerged from the silence.

Chipping glass.

Something was outside the window. He panicked for a moment, feeling an urge either to fumble for the light switch or leave the room altogether. There was no way to gauge the level of threat. The sparks had reacted to his presence, but that didn't necessarily mean they had intelligence. They could have been no more dangerous than insects. They may not even have been real.

Intrigue got the better of him and he decided to have at least a quick peek behind the curtains before he made any irreversible decisions. He advanced on his bare feet, using his memory of the room's layout to navigate. His outstretched palms found creased fabric and he worked his way towards the gap between them.

He peered outside with one eye. Clouds had gathered in the fallen night. The valley was fast asleep. Faint moonlight proved ample for his accustomed eyes, and he could see there were no dancing lights in the garden. Nothing was moving, and yet there was still that sound of scraping and scratching. Desperately curious, he felt his way to the draw cord by the window frame and slowly drew the curtains open.

There were people at the window. Standing in the garden were a dozen silhouettes, pressed up against the glass – hunched bodies of different heights and builds, all in a row, shoulder to shoulder. They were close enough to touch, yet in the darkness, Wren couldn't fathom a single detail on their faces and bodies. They formed an irregular black mass, recognisable only by its overall shape. It resembled a picket line, making contact with the glass until the latter bulged under pressure.

They were there for him. There could be no other explanation. Faint cracks riddled the glass. Something crunched, and he understood what was going to happen next. Panic returned. He staggered away from the outer wall, searching for a place to shelter. He leapt behind the sofa, landing so hard on the floor that he bounced. With a deafening crash, the window collapsed. It didn't just break. It shattered, launching bullets into the air with unnatural force.

He buried his head as the sofa almost reared up onto its hind legs. Upholstery tore with a wrenching *rip*. He heard the wall beside him get peppered with a hail of fragments. He was left with a ringing in his ears, now deafened and paralysed. For several agonising seconds, he was too scared to move, barefoot, waiting for the mob to come inside and tear him limb from limb. A chill snaked in through the empty frame and curled around his elbows. An isolated smash sounded like the ceiling light crashing to the floor.

He held his breath, then after half a minute, let it out again. Another half a minute and he dared to lift his head. No one had come inside. The shadows had vanished, nowhere to be seen. They hadn't bludgeoned him to death. They hadn't explained themselves.

The curtains had fallen off, increasing the level of light in the room. The window had completely gone. Every surface shimmered with broken glass, as though covered in a blanket of frost. He realised his shoes were on the other side of the sofa, out of reach, and themselves likely covered as well. If this was his chance to escape, he was going to have to think fast.

Leaning over the sofa, he collected the two cushions he had been using for pillows, now both torn on one side. He turned them upside down and threw them on the floor, creating a line of stepping stones that led towards the door. After giving himself a count of three, Wren hopped from one to the other and made a break for the hallway, not looking back until he succeeded in reaching safe ground.

There wasn't time to self-congratulate. He turned back to pull the door closed, but noticed something new in the distance. There was still one person out there – a familiar figure, different to the others. Beyond a damaged stone wall at the bottom of the garden lay a deceptively peaceful scene, growing lighter by the second in the pending dawn. At the foot of the hillside, by the edge of the forest, stood a woman.

His mother.

Long, dirty hair was lifted by a gentle breeze, shivering about her face. She wore a green hospital gown that sank down to her knees. He knew the hem was stained in blood, for she had been dead his entire life, frozen in her final moments, the agony still present on her straining face.

Her name was Hope. She had been watching over him for his entire life, only letting herself be known when he seemed to be at risk. Wren had only understood that in recent times. He hadn't seen her since the summer, and her appearance proved the threat was very real. Terrifyingly so.

Despite the distance, the two of them locked eyes, but then a pain tore through his foot as he drifted towards the living room. A thick shard of glass had embedded in his toe, glistening and impossibly sharp. He bent down to pluck it out, and when he looked up again, she had disappeared.

He shut the door and limped upstairs, going straight to the bathroom. He opened a small, square, opaque window and leaned out as far as he could, afforded a better view of the hillside from on high. The day seemed brighter from up there, as though minutes away from sunrise. He could tell beyond a shadow of doubt that he was alone. No mother, no crowd.

He scanned the row of back gardens, all bordered by tall fences and stone walls. He scanned the treeline of the forest. There was no sign of the mob from his garden, not a soul in sight. Anxious, Wren came back inside and rushed across the landing to his bedroom, aware of warm blood seeping from his wounded toe. Abandoning any sense of preservation, he ran to yet another window and looked down at the front of the house. Nothing.

A dozen people had simply vanished.

He needed to lean out and be certain. He lifted the catch and was pushing the window when something stirred in the room behind him. A gust of wind poured into the back of his head, coming from inside the house. The window was torn right out of his hands, almost ripped off the hinges.

He grabbed the sill to keep from being thrown outside. His wardrobe rattled as it shifted on its balance, threatening to topple down and crush him. He heard a shriek of apparent rage. Dropping to all fours, he fought his way back to the bedroom door, placing his weight behind it until it closed with a clunk. Instantly, the channel through the house sealed and the wind died, evaporating like it was never there.

In the restored stillness, he struggled to think straight. Two days before, he had stood inside a cyclone, in the garden of the bungalow. It had toyed with him, but that had been miles away, hours of driving. That couldn't be the same wind. Surely, it couldn't. Wren felt exposed. He opened the wardrobe and stole a pair of his old shoes and a padded jacket. Neither was a perfect fit. The shoes were too small and the jacket sleeves fell short of his wrists by several inches. But they offered more protection than nothing would. The morning would be there any minute, and when he had awoken with Isabel the day before, the evening's wind hadn't been there. Maybe the same thing would happen this time.

He put an ear to the door and listened to the landing. Once again, calm had descended as though nothing had ever happened. Was it trying to lull him into thinking nothing was wrong? If so, to an extent, it was working. Wren let himself back onto the landing, closing the door behind him so there wasn't a clear path for the wind to pour through the building. Then he entered the bathroom and sealed himself inside, trading one room for another with a much smaller window.

The lock twisted easily, sealing him inside. The small window hung ajar and he stole a glance through the gap at the garden below. There was a disturbance out there now, the same as he had seen all those miles away. Long grasses bent, tussled by a twisting wind that loitered almost silently where the figures had been.

Beyond the garden wall – and in every other direction – the world appeared still. He stared with perplexity as grit and loose earth circled round and round. From his vantage point three metres above, it was like the gale wasn't even there. It seemed so localised as to defy any logic he could fabricate.

The bathroom window didn't move an inch. He couldn't understand it, and for the second time in as many hours, his doubts manifested in a strong thirst for alcohol.

END OF LIFE

PART TWO: DEATH
10.FOUN|DER

An elbow landed hard in Andrew Goodwin's side, knocking the wind out of his lungs. He stumbled, but defiantly stood his ground.

The pain was worth it.

He could hardly avoid violence in the bustling crowd. The city streets were crammed with pedestrians, weaving around one another with unsettling urgency. He shuffled in a straight line, against the flow of movement. Collisions and near misses were commonplace. A woman trod on his shoe as she passed and shouted abuse back over her shoulder. He didn't care. Causing a disturbance was part of his plan.

And besides, he hated the alternative. Ever since the horrors of summer, time spent alone in his flat was the hardest part of the day. He liked to be around people, prepared to do anything to stand out in case something happened to him again. He wore a bright yellow jacket over a high-collared shirt. Beneath his thick-rimmed glasses, his stubble had been closely shaved to accentuate the scarring down his jawline.

He fought his way along a gentle decline. Andrew tried to hide the difficulty of walking, still recovering from his fall off the bridge three months before. He scanned every scowling face as people tried to walk through him. It was the busiest place he could think of – a railway station. He came there often, always at peak times, but he had no plans to travel, not today, not ever. He didn't want to run.

He was there to fight.

A man with a suitcase piled past, its metal-clad corners narrowly missing his shins. Somewhere deep down, Andrew liked to antagonise. After all, someone had ruined his life, with every chance they had got away with it. He had no faith in divine justice. He entered the main hall to find train carriages abutting sleepers on the platforms. A tannoy system echoed through the cavernous space. The departure board hung down from the ceiling and he put himself beneath it, right in the heart of the commotion.

He leaned against a pillar for some much-needed rest. This was his perch. At one time or another, every person in the room would stop to read the schedule high above him, and as they did, he would look them in the eye, trying to catch their attention. If he stared for long enough, most would see him down there, hard to miss with his distinctive scar and the brightly coloured jacket. It was a natural reaction to glance in his direction, even just for a second, and he made sure to be ready for it, looking for something very specific.

One of those days, he would find it.

Recognition.

Wren Lawton had been out of Andrew's head for months, physically extracted. But he had left a hole in his wake, a sense of emptiness that defied explanation. Some days, Andrew felt emotions he couldn't be sure were his own, making him second-guess everything he thought he knew about himself.

It was humbling. Wren was gone. He had to be. The rest was just residue. But the memories they shared hadn't simply been forgotten. Andrew could picture Wren's heart attack on the seafront. He could picture his death and his rebirth. With closed eyes, Andrew lived traumas that had never been his, like the horror of awakening in a stranger's mind. He felt violated, and increasingly determined to make his adversary pay. It seemed unlikely Wren had gone forever, which meant he was likely inside someone new and just as unwilling.

It could have been anyone. Every soul in that station was a potential threat. Andrew had developed a keen power of observation from weeks of limping around, searching at random. He didn't blink much. He rarely missed a thing. He had no other purpose in his life other than to find Wren again and somehow, by any means possible, take revenge for the pain he had caused.

Nothing could be taken for granted, nothing at all. Isabel had been attacked by a freakish turn of weather, right in front of his eyes. A grown woman had been pulled kicking and screaming across an open pavement by something invisible. It opened up a frightening new world of possibilities. Wren may not be confined to a body anymore. The rules of the living may no longer apply. He could be absolutely anywhere, lurking in the air itself.

Andrew had no way of knowing what the limitations were, which felt crippling. Beneath his thin façade, his confidence had shattered. Without clear direction, he continued to assume Wren had a physical form. Only one tenuous advantage kept him going. He had the trust of the woman Wren wanted more than life itself. The phone rang in his pocket and he answered with a grunt, without looking at the screen.

'You look well.' Isabel sounded serious, matter of fact.

He glanced at surrounding faces, straining to hear her over the bustle. 'How did you know to find me here?'

'It's the only place you ever go. Haven't you seen me yet? I've been watching you for a while.'

After a brief search, he found her nestled in a corner. Isabel looked to have taken to the station in her own way, with her head down and her guard raised, shying away from the hordes. He corrected his posture now he knew she was there. She understood the struggles he had faced, but she didn't know everything. He couldn't bring himself to open up completely. He ended the call and worked his way through the crowd until they were together.

'Are you alright?' he said. 'You look pale.'

She smiled, though he could see her discomfort. 'Can we go somewhere and talk?'

'Of course.'

He abandoned his search for long enough to escort her to a coffee kiosk near the heart of the station. A row of poseur tables ran along the front, with tall stools rooted to the ground. Only one table was available, and Isabel was about to sit when Andrew intercepted her. 'I don't want to make you any more uncomfortable, but I still need to keep an eye out in case someone sneaks up on us.'

'It's okay.' She seemed to swallow her reticence and sat with her back to the main thoroughfare, clearly hating the exposure. 'The wind is my number one concern, and we're far enough indoors that it can't get me, or so I hope.'

'You haven't seen it near a crowd yet. Maybe all these people are enough to put it off.' Andrew checked his watch, lowering his eyes for the shortest time possible. 'Do you think it followed you again?'

'Not that I can tell, but that means nothing. I don't trust my own eyes at the moment.'

'What brings you here?'

'I needed to see a familiar face,' she said. 'After spending a night alone in the house, I couldn't bear the thought of being trapped there all day.'

'What do you mean? Where's Scott?'

Isabel looked down at the table as she took a deep breath. 'He's gone away. He skipped work and went down to Jon Lawton's second home.'

'Didn't you discuss it first?'

'We had a fight two days ago. He didn't see the wind attack me so he doesn't take it seriously. When he first mentioned going to the house, I told him it was a bad idea, but he wouldn't listen. By the time you dropped me home last night, he was long gone.'

Andrew stopped scanning the room. He straightened his back and shook his head. 'Maybe the lure of understanding was too much to resist.'

'You're being too kind. Last time we spoke, he gave me a half-baked explanation before his phone died. It's been switched off ever since. It's not that I don't share his need for answers, but he took the keys and deserted me. He's never done anything like that before.'

'Well, I can keep you company. Let's see what he's like when he gets back. I wish I could offer you better advice. When it comes to recovering from trauma, I wrote the book, but relationships ... As you know, I have a poor track record with those.'

'There's more.' She reached into her bag, fumbling around with apparent urgency. 'I found this in a drawer by his side of the bed.'

Isabel produced a small notebook and slid it over the table. Andrew flipped through the first few pages of mindless, handwritten scrawl. There were spirals, loops, and random words repeated dozens of times. '*Careful, shrink, quarry, epoch.*'

The pressure of the pen was different every time. 'What do you think it means?' Andrew asked.

'I don't know.' Isabel closed her eyes for several seconds. He could see her pupils moving while she thought. 'I knew Scott better than I knew myself, but we've both changed since Wren came back. I'm doing my best to be supportive, but he keeps having these funny turns.'

'It's improving though, isn't it?'

'Whenever I think it is, something drags him back down. I feel isolated, Andrew. My whole world is condensed to a few trusted people, and one of them is … broken. I'm worried I don't look at him the same way I used to.'

He put a hand on top of hers. 'Don't berate yourself for being cautious. Maybe the doctors encouraged him to practise handwriting. Maybe it helps his brain to rewire itself.'

'I wanted to compare it against something he wrote before the coma, to see if it's just me. But I turned the house upside down and there's nothing left. Scott burned it all in the back garden.'

'Could be a coincidence,' said Andrew. 'Maybe he's having trouble with his coordination and doesn't want to worry you. The coma could have affected him more than he's letting on. Some people take years to recover. Others never do.'

'But Scott didn't used to keep secrets.' She shrugged, as though bundling up her feelings and letting them go with the drop of her shoulders. 'Maybe you're right, but I don't know. I feel like I'm losing my mind with each passing day.'

'Of course you're not,' said Andrew. 'It could be he's just doing what's best for himself. I'd be the first to say if I thought your suspicions were well founded, but I don't know about this.'

She looked him in the eye. 'Scott doesn't seem to understand me lately and it feels like I'm turning on him because of it. I'm angry he went down to that house, and angry at myself for not trusting the man I'm living with.'

Andrew could see the strain of so much uncertainty in her life. He could relate to that, and he could help. 'You deserve answers every bit as much as Scott does. So do I, for that matter. So let's not mope around while he finds them all himself. Why don't we get involved?'

She smiled. 'I really don't want to go all the way to Wales.'

He leaned forward and lowered his voice. 'That wasn't what I had in mind.'

11.DIST|RUST

Jagged lumps of shattered glass lay strewn across the living room carpet, making it sparkle in the morning light. Wren's eyes were tricked into thinking it was coated in a thin shell of ice. His childhood home had been transformed from a place of wistful reminiscence to something sinister and foreboding, the scene of a brush with death.

He had seen many strange things during his lifetime and in the period since, but nothing so imposing as the shadows and sparks. This was something new. He stood on grey flagstones in the back garden, staring into the house as the faceless crowd would have done some hours before. Not a single shard remained attached to the wooden window frame, as though every square inch had buckled under the same massive pressure.

He wore old shoes from when he was a teenager, shoes that were bought for a different pair of feet. Raised hairs along his bare forearms alerted him to the slightest movement in the air. Whatever he had encountered at the bungalow back home – with its harrowing, deafening moan – appeared to have followed him all the way to the village of Pontrhyd-y-werddon. It hadn't followed Isabel; It had followed him, as though it had switched fascination after their first encounter.

The garden was a windswept mess, littered with debris and snapped branches from overgrown shrubs. Wren had no hope of finding any footprints, nor trampled undergrowth. But neither did he expect to. The crowd at his window hadn't been comprised of ordinary men and women. That much was clear. He retraced the path they would have taken on approach, climbing over the collapsed section of stone wall at the bottom of the garden and into the field below. There were no clear signs of where the crowd had started from, nor where they had gone to when the sun had risen.

He could see the village stretching up the hillside, as though looming over the back of his father's tiny house. From any angle, the area looked dilapidated. Perhaps the decline had been gradual, and as a child, he hadn't noticed. Perhaps it had happened in the few years since he had left. Moss smothered brickwork. Vegetation hung from gutters. Metalwork had rusted. Windows were split. No one would have lived there by choice, and no one seemed to care what happened to it anymore.

He circled around to the pavement and worked his way up the hillside, straining his calf muscles on the steep incline. What struck him the most was the lack of vehicles, and of the residents themselves. With the outward appearance of a total stranger, his presence should have drawn attention. Visitors to those parts would have been a very rare thing. But he didn't see a soul. The front room of every house he passed was fully furnished, the walls and surfaces decorated with pictures and ornaments, but no one peered back out at him, no one at all.

As he reached the highest point of the village, he turned to look down. Wren could see everything from there: a hundred houses, alone on the edge of the valley, slowly collapsing. Even the forest beyond the stream seemed to have lost its vitality, like an extension of the disease that had struck the small community.

There were, however, some signs of life. A second, healthier forest rose alongside the village until it engulfed the summit, dominating the hilltop. Its branches dripped autumn colours, catching his eye every time a leaf broke loose and drifted to the ground. From within its extent, a two-storey building protruded, the uppermost in Pontrhyd-y-werddon. Upon white-painted walls, gothic lettering had defied decades of weathering.

'The Black Horse.'

No attempt had been made to protect its borders from the encroaching branches, making for a curious sight, like the building had been carved out of the trees. A short flight of uneven stone steps rose to the door, where a layer of forest debris was like a soft welcome mat. Faint wisps of smoke seeped through a solitary open window, carrying the pungent smell of cigars. He was glad, though not surprised, to hear conversation from inside.

He gripped a steel handrail and heaved himself up to the entrance, lifting an iron latch and swinging the heavy oak door ajar. He had been there before, several lifetimes ago. He knew what to expect. It was a dark space, cramped and cluttered. Lamps stood against bare brick walls, supplementing the scant light seeping in. Smoke churned in broken sunbeams. A group of six or seven men sat at a table in an uneven alcove. An eighth sat alone, loading tobacco into a pipe, while a further two – the youngest by a clear margin – nursed half-empty pint glasses by the open window. All were male, and none looked familiar. Wren would have struggled to come up with a single name. They were men he had probably grown up living right next to, yet had never once spoken with.

His shoes clomped on the bare wooden floor. Murmurs of conversation hushed as one of the younger men lowered his glass and spoke. 'Can we help you?'

Wren smiled awkwardly. 'You'd probably guess I'm not here for a drink.'

The man had a distinctly weather-beaten complexion, with leathery skin and spiny crow's feet. He didn't sound impressed. 'You've been around since yesterday. We saw you arrive.'

'I came to see one of the houses at the bottom. I'm hoping you can tell me about the man who lived there.'

'You mean the snoop?' One of the men in the larger group snarled. 'He turns up, now and then. All he ever does is spy on us.'

Wren nodded, trying not to retch from the cigar smoke. 'He died last week.'

An uneasy silence descended, but it lasted less than five seconds. 'Lawton, you call him.' Wren turned at the mention of his surname to see a man in his late twenties with hefty features. Wren didn't need an introduction. His name was Alwyn Speake. A stern set of thick eyebrows echoed a wild, bristly beard. Alwyn and Wren had been friends once, a long time ago. The schoolhouse was small enough that every child in the community had been taught in one classroom, regardless of their age. They had even shared desks.

'I was told he collapsed by the front door,' said Wren. 'Do you know who found the body?'

Alwyn stood up. He was taller than Wren remembered. Strands of wild hair brushed against the low ceiling. 'What's it to you?'

Everything, Wren thought, but couldn't say. 'My name is Scott. I used to work with his son. Out of respect for both their memories, I've come to clear the house.'

'Why? What happened to Wren?'

'He's been dead for two years.'

Alwyn seemed to pause, as though absorbing the news. Behind those chestnut eyes, Wren knew he had a spark of intelligence that he often chose not to reveal. 'Were you close?' came the eventual response. 'You must have known him well to come so far out of your way.'

Wren nodded. 'Much of our lives overlapped.'

The circle of men at the main table appeared cautious. Most of them chose not to speak, but an older man broke the second silence. His wrinkles shook with the movement of his jaw. 'How long are you planning to be here?'

'Another day, maybe,' said Wren. 'I was only intending to pack a few boxes, but I feel it's only right to learn more about the man I'm putting to rest.'

'Don't bother,' said another voice.

Alwyn was more forthcoming. 'We never saw much of him. He moved away a few years back, but returned from time to time. He mostly kept to himself, unless he needed work doing.'

'What kind of work?'

'Odd jobs, some gardening. I used to be known for it around here, so whenever he resurfaced, I'd go round and offer to fix things up for him. Last time was probably a year ago. He hadn't told me he was back.'

'But you found him?'

'We saw his car, parked where yours is now.'

'Of course. What happened to it?'

A third silence took hold, with a palpable tension. 'There's not much kept secret in this village,' said the man with the crow's feet, 'but there's not much discussed, either. We leave people to their business and I suggest you do the same.'

Alwyn Speake stepped forward, extending a thick forearm. 'Maybe you should go. I'll walk you out.'

Feet creaked on the wooden floor as the group became unsettled. 'So that's it?' Wren said. 'You're just going to shut the door and let him be forgotten?'

The elderly man in the corner slammed his pipe down on the table. 'We're closed to outsiders,' he said, 'and I suggest you think twice about staying here longer than you need to.'

'I came for insight. A man is dead. Surely one of you cares?'

122

No one rose to his challenge. Wren relented to a hand in his back and allowed himself to be escorted to the heavy front door and out of the building. He couldn't have fought Alwyn off, even if he wanted to. He was ushered outside to the stone steps and the view across the valley, but was surprised when Alwyn spoke again with a hush voice.

'You needn't worry about the men in there. They've been sat still for so long that even their words are restless.'

'Why does this place feel like a ghost town?' said Wren. 'Where's everybody else?'

'Away. There's nothing to keep people here. We're the last now, and that's by choice. We're used to it. We'd prefer to be forgotten.'

'Surely moving away involves selling up? Why are all the houses empty?'

Alwyn didn't acknowledge the question. 'If you're only passing through, make it quick. There's a town fifteen minutes up the road where you'll be more welcome if you have to stay for a second night.'

The air tasted fresh after the smoky pub, ill-befitting the send-off. 'I hopefully won't have to be here after today,' said Wren. 'There are a few setbacks I didn't see coming, that need taking care of.'

'Can I help you get finished faster?'

The tone in his voice made Wren grip the handrail, feeling vulnerable on the top of the stone steps. But he saw an opportunity, a means to get Alwyn alone and find out more. 'As it happens, I could use your extra reach ...'

12.QUES|TIONS

Wren had hundreds of memories of the little Welsh house where he grew up. As a child, he had spent hours at a time in his own company, often while his father was away from the village for work. They were innocent times and he remembered them fondly, playing alone within its walls, or in the garden, on a neat and tidy lawn.

He hadn't seen those days as lonely, but things look different in retrospect. Jon Lawton's house was an unwelcoming, dilapidated shell, and perhaps always had been. Even with a degree of upkeep that the surrounding properties lacked, it looked tired and dated. The garden, too, bore scars of neglect. Tangles of weeds choked the unkempt lawn into a knee-high mess of greens and browns, while compost in the corner let off a foul stench as it festered.

Alwyn Speake – Wren's former classmate – seemed oblivious to the sadness of the situation, and he would have been unaware of Wren's connection. He seemed much more interested in the immediate task at hand. 'The glass has blown clean out of the frame,' he said. 'What on earth happened here?'

Wren stood on the patio beside him, looking in through the living room window. The difference in their heights was marked – Scott's stocky frame was no match for Alwyn's towering strength.

'It was such an old piece of glass,' said Wren. 'Something was going to bring it down eventually. All I did was fall into it.'

'Some of it's embedded in the ceiling. You're lucky you weren't cut to ribbons.'

'Believe me, I know. That's my reward for coming out here after dark.'

The television in the lounge had remained upright, despite the barrage, and seemed largely intact. Its blank screen pointed away from the window towards the sofa cushions that Wren had used as stepping stones that morning. The lack of detail in his story should have raised all kinds of suspicions. There was clearly more than he was sharing. But Alwyn made no further comment, nodding in blind acceptance of what he had been told.

'You're not hurt?' he asked.

'Not at all. And looking on the bright side, there was nothing of any value to be destroyed. Jon didn't exactly embrace luxury, as I'm sure you already knew.'

'Actually, I'm seeing it for the first time. The old man only ever asked me to work on the building's exterior, and he never left a key when he was out.'

'He shut you in the garden?'

'I'd climb over the wall when I was done. It wasn't a big deal. Believe me, worse things happen in these parts.'

Wren turned towards the garden. A portion of the stone wall around its border had collapsed, leaving a gap large enough for a man to fit through. Pieces of rubble stretched across the wild lawn for several feet. Wren could see right down the hill towards the sprawling forest on the valley floor. They were unquestionably alone, no better time to ask probing questions.

'If you don't mind me saying, they all seem a bit ... unfriendly around here. You would have thought people of a certain age would enjoy being asked about local history.'

'Definitely not in this village,' said Alwyn. 'Even if you'd lived here for most of your life, you'd have a hard time separating fact from legend. This place has a chequered history, which I don't fully understand.'

'Did something happen here?'

'Many things, but you won't find anyone willing to discuss them. My best advice is to take care of your business then be on your way. I appreciate you've got a job to do, and I know how it feels to find obstacles to that. Just don't hang about.'

'I'm not intending to be precious about any of the contents, but this was someone's life, however worthless it seems. I need to do it right.'

'Are you planning to sell? Is that your decision?'

'It is,' said Wren, 'and of course. No one's going to want to rent it.'

'Let me ask around before you put it on the market. One of the locals might want to make an offer.'

Alwyn Speake had donated two large sheets of hardboard, enough to cover the frame before the weather turned. Wren balanced one end on the toes of his trainers while he waited for Alwyn to ready his tools. 'Which of these homes is yours?' he asked.

'I live right up at the top,' said Alwyn, 'backing onto the trees. It's only a few minutes' walk.'

'I suppose *everything* is a few minutes' walk, right?'

'There's nothing to find here apart from houses. You probably won't be used to the effort it requires to do simple things like buy bread and milk.'

'No, I get it,' said Wren. 'I didn't always live in the city.'

On the count of three, they hoisted the wood into position. Alwyn quickly worked his way along the top edge, hammering long nails right through the window frame. A single blow knocked each right down to the head, showing the strength in his forearms. The board rattled with each strike.

'What kept you here?' asked Wren. 'You're young, and you seem capable. Why not move away?'

'I couldn't leave the others. I've known these people all my life. A lot of them are simply too old to start fresh elsewhere and they need help with upkeep.'

'I suppose that's where you make a fortune mowing lawns, right?'

'I used to,' said Alwyn. 'It was regular work. People like Jon were important to me and it's sad to hear he's gone.'

'I never knew him.' Wren smiled solemnly, the lie tasting bitter. Alwyn unfolded a bin bag and produced a roll of duct tape, covering the wooden board with an extra layer of protection. 'You look like you've done this before,' Wren continued. 'Has anything similar happened to the other houses?'

'This is nothing.' Alwyn nodded to the east. 'You only have to walk five doors along the road to see what I mean. There's a bridge. The house next to it burned down.'

'By accident?'

'No one really knows. They didn't find any bodies and the owners were never seen again.'

'What did the neighbours say?'

'They left a day or two later, packed up and vanished. I think they were scared their own house was unsafe.'

Wren waded down the lawn, trying to draw Alwyn's attention to the break in the garden wall. 'What do you think did that?' he asked. 'Looks almost like a tractor hit it.'

Alwyn took a cursory glance over his shoulder. 'Driven by whom? Maybe it collapsed from old age, the same way your window did?'

Wren tried not to read into his comment. 'This thing was built to last. The force it would have taken to knock it down is unthinkable.'

Or unnatural, he thought.

'Looks can be deceptive,' said Alwyn. 'You don't know what condition it was in before. If you want my opinion, making a hole like that wouldn't take more than a few good strikes with a lump hammer.'

The long grass forced Wren to shorten his stride. He trampled over weeds, trying to flatten them down. There were pieces of broken concrete, like petrified dust, scattered all over the place.

'It must have been some impact. You think someone did it on purpose?'

Alwyn shook his head. 'All I see is a mess that needs clearing, and if you want, I'll take a look.'

Wren nodded absent-mindedly. He couldn't make sense of it. The debris had fallen into the garden, so any impact must have come from outside, and with some appreciable force. A chill passed through him, accompanied by a need to understand more. But with the locals so unwilling to cooperate, there was only one way to achieve that. He would have to tempt fate, wilfully placing himself in danger, and embrace a dauting prospect.

He would stay another night.

13.DESO|LATION

A thin window shattered on contact with the wooden log in Andrew's hand. Shards of glass rained onto a ruffled carpet and broke into much smaller fragments. The smashing noise echoed through the house, but he didn't care. No one lived there anymore.

With his hand wrapped in a piece of cloth, he reached through the gaping hole he had created and lifted the latch, swinging the empty frame wide. 'Here we go,' he said. 'That's the easy part over.'

Isabel stood close beside him, shuffling on her feet. 'Quickly. Before someone sees us.'

He struggled to lift himself up into the house, an uneven strength in his arms. He clambered into the living room, grabbing the back of a red leather armchair for support, realising too late that he was leaving a handprint in a layer of dust. He had broken into that house before, months ago, under the cover of darkness, again with Isabel by his side. Seasons had changed, but his feelings towards it hadn't – Jon Lawton carried secrets, and somewhere in that property would be something worth knowing.

He moved aside as Isabel slung her bag over her shoulder and gripped both sides of the window frame. Nimble in her pair of jeans, she scaled the wall and slipped inside, dropping onto the glass with a crunch. While Scott was away in Pontrhyd-y-werddon, they had come to the house in the city, the house they thought Jon had called his only home. Its appearance challenged that preconception. Andrew tried to wipe his handprint off the dusty chair. It prompted him to check other surfaces, looking to see if someone else had done the same.

Were they the first people to break in, or had Wren been there as well?

She shivered, then spoke with a lowered voice. 'Where should we start?'

'Anywhere you fancy,' he said. 'Scott ran off with every set of keys we know about. It's fair to assume no one's going to come through the front door.'

'We should still hurry,' she said. 'I don't want to tempt fate.'

A red carpet had faded over time to a pale orange, though it looked almost brown in the dim light. Each step produced a strong smell of musk. It was hard to believe a person could have survived for long in such an unclean environment.

'Has he made contact yet today?' asked Andrew.

'Scott? Not a word. Do you think he's found something?'

'I'd say almost definitely. He's basically at the gingerbread house while we're searching through a trail of breadcrumbs.'

'So you think we'll need to go down there, too?'

'I wouldn't rule it out.' He tried a light switch and confirmed his suspicion that the power was off. A record player sat on top of a cupboard, but when he opened the cupboard doors, the shelves were empty.

'That seems odd,' he said. 'Where are all the records?'

'Maybe someone cleared the house out already?'

'The will makes that your responsibility.'

'Wouldn't stop a thief.'

Andrew couldn't hide his disappointment at the lack of belongings to rifle through. Memories kept flooding into his mind, many of which weren't his – residue left behind when Wren had vacated. 'It's too tidy for a burglary,' he said. 'Why clear out the furniture, but leave everything on show?'

He had a different theory. It was a façade. Wren's knack for deceit had to come from somewhere. If Jon Lawton knew his son could cheat death and was capable of keeping such a massive secret, he was more than capable of fooling the world into thinking he lived somewhere he rarely set foot inside. Andrew moved to the hallway and squatted by the welcome mat, using the flashlight on his mobile phone to illuminate the carpet.

'What are you doing?' said Isabel.

'Trying to see who else has been here.'

'I know who you mean.' She put her hands on her hips. 'We're not here for that. Help me figure out Jon's motives.'

'Both are important.'

'But time is short. We don't even have an address for the second house because Scott took the envelope.'

'That part shouldn't be too difficult.' Andrew picked himself up and wiped his trousers down. 'Follow me.'

He took her into the dining room opposite the lounge. Most of the space was taken up by a large wooden table with six sturdy chairs. There wouldn't have been much room to sit around it. Andrew couldn't help but wonder whether its intended purpose was to maintain Jon's elaborate ruse.

'Remember, I've been here before,' he said, 'though admittedly after dark.'

'So have I.' Isabel ran her fingers along the polished wood, leaving an imprint in the dust. 'I used to come here with Wren sometimes. We'd bring food and sit together for dinner. The place seemed more homely back then, not much, but enough.'

Against a woodchip wall in the far corner stood a mahogany bureau with a glass-fronted cabinet. Andrew edged his way around the room. He knew what to expect from his previous visit. One knee cracked as he crouched beside it. The other refused to bend. 'Maybe Jon stopped caring about life when Wren died and didn't come back for him.'

'Or worse,' she said. 'Maybe Jon knew Wren came for me instead, and he died waiting for his turn.'

Unlike the cupboards in the lounge, Jon Lawton's bureau was full to bursting. Andrew scanned the crowded shelves, his nostrils filling with the scent of aged paper. He found a plastic tub and lifted it onto the tabletop, tipping out the contents without a second thought. Business cards, shopping lists, and scraps of paper spilled out, worthless to anyone except Wren and his father.

'What are you hoping to find in there?' said Isabel.

Andrew fished out a passport, checking the back page. 'The address you wanted, for starters …'

She took it off him and read the second line aloud. 'Pontrhyd-y-werddon.' He could almost hear her heart sink and understood why. She had no excuse not to go there now, and fell silent at the prospect. 'You know, in my darker moments, I ask myself whether Wren had a point, whether the way I treated him made him what he became. Did I give him false hope? Was I maybe too hard when I let him down?'

'Don't,' said Andrew. 'You'll go mad looking for those kind of answers. I spent the guts of two years married to someone whose moods changed with the tides. It drained me. By the end, I was a changed man, and she was probably a changed woman. We pulled each other down, and then Wren went to work on whatever pieces were left. These scars of mine are a constant reminder of the time I gave up, but that isn't who I want to be. What brought me here is determination not to be a victim, not ever again. That pair can rot for all I care, and they certainly don't deserve our sympathy.'

He carried on sifting through the scraps, stuffing anything of value into his pocket.

'What are you doing?' said Isabel. 'You can't just help yourself.'

'I'm stockpiling,' he replied. 'The fact no one else has broken into the house proves Wren hasn't been here, but don't kid yourself. If he's still around, he'll come looking for his father eventually. We need to be prepared.'

Andrew bent down and lifted something else off the shelf – a heavy box with a wooden lid, engraved across the top.

'His ashes?' Isabel put her hand over her mouth. 'That's horrible.'

Andrew slammed it onto the table, sending clouds of dust into the air, then he unceremoniously wrenched off the lid. They stood looking into a container full of grey, barren ash.

'What do you want with those?' she said.

'It's more about what Wren wants with them. Any leverage we can find is pivotal, and if I were him, this would be the most valuable thing on the planet besides maybe yourself. All that remains. If I knew it was here, he will too.'

'I don't think Wren was sentimental about himself that way. You're forgetting we had three years together. We were in love. I knew him better than most.'

'I know all I need to. He tried to kill me.'

'Then you shouldn't be provoking him,' said Isabel. 'I don't want to get in his way, Andrew. I just want to get my partner back and escape all this, to be left alone.'

He hesitated, putting one hand in his pocket. 'This is an opportunity we may not have again.'

'Please listen. I know you have my best interests at heart, and believe me, I'm grateful. But this isn't right. I don't want revenge. I just want him to forget me, that's all, and if you take that, you'll make yourself a target.'

Andrew was reluctant to listen. He didn't feel the same. His solution to extricate themselves from Wren was to go on the offensive, to lure him out. To what end, he wasn't sure, but there had to be a way …

Isabel's eyes derailed his train of thought. They pleaded with him to stop. With a sigh, he pressed the lid back onto the box of ashes then put them on the shelf where he'd found them. 'I suppose we can always come back some other time,' he said.

'Thank you.'

He smiled insincerely, and it soon faded. In truth, he was disappointed to find the ashes there at all. Their absence would have proved for certain that Wren still existed. At that moment, he had no evidence whatsoever.

'What else is in that cupboard?' she said. 'Why's it so full, when the lounge seems empty?'

'Books,' he said. 'Heirlooms and keepsakes.'

She leaned across him and folded down the bureau lid, converting it into a desk. The upper half was filled with reams of paper, most of which were blank, untouched. But three pens rolling loose suggested intent and she, like him, would have learned not to trust her eyes. He wasn't surprised when she took one of the notepads, tore off the top sheet, and held it up to the window.

'Look at this.' There were deep indentations where the nib of a pen had pressed through from the page above.

'Maybe we can do a pencil rub.' Andrew searched through the desk until he found a graphite pencil and watched her scrape the side of the point across the paper. Steadily, miraculously, handwriting revealed itself. Two lines had been drawn down the page, dividing it into three. In the left-hand column was a list of names, the first three of which were known to him – Jon, Hope, and Wren. The Lawton family.

Beside each name, in the second column, was a location. Most were legible – Loughborough, Donnington, Aberdeen …

'What do you think this is?' she asked.

'I'm not sure.'

The third column made it clear. It listed illnesses, accidents, causes of death. Beside Wren, it said 'heart'. Beside Hope, it said 'birth'. Together, they painted a dark picture. Gwen Richards had been killed by a train in Suffolk. Ellen Vaughn, who lived in Birmingham, had died in her sleep. He counted eighteen names in total, only five of which didn't have a cause of death. Three of those had been underlined, all with the surname Craddock.

'Now do you believe me?' he said. 'Jon Lawton was up to something.'

'Maybe,' said Isabel. 'We should look some of these people up, see if their loved ones can help piece things together.'

'Okay,' he said. 'But there's something else we need to think about. This is a list of people who we assume are dead, presumably with some kind of connection. But if Jon wrote this, why is his own name on it?'

'Because he thought death was coming for him?'

'I mean what if it had already happened?'

She appeared lost in thought for a moment, then she shuddered. 'Wren and Hope have more in common than their surname, don't they?'

His eyes locked on hers, and he understood. At least until the summer, both Wren Lawton and his mother had still been out there in the world, having transcended death in their own different ways. So if they had this ability, what did that say about Wren's father?

Were they alone in the house?

14.GLIM|MER

Wren was both unconscious and fully self-aware. He drifted in darkness, as though floating in space. His body was well lit and fully clothed. He seemed to glow from within. It was his perception of himself, rather than his physical form, and it looked like the body he had stolen.

This was purgatory, a place between life and death. Wren had been there more than once before. Nothing about the scene gave him cause to panic. The freedom from gravity, noise, and the sensations of hot and cold left him numb, to the point of being quite relaxed. He was, however, disappointed with what he could see. Even in such an unearthly place, it seemed he couldn't escape from his connection to Scott. The two had merged almost completely and a piece of his identity had been lost forever.

Months in complete control had given Wren an overfamiliarity with traits he used to find obnoxious – the foreign smell of sweat, the crick of stiff joints, and the subtle wheeze of a nasal exhale. He didn't stumble when he walked anymore. He didn't struggle with his grip. He was used to having a flatter stomach and a shorter stature. He couldn't even remember what his old life had been like.

Even in the void, however, there were phantom pains. Something jabbed his thigh, a reminder of when he used to inject himself with adrenaline to stay awake. Losing consciousness would always carry a risk that Scott might assume control while his guard was lowered, as he had found with Andrew Goodwin. The doctors had thought Scott brain dead, but what did they know?

Could he ever be sure?

A dull ache rose behind his temples. He raised an arm on instinct, which swiped through the darkness with unnaturally low resistance. But somewhere along the way, his muscles stopped responding, as though his commands were being ignored. Wren became paralysed, stranded. His only free action became thought, and even that was tainted as a voice emerged from somewhere behind his eardrums.

'*You hijacked my life,*' it said. '*You took everything.*'

It sounded sharp and scratching. He assumed it was Scott. *'I reclaimed what you took first,'* he responded. *'You got what you deserved.'*

There was a swift reprisal. Another sharp needle dug into his thigh, then another. It was like a handful of claws trying to gouge his flesh. Shreds of clothing tore away from his body and spiralled out into nothingness, followed soon after by skin and muscle. A mist of blood expanded from his midsection, bright scarlet in the ubiquitous light. The pain overloaded his senses until he knew nothing else.

The two identities began to separate. Wren became the passenger, watching Scott pull himself apart, as though self-destructing. His physical form was carved into strips and slices, twisting entrails mixed with shards of bone. Wren couldn't think straight, agonised to the point of insanity. He couldn't tell whether Scott's actions were a disaster or a mercy. He couldn't tell whether this would bring about his final death, or whether he would simply wake up inside another host.

He couldn't tell which outcome he wanted.

***

He woke up screaming. Wren's heart lurched as he sat up in pitch darkness and felt for a light source. Only by turning on the shaded lamp by the bedside and bathing the room in soft yellow tones could he finally get a grip. There was no need to panic, or at least not yet. He was in the upstairs bedroom of his father's house, in the same bed he had used since he was a teenager.

Still in Pontrhyd-y-werddon.

Sweat ran down his back. Familiar surroundings had lowered his guard, allowing his demons to creep up on him. The nightmare was disturbingly real, enough to seek proof that it was over. He took deep breaths of stale air and patted his stomach, relieved when his hands responded to their instructions, and to find Scott's body was fully intact.

The bedcovers hadn't been changed since he moved out several years ago. The whole room was a shrine to a life he felt detached from. Wren had been away long enough for it to become an impersonal space, filled with hoarded relics that had lost all sense of value. In many ways, he had been more comfortable on the sofa downstairs with fewer sad reminders, and he wished he still had the option.

An unnerving silence seemed to fill the property. Alwyn Speake had finished helping him to board up the rear window that afternoon, but Wren hadn't stopped there. The living room door was nailed shut and barricaded with the washing machine from the kitchen. Nothing would find its way into the property that way. The kitchen had French doors into the garden, again decades old, but all six panes of glass were smaller than those in the lounge. He didn't think they would break so easily.

Nevertheless, Wren was hiding upstairs in the front bedroom. He hoped that the shadows and sparks would give fair warning before they attacked, as they had done the night before. He would know to run away this time. The goal was to learn more about who or what he was dealing with, to understand their strange behaviour. He just didn't want to die in the attempt.

Now that he had switched on the bedside lamp in an absent-minded moment, the villagers would know he had ignored their warning to leave. He put on the faded trainers that cramped his toes and the jacket that didn't reach his wrists. He slipped his car keys into his pocket and turned the light back off. Wren could easily manoeuvre in the darkness, guided by instincts honed throughout his childhood. He clutched his mobile phone in one hand and felt his way towards the landing, twisting the door handle slowly so it hardly made a sound.

He ran his feet along the skirting board to avoid the floorboards he knew would creak. His imagination fed off the silence, hearing thumps and voices through the walls. As he crept down the stairs, street light passing through the opaque front door left no impression of the time. He found his way to the washing machine blocking the living room and reassured himself of its weight. Then he went on to the kitchen. A brief pause to build up courage ended when he eased the door open a crack.

There were sparks on the other side.

He had known what to expect, but was shocked to be proven right. Wren's eyes were drawn to tiny specks drifting through the floor, just as he had seen on the previous night. Points of dancing light let off a dim glow, snaking around chair legs and beneath the rounded kitchen table. They were mesmerising, at once terrifying and fascinating. They seemed to explore the room, each with their own personality. Some drifted, some darted, some circled, others spiralled.

Using the door as a shield, Wren extended an arm into the kitchen. He made no sound, but they still reacted to his presence. At once, the sparks withdrew to the back wall, as though swept away by a fierce current. Some vanished through the peeling wallpaper, but others tried to resist, leaping towards him like salmon fighting against a rushing river, only for unseen forces to repeatedly push them back.

He found the light switch and flicked it on. The colours in the room inverted, bathing the kitchen in a blinding white. The sparks were no match for the new intensity and seemed to disappear. Wren abandoned his cover and ran to the French doors, cupping his hands against the glass. There was no trace of them outside, nor any sign of life whatsoever, as though the sparks had only existed within the building's walls.

The light from the kitchen formed a yellow column that stretched down the lawn, illuminating every blade of grass. Beyond its limits, the rest of the valley was impenetrably black. The clouded sky was an ominous grey. He had no desire to set foot out there. Instead, Wren retreated to the doorway with trepidation, braced himself once more, and turned the light back off.

Shadows at the window.

A handful of silhouettes now stood packed together on the other side of the pane. They were silent and unmoving, as on the night before. By the time he saw them, they certainly would have seen him, and there was no point hiding. He was there to make contact.

'Hello?' His mouth was dry. 'Can you hear me?'

One of the shadows leaned forwards, as though peering through the glass. Wren waved his arm slowly. 'If you can understand then give me a sign. Maybe we can communicate.'

It had no discernible features. It stood with its hands by its sides, as close to the door as it could get. It was too solid to be imaginary, but not defined enough to be considered real. Again, Wren had a plan. He raised his mobile phone and tried to take a photograph. The flash flooded the room with light. During that instant, the shadows all vanished, as though they had never been there, only to return along with the darkness.

It was immediately clear he would struggle to gather any evidence. After one more attempt, he gave up. 'What do you want?' he asked. 'Why are you here?'

There were more of them than he had expected, stretching right down to the end of the garden. He saw one climbing through the gap in the wall. It sifted – not walking, but not exactly floating. It was, in equal parts, both terrifying and hypnotic to watch, unlike anything he had seen before. He likened it to the memory of a walk, an imitation from a thing that didn't really need to move its legs.

The French door frame creaked. He stepped back, the handset slipping through his sweaty fingers. It didn't make sense how they could impress upon the structure when they had no physical form, but he had seen enough. Trying not to panic, he withdrew from the kitchen and closed the door behind him before moving to the empty dining room. There were no sparks in there, nor did there look to be any shadows at the front of the house, but were they hiding under the artificial light? Could he trust his own eyes?

It was an impossible choice – either go back to hiding and hope the wind didn't penetrate the house again or take his chances with the ten-metre dash to the Range Rover. He chose the latter. There would be more than an hour before daybreak and he couldn't rely upon the sun for a rescue. He had to make his own luck. Wren took himself to the front door, his wet palms slipping on the handle as he turned it. A rush of cold air struck his face, and he plunged headlong into the night.

He braced himself for his balance to be challenged, but what he found was quite unexpected. He did, in fact, appear to be alone. There were no strange sights or sounds, but an exhilarating sense of openness. A man appeared from higher up the hillside. An ordinary man, just like him. He had form in the orange streetlight, standing out as the only thing moving in the abandoned village. He was dressed in a black shirt and dark, denim trousers. He looked hurt, sprinting down the hill with an uneven stride and wild eyes.

Wren waved his arm to beckon the man closer, fumbling the car keys out of his pocket. Wren recognised him, even from a distance. His name was Rees Franklin, another historic resident of Pontrhyd-y-werddon, someone he had known since childhood. Rees would be around thirty-three years old and stood almost as tall as Alwyn, with short, fair hair that seemed almost white.

Wren could tell what he would be running from. 'Get to the car,' he shouted. 'Quickly.'

He looked down at his key fob long enough to find the right button to unlock the Range Rover. Indicator lights blinked reassuringly. When he raised his eyes again, Rees had halved the distance between them, covering fifty metres in a few seconds. There was something odd in his movement, more apparent from much closer. He had no real sense of weight. Wren realised with a jolt that Rees was moving as the shadows did. He wasn't like Wren after all, but something altogether more frightening. He was more reminiscent of Wren's mother – *dead* – and he wasn't being chased.

He was in pursuit.

Wren snapped out of his trance and made a dive for his vehicle. Rees was close enough now to make out the whites of his eyes and his yellow-stained teeth. There looked to be dirt all over his clothing and red scratches on his face and arms. Wren opened the driver's door, but Rees was accompanied by a powerful gust which got there first, sucking him two steps backwards onto the pavement.

Wren was surrounded by wind, as with that evening in Isabel's garden, half a world away. It formed a near-invisible blockade which jostled him into its centre. Powerless to move more than a few inches, he watched Rees slow his approach and lose all apparent urgency, passing through the cyclone like it wasn't even there. The two men stood face to face – two aberrations of natural laws. Wren couldn't find the words to speak, and Rees didn't attempt to. An outstretched arm made contact with Wren's jacket, and to his horror, passed right through it. Fingernails disappeared into fabric.

A chill shot through his body, as if from a plunge into icy waters. It felt exactly like a heart attack, something he knew all about. Rees appeared to shake with exertion as the hand disappeared into his body, right up to the wrist. Wren's muscles tensed, arresting a scream. Everything grew distant, turning black. His legs buckled. The ground raced up to meet him, but gravity proved to be his saviour. As he fell, icy fingers were drawn back out of him.

He managed to take a breath.

Wren mustered all the strength in his tensed-up body. Terror gave him momentum, the instinct to survive. He found less resistance from the wind so close to the tarmac, as though it was weaker below the knees. He scrambled forwards and dived through the open car door. Once the latch had clicked shut, no effort could have pulled him back out.

The vehicle rocked on its suspension. The wind roared. Wren started the engine, lurching back into his seat as he accelerated up the road to thirty miles per hour, then forty, then fifty. He watched Rees Franklin shrink in the mirror, left standing on the edge of the pavement, surrounded by turmoil. He turned down the hillside and left Pontrhyd-y-werddon altogether, not stopping until the sun was on the horizon.

There could be no mistake – one of his childhood friends still had presence in death, and something in the transition had changed a once-placid man to someone hostile. His mind raced faster than the car. Of course there were other spirits out there like his mother. Of course there were. It would have been naïve to assume she was the only one. And yet, for his entire life until that point, he had never given it a second thought. Counting Wren himself, that made three of them who had cheated death, all from the same village. It couldn't have been a coincidence, no way.

So what was happening there?

15.THRE|ATS

It was midday before Wren dared return to the village. The weather had taken a marked downturn. An intermittent drizzle dampened the grasses, obscuring the distance with a fine, hazy mist. Low-lying clouds made everything seem dull and unwelcoming, but mercifully removed all trace of shadows.

As he retraced his exit path, the night played over in his mind like a skipping record. He wanted to be anywhere else, back with Isabel in the city, planning their new life together. The problem was he couldn't leave, not now. Pontrhyd-y-werddon was the only place to answer so many burning questions. He would never understand his parent's fates if he simply gave up.

Tension built in the air as he came in sight of the little house, returning to the scene of his own attempted murder. The front door hung open, the hallway beyond it still and silent. He could see the washing machine blockading the living room, but otherwise no trace of the horrors he had experienced.

It didn't feel like home anymore. Without wasting a second, he hurried inside, relieved when nothing challenged him in the daylight. The house was colder than when he'd left, as though the building was trying to get rid of him. It was even colder than the outdoors.

A sense of dread lingered in the kitchen. His mobile phone lay untouched on the floor where it had slipped from his hands. His father's research littered the table. By a miracle, the French doors had managed to resist the shadows' crush. Upon close inspection, the glass was covered in a criss-cross of hairline fractures. It had been a near-miss, and he was lucky to be alive. Before the sun went down and Rees Franklin returned, he needed to either be hiding somewhere safe and remote, or else gone for good. He wouldn't make the same mistake again.

He let himself back out of the house and closed the door behind him, glad to be leaving its four walls, but nervous of being in the open. He headed east. After a few hundred yards, the road sloped down towards the stream at the base of the hillside, and where the two intersected stood a short bridge made of stone. No vehicle could have crossed it. The roadway was too narrow, perhaps another factor in the decline of the small community.

Beyond it, the path continued as a gravel trackway, which acted as the dividing line between the vibrant forest and the dead forest. An undisturbed blanket of browns and oranges carpeting its surface suggested no one had been down there for a long time. This was the view from a pair of semi-detached houses on the nearside of the crossing. They were the oldest and lowest properties in Pontrhyd-y-werddon, with no driveways or gardens. Instead, a retaining wall ran along the rear, eight feet from the bricks, as though holding up the hillside. One house, it was evident, was empty, though it looked for all the world like its owners could return at any moment. The other was in ruin.

Alwyn Speake had mentioned a fire in one of his neighbouring properties. Even without prior knowledge, it would have been easy to find. Flames had gutted the house on the right. Charred brick walls had collapsed inwards, bringing most of the top floor down with it. A section of roof frame hung precariously over the empty space. Exposed woodwork had turned a dirty shade of blue from years of weathering.

Wren hadn't known the people who lived there, despite growing up only a few minutes away on foot. He regarded the scene coldly, more interested in what could have happened to the house than its inhabitants. Alwyn had said that no bodies were discovered, but he doubted anyone had searched for long. Through an empty doorway lay a thick pile of bricks and splintered beams, laced with broken glass. He saw no evidence than anyone had attempted to sift through it.

He approached the adjoining home. Alwyn claimed the owners had packed up and left, but Wren discovered it was fully furnished. There was a plate full of crumbs on the coffee table and a magazine folded over the arm of the settee. Squinting through the glass, he saw a painted portrait of a girl no older than nine or ten, an item unlikely to be left behind in a planned escape.

Something crunched underfoot. Wren glanced up to see a broken front window, shattered by the roof as it dropped. Curtain fabric hung through the hole, shivering as a sudden gust moved quickly through it. Hairs rose on the back of his neck. He turned and retreated up the road, a third of the way home in a matter of seconds. Looking back, he saw the dreaded wind rouse from slumber. Rubble shifted, wood creaked. He became aware of an unnatural distortion in the air, like the shiver of heat above the flames of a raging fire.

Life returned to the house. He could see air pour out of the window and whip around the structure, unsettling the leaves all around it. Wren stood high enough up the slope to be level with its rooftop. He felt no breeze. The curtain tails billowed outwards, pointing almost horizontally. And it wailed – the same deep moaning he had heard the first night he stayed there, carrying far in the calm.

Disturbed by his presence, it seemed the wind was staking its claim, twisting out through the roof cavity then in through the hollow front doorway. He realised the house was far from deserted. Its original owners had been expelled and it was now home to something unnatural. They would have been able to hear it from all the way at the top of the village, through the open window of The Black Horse. Any claims of ignorance seemed ridiculous.

He turned and marched up the hillside, passing silent houses with their own curtains closed, even at midday. Again, there were no vehicles parked anywhere, not so much as a bicycle. He climbed the stone steps to the front door of the tavern and flung it wide open. The aging crowd of locals sat as they had the day before, around tables in alcoves where the sun didn't reach. They looked as though they hadn't moved an inch during his absence. Speake sat with another younger man beside the window, distancing themselves from the tobacco smoke. Everyone looked round as he entered.

'What are you still doing here?' said the man with the pipe, looking surprised to see him back.

'You mean how come I'm still alive, or are you wondering why the wind hasn't driven me out yet?'

'That makes no sense,' said Alwyn.

'You know damn well it does.'

Wren scanned hostile faces and saw no trace of denial. It cemented his suspicions. The man beside Alwyn seemed to glance at the others for permission to speak before he dared to respond. 'We warned you to mind your own business. We don't ask what you're really doing here, and we expect you to pay us the same respect.'

'I was attacked last night,' said Wren, 'by the ghost of Rees Franklin.'

There were gasps. 'Where did you hear that name?'

'Never mind that,' said Wren. 'I know Rees lived locally. I need to understand what killed him.'

'Don't get involved,' said Alwyn. 'Whatever you think you know, you're still an outsider.'

'It's too late for that. I've seen him, clear as day.'

A pair of men stood up, their stools scraping across the wooden floorboards. One of them – mid-forties – looked fit to heave his table clean off the floor and hurl it in Wren's direction. 'Liar,' he yelled.

'You all know I'm right, and Rees isn't the only one, is he? The dead are all over this village, walking around like the rest of us.'

'You don't know what you're talking about.' Alwyn was less accommodating with the others listening in.

'So why are there so many empty houses? Why are they abandoned if people aren't being scared away? Where are your wives and daughters?'

A third man stood and clenched his fist. 'You watch your tongue. What gives you the right to come in here and start throwing accusations? You need to leave.'

'That's exactly what I plan to do,' said Wren, 'but not without hearing what this is really about. You know what's going on. I can see it in your faces.'

Alwyn remained seated, his tone unthreatening, but he sided with the others. 'What happened here is complicated, and none of your concern. You're just passing through, remember?'

'You saw the window,' said Wren. 'Something was trying to get into the house and I'm willing to bet that's happened before.'

There were unsure glances all around until the eldest shook his head. 'Just get rid of him.'

Those already on their feet advanced together. Wren raised his guard. 'You're proving me right.'

'That's enough,' said the man with silver hair and deep-set wrinkles. 'Quit this village, for your own sake.'

'Because of the wind? What is it? Why's it in the burned-out house?'

Someone seized his arm. He shrugged them off and raised a finger to point, but it was snatched out of the air and twisted behind his back. He was bent over and a swift knee landed in his stomach. Even in Scott's body, he wasn't strong enough to resist. He was dragged, kicking and yelling, towards the door then propelled into the open. The stone steps jarred his back as he tumbled down them.

'Forget what you saw,' shouted the youngest man. 'You may think you're the first, but there have been several like you. Even if you knew Franklin, don't push your luck. That man's not for saving.'

The villagers went back inside and slammed the door shut, leaving Wren alone. He carefully pulled himself up, struggling to hold his own weight on a bruised ankle. If nothing else, his suspicions were confirmed – the people of Pontrhyd-y-werddon knew exactly what was going on. They just weren't prepared to share it with a stranger.

The settlement seemed colder and more hostile than ever. Mist continued to obscure the distance. The burned-out house at the bottom appeared still and silent. He felt no attachment to the place he had known for over thirty years. It was nothing like he remembered. Prying eyes at the tavern window would be willing him to depart so he limped back down the hillside. He fully intended to give those people exactly what they wanted. He would get his things and leave. He wished his father had done the same, then maybe he would still be alive. Jon Lawton's stubbornness had sealed his fate, struck down on his own front doorstep.

Wren couldn't allow himself to follow suit. He hobbled towards his childhood home, looking over his black Range Rover parked close to the door. Beside it, he saw another car – a red Honda Civic. He stopped dead, staring down the embankment. Two people stood by his front window, peering through it like the shadows had overnight. These two figures were unquestionably alive, and he recognised them both. One was Isabel … his Isabel, right there in Pontrhyd-y-werddon. She had come all that way to check up on him, arriving at the worst possible time.

The other was Andrew Goodwin.

16.CAPT|URE

Whenever Isabel examined something, she seemed to have an urge to touch it, as though a little of its mystery would rub off on her. As she walked around the kitchen of Jon Lawton's house, her hands reached out to one thing after the other, feeling their texture. Wren found it unsettling to watch.

'Deep down, this is better than I expected,' she said. 'Under the neglect, I mean. Someone with the right vision could do a lot with it.'

He stood in the doorway, his hand on the frame, trying to take the weight off his bruised ankle without revealing he was hurt. 'Most of the village is a similar age,' he said. 'This was probably a nice place to live, once upon a time.'

Isabel had never been to that house before. He didn't like her pawing over the relics of his childhood, something that would have seemed impossible four days ago. And glimpses of his reflection unnerved him even further. Dirty hair clung to his scalp in greasy clumps, unwashed since she had seen him last. His jacket and shoes were too small, and she would know that neither belonged to him.

'Tell me again why the lounge is sealed off?' she asked.

He tried to think quickly, struggling with the effects of two nights without sleep. 'The window collapsed. I fell against it soon after I arrived and the damned thing near-exploded. There's glass everywhere.'

'So you blocked the door with a washing machine?' Andrew Goodwin's interjection was profoundly unwelcome. He sat at the kitchen table, his nose upturned to the filth. The two of them had rarely crossed paths since they had fought in the summer. Seeing him felt strange, like an out-of-body sensation, as though Wren was looking at himself in a mirror. Goodwin wore thick glasses and had a prominent scar along his jawline. He looked diminished, but his continued life was an affront to everything Wren had survived.

'I needed to move the washing machine anyway,' he replied. 'I was looking for the stop tap. The point of my being here was to determine what was worth trying to salvage so Isabel wouldn't have to. I'm not here to carry out repairs.'

'Well, she's more than capable of making those decisions herself, now that she's here. It's her inheritance, right? So it's her choice.'

'Fixing doors and windows is a given,' said Isabel. 'No one will buy this house if it's falling apart. You, Scott, should be resting. I haven't heard a word from you in almost two days. We've been worried.'

Wren folded his arms. Being home again had made him revert to old ways of thinking, forgetting his life of deceit. He hadn't even thought about keeping in touch, nor how his silence must have looked. 'Like I explained to you once before, my phone doesn't work in the valley. Besides, I've been busy.'

She stepped back and leaned against the counter, increasing the distance between them. 'I don't know how you could stay a minute longer than you have to, given who grew up here.'

'I was trying to spare you any burden. My heart was in the right place.'

It took a great deal of effort to bury the urge to defend his memory. He was painfully aware of Goodwin's watchful eye, and there was more at stake than his reputation. He bit his tongue and allowed the countryside silence to take over. It was stark, devoid of even the slightest murmur.

'Is there anything to drink?' asked Isabel, softening her tone. 'The two of us have driven for hours and I'm dying of thirst.'

'The cupboards are bare. I've hardly eaten myself, and I can't recommend the tap water. We should head further afield in search of a meal.'

'Suits me fine.' Andrew put his head in his hands and rubbed his temples like they hurt. 'We shouldn't hang around here anyway. This place makes me uncomfortable.'

'Agreed,' said Isabel. 'We can talk through what we've found before we decide our next move. Where are you staying, Scott?'

Wren took a deep breath. 'I know how this will sound, and it was never my intention … I've been sleeping upstairs.'

Andrew's jaw dropped. 'Here in this house? What could you possibly be thinking?'

'The situation sort of developed.'

Wren caught Isabel staring at red scrapes along his forearms, wounds he couldn't hide. 'Is there something we should know about?' she asked.

'I'm not in any trouble, though the people around here aren't exactly friendly. I thought they might know what happened to Jon Lawton.'

'And did they?'

'No one's sharing if they do.'

'Maybe I should try,' she said. 'You can be quite heavy-handed at times.'

He felt the muscles tighten around the tender skin on his stomach. The locals wouldn't hesitate to use violence, if tested any further. He couldn't let her go near them. He crossed the room and tried to hold her hand, but she withdrew.

'I still don't know what possessed you to come down here,' she said. 'You just upped and left me, even after we discussed—'

'It wasn't planned,' he said. 'I came for a quick look, but you can see how big a job it's going to be sorting through so much rubbish.'

'I don't know why you're even trying.' Her focus shifted to Goodwin, as though seeking support, then came thundering back. 'I've tried to be understanding, but you're acting strangely now. You look like you haven't washed since you got here, and what are those on your feet?'

Wren looked down at the ill-fitting trainers he had raided from the wardrobe upstairs. His own pair were still in the living room where he had kicked them off on the first night. They were covered in glass.

'It's a very long story.'

He cast his eyes downwards, trying to invoke sympathy, and it seemed to loosen her resolve. 'Listen, we're worried about you,' she said. 'I brought you a change of clothes in the car.'

'What's with all the paperwork?' said Andrew. Distracted by the shadows and the villagers, Wren hadn't taken the time to move his father's notes from the table. They had lain almost untouched since the day of his arrival. To his dismay, Andrew was sifting through them.

He felt violated.

'They were like that when I got here,' he said, lying. 'I was hoping to learn more about Wren's background.'

'What can you tell us so far?' asked Isabel.

'That we're judging him too harshly. Wren wasn't evil and neither was his father. They seem like normal people with a normal home. Normal enough, anyway.'

Andrew dropped his fist onto the table, where it landed with a clunk. 'I'm sorry, are you joking? He's a monster. Let's not forget he tried to strangle the life out of you, and he launched me off a bridge. He deserves no pity.'

'I'm just saying this trip is helping me to understand him better.'

Isabel approached the table and picked up one of the few photographs he had discovered amongst the handwritten papers. 'I've never seen his mother. If this is her, she's pretty.'

'It's her.' Andrew's lip curled with apparent disgust. 'Not that I've ever seen her smiling.' Quite unexpectedly, he swept the entire pile of papers aside, casting them to the floor. Beneath them, he uncovered the large map of the village that both Wren's father, then later Wren himself, had been using to assemble a regional history.

Wren felt his stomach lurch, aware that neither set of handwriting would match Scott's. 'That came from upstairs,' he said.

Goodwin's eyes flitted left to right as he scanned over the detail. 'What have you learned from it?'

'Precious little. I tried quizzing the locals, but like I said, they weren't helpful.'

Isabel frowned. 'Are there any hints as to why he kept this house a secret?'

'Not yet.'

'And what else do you have to show for two days of being here?' Andrew asked with no sympathy. Wren swallowed, deciding to play the only card he had left.

'The wind is here.'

Isabel lifted a hand to her chest. 'So that's where it's gone. I haven't seen it since you left. Did it try to attack you?'

'I didn't give it the chance.' Again, Wren lied. 'I've stayed indoors as much as possible.'

Her demeanour changed completely, stripped of any confidence. She hurried to the window and peered down the misty garden, seeming not to notice the hairline cracks across the pane. 'Do you think it could be Jon?' she said. 'If it followed you across the country, no other explanation makes sense.'

'I haven't worked it out yet,' said Wren, 'but let's not take any chances. We should leave while we can.'

'Soon enough,' said Andrew. Wren turned to see him draw a line across the map with a red pen, defacing it. He took offence.

'What are you doing?'

'Matching surnames, looking for patterns. It surprises me you haven't done this already.'

Wren gritted his teeth. 'I was trying to preserve what's there until I understood it. How can we look for patterns with your notes on top of his?'

'Let him work,' said Isabel. 'Everything's getting thrown out anyway, as soon as I can arrange it. Andrew could draw on the walls for all I care.'

Wren bit his tongue, his situation too delicate to protest. With too many other distractions vying for his time, there was a very real threat that Andrew would unlock the secrets of the house before him. It was a thought he couldn't abide, so he turned to Isabel.

'Why is he here at all? I've told you before that I don't trust him.'

'But I do,' she said. 'He's quick and he means no harm.'

Wren didn't understand her relationship with Scott well enough to stay in character when they argued, afraid of being exposed. Instead, he continued to exploit her fears. 'Listen to me about changing location, at the very least. It was one thing to be stranded in this house alone, but now that you've arrived, the risk is too apparent. I want you somewhere safe before nightfall.'

'Is that when the wind comes back?' she said.

'Could be any time, really, and when it's here, we'll be trapped.'

That was all it took. Isabel left his side and approached the table. 'We should take those notes somewhere safer while we can.'

Andrew looked bemused. 'Can't I have just half an hour?'

'Please, Andrew.'

He put the pen down without objection, irritating Wren even further. The pair seemed to have developed a rapport that made his skin crawl. But he was glad to regain control for a short while, keeping the village's secrets from being unlocked. He would keep stalling until he could work out how to give his antagonist a fitting send-off.

Andrew picked the research off the floor and tucked it under his arm, making it clear he didn't intend to let go of them any time soon. Wren held the door for Isabel, making sure he was the last person in the room. Her presence in the village was an unlikely opportunity, a way to soften her feelings towards his true self. With a little more time and no more interference, he could prove his father's innocence and clear his own name. Then maybe one day – in a perfect world – she might be ready to hear the truth.

17.FATH|ER

Jon Lawton's wake should have been one of the defining moments of Wren's life. It should have been a heartfelt affair, or at the very least respectful. It should have been a chance to pay tribute to a man who, although distant, had provided him with a secure and stable home. It should have brought a sense of closure.

Instead, the wake functioned as something far less dignified: A means to cause a distraction. Pontrhyd-y-werddon had been exposed as a dangerous place, somewhere Wren couldn't let Isabel within a mile of. He would have taken her right back to the city if he thought she would have gone, but he could see her sheer determination, mixed with her resentment at having to come down there in the first place. She would see the house was emptied, all memories either buried or burned. To resist would only make it happen quicker.

And she had willing help. Somehow, in Wren's two-day absence, Andrew Goodwin had kindled her suspicions to the point where she questioned every word out of his mouth. The two had already managed a hushed conversation, communicating in signs and whispers, while he checked the three of them into a small hotel on the coast. Coming up with valid ways to shield her from the truth seemed more challenging by the minute.

'To a man we all could have known better.' Wren raised a glass of watered-down whiskey from a wooden table, glancing at the shadows of an unlit bar, trying not to be spooked by the low light.

Goodwin sneered at his words. 'What a dreary place. Are we really staying here?'

'Only for a night,' said Isabel. 'Then in the morning, assuming there's no wind at the house, we'll root through what's there before we go back home. I can't imagine there's much worth salvaging and I'm sure none of us can wait to leave.'

Through the window, fog restricted visibility to half a mile, making the sea seem endless. 'I wonder if it's worth asking around the town while we're here,' said Wren. 'Maybe someone has insights, not only about Jon, but the village itself.'

'Feel free,' said Andrew. 'But if you want my opinion, you'd be wasting your time. I'm more interested in how the man died than how he lived.'

'I'm sure there's more to his story than we're giving him credit for.'

Andrew frowned. 'As we've already established, you and I see him differently.'

Isabel sat sideways to the window, midway between the two men. She showed no outward allegiance to either. 'To be fair, in the few years I knew him, Jon seemed quite decent. I know there's no excuse for keeping secrets, and this second life came as a shock, but he could still be a victim of circumstance in a similar way to the rest of us.'

'A victim of his son, you mean,' said Andrew.

Wren set his drink down hard on the table. Somewhere behind the bar, one of the staff members turned up the lighting. He hoped Andrew could see the disapproval on his face. 'You've no basis for that kind of accusation. You know as little as we do.'

'Which comes as a surprise,' said Andrew. 'You've been here for two days. Have you learned nothing?'

Isabel intervened. 'It's okay. You've been busy with the wind. I'm not angry about that. But Scott, for the record, Andrew and I have made progress of our own. We have ideas about what's happening.' Goodwin shot her a look, but she continued. 'The empty houses in the village … we think they're all dead. Not just Jon and his family; their neighbours, and their neighbour's neighbours. It would cast new light on the village if the Lawtons weren't the only ones.'

'How do you know this?' said Wren.

'We found a list in Jon's other house, the one in the city.'

'You went there without me?'

'You wouldn't answer the phone,' she said, 'or at least I couldn't get through. You're not the only one who needs to heal, Scott. Don't forget that.'

Wren struggled to hide his displeasure. He wanted both houses for himself. They were his birthright. 'Can I see this list?'

There was a stony silence, too long for his liking. 'We're going to pair it to Jon's research, once we're settled in. We think he was onto something.'

'Or involved in something,' Andrew clarified.

'What's on it?'

'Eighteen names,' she said. 'All of them are dead. The oldest happened fifteen years ago. The most recent was at Christmas. Most died within the last five years.'

'You think it's getting worse?' asked Wren.

'Right now, all we have are questions. We're going to search for a common thread. But also, why did Jon care? I mean, why was he working so hard on this?'

'Because he was grieving for his son?'

'Seems unlikely.' added Andrew. 'Anyway, the only question that matters right now is what can we do about it?'

Wren felt his eyes widen. 'Well, nothing. Don't even think about going near that place again, Isabel, especially not now. If the loss of life is so widespread then call the police or walk away.'

'They'll already know,' said Andrew. 'These appear to be natural deaths, so there's nothing to investigate. And every cause of death is different, almost suspiciously unique. Remember Wren himself supposedly had a heart attack in broad daylight.'

'Wren is on the list?'

'So is Jon, bizarrely.'

'I thought Wren was hit by your car,' said Wren.

'That's not true,' said Isabel.

'His own father wrote "heart attack" on the list, so that's what he believed. But what if there was more to the story? It's worth finding those answers, even if all we do is shove it down Wren's throat if he ever resurfaces.'

'So you're investigating his death to use against him if he returns?' Wren's hand started trembling. He had to force a sudden rage beneath the table before the others noticed, diverting energy into his jiggling leg.

'I suppose so,' came Andrew's reply. 'But if you're worried, you don't need to come on this journey. You've had things harder than anyone in the last three months. We can see you struggling, and you needn't be ashamed.'

'Excuse me?'

Isabel leaned forwards. 'Did you think I didn't notice how hard Jon's death hit you? That's someone you didn't even know. This stress is going to put you over the edge. You can't deny it. Let us help you.'

Wren scowled. 'You mean let you treat me like an invalid.'

She put a hand on his arm. 'Don't be like that. You weren't the only one affected by Wren's lies. Andrew came as close to death as you did. We're all going to head home in the morning, together, then you're going to focus on finding a new job and forget this mess. Andrew and I will get the houses emptied, then sold if possible. We can use the money for a fresh start.'

'But I was the one who found the research in the first place.'

'Only because you raced down here before anyone else had the chance,' she said. 'This is for your own good.'

A gentle rain began to fall against the window. Her eyes were cold, her jaw stiff. Wren held her gaze, but he couldn't match her conviction. She was right about that much – he just didn't have it in him.

'We'll need Jon's keys back.' Andrew's voice was calm, with a deeper connotation – *keys you stole from us in the first place.*

'I was never keeping them from you.'

'All the same …'

Wren stood up on his restless legs, unable to contain his anger any further. He hurriedly dug the keys out of his pocket and threw them onto the table before storming out of the restaurant. He couldn't fathom the betrayal. They had conspired to exclude him, even after all he had done.

He stood in a narrow car park with tiny raindrops speckling his face with cold. If they had their way, he would never again see the inside of his childhood home, all trace of his former life erased. And not just his own – Jon and Hope, his parents. Everything they had left in the world would be gone, dismantled with blithe contempt.

He took a deep breath and held it, counting to ten under his breath. Goodwin would light a bonfire, as Wren had done in a barrel, three days before. He would burn photographs and documents with a smug sense of satisfaction. Any attempt to intervene would reveal Wren's true identity, throwing away his last remaining chance of happiness.

He bunched his fists tightly, his fingernails digging into skin until the pain eased some of the tension. On the count of ten, Wren tuned into his environment, making a conscious effort to notice his surroundings. A vehicle stood in the car park – a Land Rover Defender, old and rusted. He became aware of someone watching him from inside. Their sheer size gave them away. With a glance over his shoulder to make sure the others couldn't see him through the window, Wren went over to investigate.

He found Alwyn Speake.

'What are you doing here?' Wren spoke before Alwyn had chance to lower the window.

'No one needs to know we're talking,' Alwyn said with a solemn expression. 'How are you?'

'You stood by while the others attacked me.'

'Hop inside and I promise to make up for that.'

Wren stormed around to the passenger door. Alwyn's car was caked in dirt both inside and out, with a trace of foul odour. The bearded man kept his eyes on the distance, where the fog met the sea. 'I can't tell you what destroyed the wall in your garden,' he said. 'But I know why. Everyone does.'

'It was to let the shadows in, wasn't it?' Wren didn't need confirmation. He slid onto the seat and pulled the door closed. 'What happened to Rees Franklin?'

'Rees was my oldest friend. I knew him better than anyone. What happened to him was the same thing that happens to anyone who goes out after dark.'

'But why?'

Alwyn drew an uncomfortable breath. 'If you can put the wall back together, they'll stop coming to the window, or at least you'll slow them down. We know this from trial and error. It won't change the outcome, though. If they want into a property, they'll get there eventually.'

Large spots appeared on the windscreen as falling rain gathered pace, slowly obscuring the view with a *tap-tap-tap* against the glass.

'Did they kill Jon Lawton?' Wren asked, though he worded the question differently in his mind.

Alwyn nodded. 'Sooner or later, they'll get everyone. No one knows the full reasons for it. They don't talk if you ask them.'

'And the wind?'

Alwyn's eyes shifted nervously, looking up and down the road. 'That's been stalking village folk for as long as I can remember.'

Wren nodded. 'It followed me halfway across the country. It's been terrorising me and my partner.'

'Unless she's from around here, I doubt that.'

'Maybe I'm … different.'

'You're a fool if you go anywhere near it.' Alwyn took his eyes off the horizon. 'Look, you can't understand how this place has degenerated. Every day, we lose another piece of it. You're right about The Black Horse – we stay in there because we've nowhere else to go.'

'So leave altogether,' said Wren. 'If you're afraid for your lives, pack up your bags and relocate.'

'To where? We can't afford to just abandon our homes and start over. Few of us can even work. Don't you see we're trapped?'

Wren leaned over the gear stick, making sure the bearded man could see his sincerity. 'I need to understand what killed Rees Franklin.'

Alwyn closed his eyes like he couldn't believe what he was about to say. 'Turn right at the steps to The Black Horse and you'll find a house at the end of the road, set back in the woods. Someone there can tell you more than I dare repeat. Don't ask me any more questions. I've already said too much.'

'Fair enough.' Wren pulled the door handle and a gentle gust tugged against the hinges.

'Understand, I'm not doing this out of sympathy,' said Alwyn. 'This is for the Lawtons, and in the hope you can bring sense to what happened to them.'

Wren slid out of the car and looked back at the man he had known since childhood, who could never have seen through his perfect disguise. 'If I can, Alwyn, that's exactly what I'll do.'

He didn't bother going back into the restaurant, unwilling to trade more insults with Isabel and her vile companion. Instead, he unlocked his own car, climbed in, and backed out of the parking space. There was less than an hour before the sun went down, and he needed to get there and back before dark. He doubted they would even notice.

A voice of doubt rang in his ears. Someone the size of Alwyn, with all his knowledge of the area, with favour from the locals, and unburdened with disloyal companions … if Alwyn couldn't fix those problems, it seemed unlikely that anyone could. Wren felt underpowered, but not powerless. He had some knowledge of his own. He knew exactly where Alwyn was sending him, and exactly what he would find there.

18.MALI|GNANCE

Damp leaves and soft moss formed a carpet underfoot, allowing Wren to move silently through the forest. The slightest noises seemed to echo through the twilight. He made a conscious effort to steady his breathing as he pushed through supple branches.

Sneaking up on an empty house.

In the highest corner of the village, a long and narrow driveway ended abruptly at the woodland's edge. A tiny two-bedroom cottage lay beyond, obscured by drooping overgrowth. Brown leaves stole most of the sunlight, leaving its windows in perpetual dimness. Shallow roots had created cracks in the walls, which had then filled with green moss.

The house resembled a tomb. Wren had been there as a child, but it had since changed beyond recognition. Back then, there had been a recognisable front garden and any leafy incursions had been kept at bay. He crept along an uneven pathway smothered with forest debris. The front door hung open. Gnawed, scratched wallpaper ran along a dingy hallway, as though the place had been – or still was – infested with vermin.

It seemed so derelict that he had no reservations about stepping over the welcome mat and heading inside. 'Hello?' he called. 'Is anyone in here?'

An unnerving breeze flowed through the building. He felt his hair ruffle against his forehead. The first room he encountered was a lounge, fully furnished. The pattern on the fabric of a blue sofa looked vaguely familiar. The air smelled of mould. Grey wires hung from the ceiling rose and ended in bare conductors. A large crack reached across the window.

No one could have set foot in that room for several years. He felt no need to enter, himself. Next, he found the kitchen. White walls and a large window made it light enough to navigate. The wallpaper had puffed out over rising damp. The stench almost made him gag.

As he walked through the room, linoleum flooring crackled beneath his feet. He was compelled to try running the tap. Rattling pipes confirmed his thoughts as copper-coloured water spilled out, filled with sediment. No one could have drunk it and survived.

There were, however, some unexpected signs of life. He found knotted plastic bags on the edge of the counter, beside a cupboard filled with boxes of biscuits and cereals. Someone had spent time there recently, someone with an even lower standard of living than his father. He was looking out towards the front garden when he heard a sound.

Coughing.

Wren swallowed his breath. Someone was in the house after all. He became aware of other items in the kitchen. Clean plates had been stacked by the cupboards. An opened jar of coffee sat beside a cheap kettle. He turned around to discover a light was on in one of the other rooms.

Wren almost gasped. He retraced his steps to the hallway and peered through the half-open bedroom door.

'Hello?' he said. 'Can I come in?'

He could still smell decay. There was a murmur from inside the room, so quiet that he would never have caught it from outside. 'I'm sorry to intrude,' he said. 'I wondered if I could talk to you.'

He stepped forwards and gave the door a gentle push. It drifted open to reveal a bedroom, lit by a pale glow from a bedside lamp. His image was reflected on a bare window with no blinds or curtain rail. Also mirrored in the glass, he saw a wardrobe leaning dangerously off-kilter, and a single-sized bed with a wooden headboard. Under a thick set of blankets sat an elderly lady, so tiny as to barely raise them.

Rees Franklin's mother, Eira.

She looked withered, as though the slightest knock could have smashed her to pieces. White hair fell about her shoulders. Faded, blue eyes stared blankly at the window.

'Mrs Franklin?' he said. 'My name is Scott.'

She took a moment to register his approach, then smiled. Her quiet voice was gravelly. Her dialect was heavy. Her words were calculated. 'Now, Wren, we both know that isn't true.'

This time, he gasped out loud. 'How?'

'I can see right through that shell of yours. You're Jon Lawton's boy, however you may appear.'

'Someone told you?'

'I hear all sorts of things,' she said.

'Then you'll know what Rees tried to do to me last night.'

She never once turned her head. She continued to peer over the foot of the bed towards the window. Her reflection made an approximation of eye contact. 'Why don't you sit down?' she asked.

He didn't comply, but despite himself, he entered the room. 'My father died. No one's willing to tell me the circumstances, but you probably know what I think.'

'I do.' She sounded unsympathetic. 'But what you think is unimportant. How do you feel?'

He sighed. *Enraged, adrift.*

'It hurts,' he said.

'That's grief. Good for you. I was wondering if you'd feel any.' Her withered hands smoothed out ruffles in the sheets. She spoke slowly, as though savouring every word. 'Grief is a powerful emotion for those who experience it. You'd be surprised what it can do.'

'Rees attacked me.'

'I know.' She pursed her lips. 'I'm glad you recognise him. He's changed since you were both young. He and I share a close bond, even now – two-sided, not like that mother of yours.'

'You know about my mother, too?'

'Don't interrupt,' she snapped, and he was quiet. Eira turned her head, and he wished she hadn't, for without the buffer of the reflection, he could see the hidden intensity of her glare. It petrified, like Medusa's curse. It was almost inescapable. 'What happened to your mother was tragic,' she said. 'But if you ask me, not mourning her loss makes it even sadder. She was always such a kind little girl. She deserved more.'

'She died giving birth to me. I can't grieve for someone I never knew.'

'And your father? Your grief for him is superficial, that much is obvious. Real grief knocks you sideways. Real grief wears you down. But it can also feed.'

'Feed what?'

'You should sit.'

'Please,' he begged, but the word caught in his throat. Eira Franklin seemed to know everything that had happened in his life, as well as he knew it himself. He formed an escape route in his mind, ready to run at the slightest provocation.

'There's a power in these hills, Wren. It's something unnatural and invisible. To stand in its presence is to absorb it, to hold onto it. We become charged, and living here for so many years, like you and Hope … you have so much of it inside you that even death can't take it away.'

'What is it?'

'A blessing. It nourishes and sustains. Those who die with some of its influence, they become the ysbryd. The most affected remain so close to life that we can almost touch them. Others are faded, but still very much there.'

'I've seen shadows in the back garden, twice now, maybe a dozen of them.'

'You could never count them all. The moment you leave these walls, you'll be surrounded.'

Wren had a sinking feeling in the pit of his stomach, a sense of having blundered into the path of danger, taking Alwyn's direction without questioning his motives. He glanced back to the window. There were no signs of activity at the side of the house, but he couldn't trust his eyes.

'Why don't they come inside?' he asked.

'They can't. Alone, they're easily repelled by light and heat and sound. Sunlight drives them back, so do crowded places. Their energy isn't infinite. Once spent, they cease to exist.'

'But they want in. That's why they stand there?'

'They want lots of different things, but mostly more life.'

'Are we safe here?'

'Even an empty house has power soaked into its walls. The only way for them to enter is to force that energy out. If you've ever been to the home of the recently deceased then you'll know what I mean. It's not just empty; the house is depleted.'

'Did they kill my father so they could take his house?'

Her eyes burned fiercely, as though someone had stoked the fires of her hatred. 'No,' she said. 'Your father brought attention to himself. Our secrets need to be protected. He chose to be an outsider, and now you've done the same.'

'I just want to understand.'

'That's not your decision.'

Wren towered over the fragile woman, but he was the one who felt intimidated. 'Did Rees tell you all of this?'

She nodded slowly. 'Rees can see things that we're blind to. The air outside this house glows with negative energy. So do you.'

'Because I'm ysbryd, too.'

She wet her lips, as though savouring her next words before she spoke them. 'You have so much energy inside you, Wren, maybe as much as Rees. That power could sustain you for years, but it can also be repurposed. Grief drains. It releases that power for others to use.'

'You can't force me to—' He baulked. 'Isabel.'

'That poor deluded girl who thinks you're someone else.' said Eira. 'It's such a terrible shame she doesn't listen to you. She's right back in the house you lured her away from.'

'Here in the village?'

Eira grinned, and Wren knew she wasn't bluffing. Someone must have told her, someone close. He looked again to the window, stumbling backwards into the doorway. 'You kept me here on purpose.'

'I wanted you to know why this is happening,' she said. 'Run if you want. It won't matter. You'll never escape. They can't outshine the sun, but they're watching from the shadows.'

He found his footing and fled, unable to take another word. He left the room in a cold sweat, holding the walls to stay balanced, swallowed up by a sweeping panic. He needed to be far away. He needed it now.

He needed Isabel.

19.DOWN|FALL

Wren burst out through the front door of Eira Franklin's house without a second thought for his safety, leaving the energy of its four walls behind. He plunged headlong into darkness. The forest carpet that had masked his approach now worked against him, denying him sound with which to navigate. He fanned his arms out and felt for the scratching claws of low-hanging branches, grabbing each one like rungs on a ladder until he could find the next.

His progress was painfully slow. The distance to his father's house might only have been two or three hundred metres, but it felt like miles. Isabel must have watched him leave the hotel on the coastline and come after him, straight back to the village, the one place he had warned her to avoid. Her distrust had reached a level where she did the opposite of whatever he said.

Eira Franklin had inverted his world. If she was right, then there were so many more spirits than he had seen at his father's window. It was a number he could only guess at. *Hundreds more? Thousands more? Tens of thousands more?*

Whenever a branch touched his shoulder or a leaf caught his hair, he imagined fingertips reaching through the darkness. As he broke into the open and saw the first streetlamps, his eyes played tricks. Crouching figures seemed to lurk beside every building, waiting for their chance to strike.

He made a beeline for Scott's car, hoping the warmth of the engine would hold them back. *But how many would it take before they could pass through any barrier? Was that the wind ... spirits combining their strength?* The car jostled him around as he sped back down the hillside. He thought he could see movement in the corner of his eye. *'You'll never escape,'* Eira had said. *'They can't outshine the sun, but they're watching from the shadows.'*

Goodwin's car was parked outside his father's house. He screeched to a halt beside it, blocking the road, as close to the front door as he could get. Those walls had barely held a dozen spirits at bay, the house depleted by his father's death. He ran to the door and banged his fist against the wood, yelling at the top of his lungs.

'Isabel, let me in.'

It was a stranger's cry, one he had never heard before. He could almost feel the night closing in around him, swallowing the sound. He screamed again until the door clicked open, then he barged inside, slamming it closed behind him. Isabel stood nervously, stirred by his tone. One hand was clenched into a fist, clutching something beneath her fingers. He saw through to the kitchen table, where under a bright ceiling light, Andrew sat reading through his father's notes.

'What the hell are you two doing here?' Wren snapped.

Andrew removed his glasses and set them down before responding through gritted teeth. 'We're trying to concentrate.'

'I left you miles away, where it's safe. You agreed not to come back.'

'Then I suppose we're all hypocrites, aren't we?'

One of them had taken the map of Pontrhyd-y-werddon and pinned it to the kitchen noticeboard. It was covered in fresh scrawl, linking names to different properties. Ruined. Wren made a conscious effort not to lose his temper.

'We can go through this at the hotel.'

Isabel came marching up the hallway. 'We were planning to. We saw you leave the car park and wrongly assumed you were coming straight back here. Where have you been?'

He turned to face her. 'I was on my way, you're right, but I got sidetracked.'

'Scott, I can tell when you're lying. What's this really about?'

Her rising suspicions seemed to override any sense of immediate danger, despite his agitation. 'You were right all along,' he said. 'There's something dangerous out there. Isabel, please. You wanted to go home and I agree with you now, so let's go.'

Andrew put his finger on the research to keep his place, then interjected. 'Nobody wants to stay here for a second longer than necessary, but we've started something while you've been missing. We need time to see it through—'

He cut himself short with a grimace, rubbing his temples with his thumbs.

Isabel asserted herself. 'Do you see the trouble this house causes? I told you we should have nothing to do with it.'

'You were right. I was wrong. Come home where it's safe.'

'But home isn't safe.'

'Please,' he yelled, altogether too loud. Andrew and Isabel exchanged a sideways glance.

'Scott,' she said with emphasis, unaware of how degrading it was to hear that name. 'We're all upset, but we need to work together. I'm sure you're trying to protect me, but you need to explain what's made you like this.'

Andrew rolled his eyes. 'It's less of a mystery to me. A single night in this filth would drive anyone crazy, let alone two nights.'

'This isn't about filth. It's not about my father's work. It has nothing at all to do with you. It's about saving someone I care about.' Wren glared, aware he was shaking. 'Someone in this village just told me Isabel's a target and I believe them. You, I don't care about, but I can't lose her. I won't.'

No one challenged his words, which echoed off the walls, filling the room with an icy silence that persisted for several seconds. It caught him unprepared.

'What's wrong now?' he asked.

'You just referred to Jon Lawton as your father.'

A bolt of lightning coursed up his spine. He saw a chain reaction start behind Isabel's eyes. Pieces of the puzzle fell into place – the mistakes he had made, his strange behaviour, his poor excuses, and his feigned forgetfulness.

'You know what I meant,' he said.

She visibly shrank, as though retreating into herself. Her skin turned white. 'Who are you?'

He swallowed hard. 'It was just a slip of the tongue. Can we please just go?'

'Where's Scott?' She made no attempt to disguise her hurt.

'I'm Scott,' said Wren.

'Let me speak to him.'

'You *are* doing.'

'Stop it,' she yelled. 'Stop talking to me like I'm blind. I can … I can see you now.' She didn't say his name. 'I don't know why I didn't see it sooner. Where is he?'

Wren's eyes sank to the floor. He knew it would be pointless trying to hold onto the lie, now the truth was out there. He felt as though the words leaving his mouth belonged to someone else. 'I don't know.'

It was the end of everything. An enormous weight unburdened itself from his shoulders, to be replaced with something much worse. He couldn't think fast enough to repair his slip of the tongue. He couldn't save himself. For a time, no one spoke. Isabel covered her mouth and he could hear her laboured breathing.

'That's impossible.' Andrew rose to his feet, his expression shifting between denial and terror. 'You were right under our noses the whole time. How have you done this, and why?'

'I don't control it,' said Wren. 'I can't say what happened, any more than you can.'

Isabel leaned against the table for support. 'Show me what you've done to Scott. Let me speak to him.'

'I can't,' said Wren. 'He … he isn't here, Isabel. He hasn't been here for a long time. After the hospital, he just … never woke up.'

'Liar.'

'I wouldn't lie about something like that,' he said. 'Scott's gone. I can feel it.'

Isabel's eyes widened even further. 'Then you killed him after all. My God, you killed him.'

Goodwin offered her the chair and she collapsed onto it, her face now dangerously pale. Goodwin, himself, had the opposite reaction. He raised a hand and marched forwards, smashing his fist into Wren's borrowed jaw.

'Will you ever leave us alone?'

Even though the attack was loaded with emotion, the impact was weak, as though Goodwin's injuries had left him underpowered. But Wren saw red. 'Don't you dare play innocent. You're the one that dragged her down here without a clue what you were getting into. We were doing fine before you interfered. We lived in peace.'

'I stuck around to keep her safe,' said Andrew. 'Safe from you. I didn't know you were hiding in plain sight.'

Wren snarled. 'More like you've been trying to steal her for yourself.'

'I'm not surprised you'd see it that way.' Andrew lashed out for a second time, but he was no match for Scott's physique. Wren tripped him up, sending him crashing into the worktop. It made such a noise that Isabel jumped out of her seat in fright and fled into the doorway.

'You ruin every life I create,' Wren barked.

'You shouldn't have a life, full stop. You're a thief. Be honest with yourself.'

'The bungalow was mine before Scott moved in. This house is mine, too. All of these possessions are worthless to anyone else. I'm trying to salvage what I can.'

'Scott didn't deserve to die. Don't you care?'

'What about me? What did I deserve?'

Andrew tried to right himself, but something made him clutch his scalp, as though struck down with immense pain. Wren only had to exert a gentle push to send him crumbling to the linoleum floor. 'You didn't see Scott for what he was,' Wren continued. 'He pulled the wool over Isabel's eyes, much worse than I ever did. He controlled her.'

Andrew struggled to pick himself off the floor. One of his legs didn't seem to bend.

'Stop,' Isabel screamed at the top of her lungs, so loud that Wren froze. It seemed to take something out of her, and there was a lengthy pause before she continued. 'Don't fight. I can't watch you kill one another again.'

It took all of Wren's inner strength to hold himself together, but in the end, he couldn't go against her wishes, not now, not ever. He took a long step backwards. 'Okay,' he said, then again in a softer tone, 'okay.'

Isabel crossed the room and helped Andrew to stand, examining his forehead as she spoke to him. 'I need you to give us a minute alone, please.'

'Are you sure?' Andrew replied. 'You don't know what he's capable of.'

'Please. He won't hurt me.'

Through gritted teeth, Andrew complied. He hobbled across the kitchen and closed the hallway door behind him. Isabel kept her back to Wren, facing the map on the noticeboard. Her shoulders rose and fell as he heard the familiar hiss of her asthma inhaler, but all he could see was her blonde hair.

'I wanted to tell you everything,' he said. 'I never asked for Scott to move aside. It just happened that way.'

'This has been a horrible, horrible lie.'

'Don't say that,' he said. 'I couldn't be honest with you because I knew how you'd react, but everything else in the last three months … All of it was real. The time we spent getting to know one another again. You can't tell me you felt nothing.'

'What does it matter what I felt? I thought I was with someone different. Doesn't that bother you? Every conversation we had, every look we shared.'

'It was good,' he said. 'Back to how it was before.'

'Why would I want that? I've been hiding from you for months and it turns out you were right in front of me the entire time. And you knew. *You knew.* You manipulated me.'

'I didn't ask for this body.'

'Didn't you?' She buried her face in her hands. 'You left me with nothing, then made a fool out of me for three months by parading that deceit in my face. I lived in fear of you, every minute of the day.'

'I know, Isabel. There were nights I had to listen to you dissect and disown everything we'd shared like you were rewriting history. You must realise how that felt.'

She closed her eyes and held her breath, but after a few seconds, she exhaled with a gasp. Her throat sounded restricted, a scratching tone to every passing of air. She slumped down into the chair with a hand extended to steady her descent. He caught a glimpse of her face in the reflection on the French doors. Against the backdrop of the fallen night – half hidden by her clean blonde hair – Isabel was crying.

'Are you alright?' he said. 'Did you bring an adrenaline shot?'

She took another hit of her inhaler, closing her eyes until she appeared more stable. 'You know, the whole reason Scott and I got together was because you kept pushing us both away. Your fear of it happening, made it happen. There was no conspiracy. But when I caught you in the garden, burning photographs and paperwork … When you told me you were trying to reduce the baggage in our life … That was a lie, wasn't it? That was you, erasing him.'

Wren's anger ebbed away. She was right. He had lied, and it hurt to hear her say it. He felt his own heart break along with hers, realising what he had done to her. Scott hadn't deserved a moment of her love, but maybe he didn't deserve it either. He was trapped by impossible circumstances, lacking the words to make things right.

He drew breath for a fresh attempt, one laced with apology, but the words had no time to form in his mouth. He heard a crack. Behind her reflection, out in the garden, something moved. Beyond patio flags and overgrown grasses, at the very limit of the visible light, Wren caught the smallest trace of something sifting through the air. Shadows. A crowd had gathered on the lawn, a mob of dark figures. One member stood out more than the others, more defined, as though glowing with more energy. They snarled with yellowed teeth and wicked, piercing eyes. Pockmarked cheeks glistened with oily moisture.

Rees Franklin.

Wren's blood ran cold. He stepped back and flipped the switch on the wall, afraid of the light as much as the dark. They were already at the window.

'Who's that?' Isabel whimpered.

Franklin approached them, half floating, half walking, and barely touching the ground. Time almost stood still.

'Don't talk,' said Wren. 'Stand up right now and get away from the window.'

20.FRAG|MENTATION

For reasons he didn't understand, there was silence. Isabel wasn't quick enough to react. She leapt off her chair, but froze beside the window of the French doors, as though petrified by fear. A featureless mass of determined spirits threw themselves forwards with astonishing force. Each became a tiny spark upon contact with the glass, but their combined power was greater than any window could withstand.

There was a muffled crunch. In the split second it took Wren to lift an arm to his face, the air was filled with tiny shards. He was pelted with a wave of glass and light. The skin of his forearm split open like butter sliced by a heated knife. A shard the size of his thumb dug into his cheek, puncturing right through into his mouth. He felt it pierce his tongue. He could taste it.

The combined impact lifted him right off his feet. His head was flung back over his shoulders until his windpipe was exposed, and then a hole was blasted clean through it. In his mind, he fell for several minutes. With his eyes tilted upwards, he saw glass ricochet off the ceiling then rain back down, sparks weaving between them.

Isabel bore the brunt of the attack. Standing closest to the door, everything seemed to pass right through her. Wren looked down to see blood pouring through exit wounds like so much sweat. He tried to scream her name, but the sound poured out through the hole in his throat – a horrific, contorted wheeze.

He came to rest on the kitchen floor, broken and helpless. Through sideways glances, he saw spirits approaching the door frame. They needed fresh death to drain the house so they could enter. It seemed they would get what they wanted. The kitchen door rattled, and Andrew Goodwin burst into the room. At his presence, sparks exploded from every square inch of the linoleum floor, hundreds upon hundreds of tiny flecks repelled. Andrew ignored them all. He flipped the light switch and scrambled to his knees beside Isabel, as though oblivious to the glass strewn everywhere. He raised her off the floor and cradled her in his arms.

'Isabel? Can you hear me? Oh, God.'

Andrew wrapped an arm around her neck as he picked at the embedded glass with his fingertips. It blocked Wren's view. All he could see were her eyes, which were wide open with terror, staring not at him, but at his adversary. His borrowed body lay broken, its skin and flesh torn to shreds. Scarlet blood soaked his clothing and began to flood the floor.

He began to feel detached, like the wounds had been inflicted on someone else, and he was merely an observer. He kept glancing at Isabel's red-stained hair, wishing she would look back at him. A cold draught snaked through the broken window. Darkness welled from deep within. He began to lose awareness of his surroundings, his consciousness fading. He knew that to fight it was useless. The void was coming, the void he knew.

And it wouldn't even grant him one last glimpse.

END OF DEATH

PART THREE: REVOLUTION
21.VANI|SHING

'Couldn't you lie here forever?'

The cogs ticked inside a mechanical watch on the bedside table. It was such a gentle sound that Wren only ever heard it in the greatest calm. He lay perfectly still, the bed covers drawn up to his chin. Isabel lay behind him with an arm draped across his torso, her words so softly spoken that he could hear the parting of her lips.

'When I was young, my parents used to climb into bed with me on cold mornings. We would cuddle to keep warm. They're some of my favourite memories. We didn't speak; we just held one another. It felt so safe and homely. Little me, wrapped in their massive arms.'

Sunlight seeped into the room through minuscule gaps in the curtain fabric, intensified by the opacity of visible frost on the window behind. Emotions didn't come so easily to Wren Lawton, the product of a very different kind of upbringing.

'My father wouldn't have dreamt of doing that.' His voice was croaky, and hard to control. 'Whenever it was too cold to go out, he made me cordial drinks with hot water. It may not sound like much, but as a child, it was a treat. I still smell blackcurrant in the depths of winter.'

He rolled over to face her. Her blue eyes were dilated. Blonde hair was ruffled from a night of tossing and turning. 'Do you miss those days?' she asked.

'Not really. Deep down, he always meant well, but my life is better now. I wouldn't go back. Though having said all that, I really need the bathroom.'

'Oh, me first. I've been needing to go for ages.'

She took three rapid breaths, and before he could object, she threw back the covers. She pulled her long nightshirt down over her legs and hurried to the doorway. In her wake, she left a cold breeze that made the hairs along his pale arms stand erect. He couldn't leap after her. It wasn't in his nature. The two lovers were never more of a stark contrast than at the start of the day. He lumbered, whereas she seemed to float, half naked and unabashed. His body remained hidden under a set of green pyjamas, concealing a belly that wobbled as he climbed off the mattress. A worn paisley carpet offered no welcome to his bare feet.

He saw the ghost of his face reflected in the window and it gave off the illusion of a thick fuzz of head hair, something he hadn't known since his teens. He went to the lounge and paused by the radiator, relishing the warmth against his shins. The trees in the garden were caked with ice, frozen in position, deathly still.

'Hello?' came a voice. 'Can you hear me?'

'What's that?' he called through to the bathroom.

The reply seemed to come not from behind him, but through the window. 'Focus on your breathing.'

Something pricked his forearm, like a needle piercing through his skin. He rubbed it until the pain subsided. Phantom pains were a hallmark of his questionable health, so he didn't give it a second thought. Moments later, Isabel emerged from the bathroom.

'Did you say something?' she asked.

'No, I thought you did.'

'Fair enough. I'll boil the kettle. Are we going to see your father tonight?'

Wren shook his head. 'There's no point. I tried dropping by twice yesterday, but he wasn't in. The phone rang out, too.'

'Should we be worried?'

'I doubt it,' he said. 'He'll resurface in a day or two and we'll never get an explanation. He's always been like that.'

Isabel's bare feet caught his eye. Painted toenails stood out against the dull floor. They were crimson red. She skipped off towards the kitchen, and again, the displacement of air felt like a weak gust of wind. For a second or two, it stirred a foreboding that Wren had no cause to feel. He paused before he reached the doorway, watching her root through the cupboards.

'I thought we'd try something new.' She laid a courgette and a parsnip on the countertop. 'I've never made my own soup before, but I'm told it's really easy.'

Wren frowned. 'What about your Good Friday soup?'

'What's that?' She picked up a carrot, then stopped. 'Will you eat these if I cook them, or have you changed your mind about them again?'

'The soup we made together. Was that me, or was that someone else?'

He felt a strange metallic taste in his mouth and a tingling sensation along both his arms. A heavy weight seemed to linger in his stomach. Isabel came across the kitchen with a look of deep concern. He welcomed her embrace with mixed emotions.

'Are you alright?' She felt unnaturally cold.

'Something's off,' he said.

'You must mean the hob. We'll need the biggest pan we have.' She moved to the appliance and turned a dial, watching one of the rings burst to life. The flame burned several inches high, shooting tiny flecks into the air. 'Seriously, though, you look like you're sweating.'

'I'm cold, actually.' Now Wren's arms felt like they were covered in ants. He looked past her – through her – and caught sight of his reflection in the glass of a framed painting on the wall. The face looking back was unfamiliar. The skin was too dark. The nose was too large. The silvery hair didn't belong to him.

To his surprise, the image distorted. Glass bowed, folding inwards like a convex lens, without a clear reason for it. A thin web of fractures spread across the surface, then in defiance of logic, continued onto the painted walls. Any illusion of normality ended abruptly. The wooden frame split open, torn into splinters. Plaster cracked like an eggshell. Wren gasped as a clump of drywall fell to the floor and shattered.

His world was literally falling apart. Isabel stood there, oblivious, her eyes locked onto his. They glistened with tears and obvious hurt. Everything came flooding back. She knew his secret. She knew everything he had done to deceive her. She knew what he had done to Scott, how Wren had strangled him, and he had never recovered.

She was dead. Dead.

She was dead, and none of this was real.

With that revelation, everything collapsed like a house of cards. Kitchen counters dissolved like sandcastles in the tide. They sifted and shrank. The ground beneath his feet evaporated, leaving him suspended in darkness. There were flashes of light, so strong that he should have been blinded. Each one of them stripped another detail away – the stripes on the wallpaper, the scent of Isabel's skin – until only the two of them remained.

To his horror, she looked white and unresponsive, but still her expression carried such an awful sense of betrayal. He could barely stand to look her in the eye, but he also couldn't bring himself to turn away. She was the only object left in what had become a total darkness.

She was his totality.

He knew, now more than ever, how much he needed her. He had no meaning without her. He tried to close the short gap between them – to swim through the void – only for it to expand, pushing her further into the distance. He had lost her, in every sense. From the depths of his mind, he felt it.

Nothing could be worse.

22. TRAN|SITION

Wren heard voices in adjacent rooms, reduced to muffles and murmurs by the intervening walls. He was acutely aware of their distance, isolated, cut off.

Blind.

He could feel the warmth of daylight against his face. He could feel his eyelids open. But he couldn't see a thing, not even the suggestion of patterns and shapes. He should have panicked, he knew, but having no sense of location addled his thoughts. He didn't have a clue where he was, what his surroundings looked like, nor how he got there.

'Hello?' He spoke in a thin, croaky whisper, possessed by a dream-like calm. He shut his eyes tightly and tried to open them again. Nothing. He could feel a mattress beneath him, and a bedsheet wrapped around his midsection. Under his head was a pillow.

'Can anyone hear me?' he asked.

A soft hand made contact with his. The parting of a person's lips sounded loud against the stillness. A voice spoke tenderly. 'Welcome back,' it said. 'You gave us quite a fright.'

He sighed. 'Isabel, is that you?'

'It's Sarah.'

'Where's Isabel?'

'I don't know anyone by that name. Is she a nurse?'

Soft fingers stroked gently over the back of his hand, which unnerved when it could have been intended to soothe. 'Why am I blind?'

'Because you collapsed,' said the voice. 'Don't you remember?'

'I don't.' A mental block obscured the truth, as though allowing him to adjust before he could see the full picture. 'Who are you?' he asked.

There was a lengthy pause. 'They told me you'd have trouble with your memory, but try to concentrate. You should know me, of all people.'

'Are you from the village?'

'Lloyd,' she sighed. 'I'm your wife.'

Lloyd. The word echoed inside his skull like an angry wake-up. *Lloyd.* A name he had never heard before, not even once. The disorientation became too much. Wren felt his heartbeat accelerate. His breathing became fast and staggered.

'Keep still.' The woman spoke with urgency, her voice unfamiliar. 'Try to relax or you'll make it worse.'

He didn't listen. *Lloyd* was all he could focus on. *Who the hell is Lloyd?* He clawed at the bed linen, trying to pull himself up while his body refused. It was like trying to climb out of a slippery well.

'Does something hurt?' said the woman. 'Should I call a doctor?' She was verging on panic, which only fuelled his own.

'Why can't I see?' His own voice became much deeper as his throat cleared, sending tremors down his windpipe.

'They think you've had another stroke. The doctor said you might lose your eyesight for a short while. It's common. It'll come back when it's ready.'

'How long?' he spat, afraid of the darkness.

'That depends on how well you rest. Please try to calm down.'

Drained of his energy, Wren didn't fight for long. He had no means to suppress the images poisoning his mind, reliving the horrors of what had happened at his childhood home. He saw exit wounds seep blood like so much sweat. He saw blonde hair, stained crimson. He couldn't escape.

'What's happened to Isabel?' he pleaded.

'I still don't know who you're talking about,' the woman replied. 'Should I look—'

'*Isabel*,' he shouted, his voice echoing off the walls.

'There's no one else here,' said the woman. 'I should … I should get someone who can help.'

He cried in distress, in frustration, and in grief. The images were harrowing: Blood everywhere. Wren needed to get back to Pontrhyd-y-werddon and find Goodwin, or anyone who knew if she was alright. The hand on top of his held firm while another gripped his arm.

'You were in the living room,' said Sarah. 'One minute you were fine, then you took a turn. I know how you must feel, but you'll do yourself more damage if you don't calm down. We can't rush your recovery.'

'This can't be happening.' He tried to tense weak arms, but failed every attempt. She held him down almost effortlessly, doubtless thinking it was for the best. Wren saw it differently – it prolonged his anguish. If he could have seen the walls, they would doubtless be spinning.

'I brought you to a hospital so they can help you.'

'They can't,' he said. 'No one can.'

'At least let them try,' she said. 'I know it's not in your nature, but please.'

The grip on his arm relaxed as he lost the power to fight, but behind his useless eyes, the torment went on. Wren Lawton had died again. Scott was gone. Andrew Goodwin had ruined his second chance. And he didn't even know if Isabel was still alive.

***

Sleep came in short, staggered bursts. His mind worked overtime, haunted by the inescapable image of Rees Franklin, sneering from the back garden. He saw shattering glass. He saw weaving sparks. It pushed him to the brink of insanity.

Lloyd's weakness proved both a curse and a saving grace. For a time, the only thing keeping him alive was the lack of strength to tear himself apart. He was definitely in a hospital. Wren recognised the clinical smell and the scuffing of flat-soled shoes on shiny floors. Every few hours, someone would come by to check on him, and Sarah never strayed too far from his bedside.

For five entire days, he did little else than re-experience what had happened to him, waiting for his sight to return. He cursed the hostile villagers who chose to protect their secrets at his expense. He swore revenge against the bedridden mother of his childhood friend. He vowed to stop the sparks that had invaded his home, the lost souls reaching out for him.

Death, everywhere he turned.

He refused all food that came to him. He became aware of the transitions of day and night, of warmth and cold. Rainstorms pattered against the windowpanes as he gathered information from his unfamiliar senses. His arms were coated with coarse hairs and loose flesh. There was a wedding ring on his finger.

He couldn't stomach the thought of a new beginning. He tried with all his might to reject his host, praying that his mother's spirit would extract him again and return him to Scott, still lying on the kitchen floor. When nothing seemed to work, he succumbed to a new level of madness. He spent more and more time asleep – commanded by his frailty – until, through haunted dreams, he eventually, mercifully, got the rest he needed. After a week of starvation, he ate ravenously, and found his pulse growing stronger with each subsequent day.

***

Flashing blue lights poured in through a set of double doors, making the walls appear to shimmer. Wren regarded the performance with disinterest. He could see colour distinctly, but little more beyond that. After eight days, there were still no details in his world. Everything was a blur, which seemed crueller than having no sight at all. He couldn't see his own hands well enough to know what they were really like. He couldn't see his own face in the mirror. When he stood, the ground was seemingly eight feet below him, but that could have been Lloyd's height.

Who could say?

He gazed blankly through the double doors, drawn by commotion like a moth to a flame. A cold draught touched his face. He would have given anything to go out into the world under his own power, but his frailty shattered his confidence. He couldn't bring himself to commit.

Wren had sneaked out of his bedroom and shuffled down the corridor, choosing his moment carefully. Feigning a complete recovery, he had asked the nurses if they had seen a woman admitted earlier that month with wounds from broken glass. No one had been able to help. He stood at the edge of a crowded waiting room, daunted by the prospect of having to fend for himself, hoping beyond logic that he would hear a familiar voice.

'There you are.' Sarah's tone was both unmistakable and unwelcome. She spoke as an adult to a child. After so many days of one another's company, her real personality had begun to emerge. His heart sank. She would never let him leave. Her hand took his arm in a manner not meant to reassure. Wren turned to face her, seeing little more than a smear of brown hair and white clothing.

'I was exercising,' he said.

'You worried me sick. You must have wandered halfway across the building, and for what? You know you can't go anywhere.'

He declined to answer. Wren didn't like the way his booming voice rattled his skull.

'You're taking things too fast, as ever,' she continued. 'They told us to expect several weeks before you have your independence back. And they said to rest, not go on expeditions.'

He honestly didn't care for her lectures. He wasn't the person she thought she was scolding. Where that man had gone to, he cared about even less. The grip on his arm tensed, trying to squeeze a reaction out of him. 'Why won't you talk to me? They'll never let you out if you don't communicate.'

He stiffened his upper lip. He didn't want her opinions, nor anybody else's. There wasn't a person alive who could have brought him out of his misery. If he had garnered his nerve a few moments sooner, he would have walked out of the door and left her for dust, but that was no longer an option.

'Just take me back to the room,' he said.

'I can tell the difference between something wrong with you and when you're just being difficult, Lloyd. If you won't talk to me, then God help us both.'

She turned and marched away down the corridor, lost in a blur of movement. Wren lingered until she returned with a clash of metal. Something rammed into the back of his knees and she took his shoulder, physically forcing him into a seat. Wren extended his elbows to feel wheels on either side of him.

'So you know,' she said, 'I could have put you into one of these from the start. I've used all my leave to be here for you. God only knows, I didn't have to do that. It's only for the sake of our children that I came at all.'

He drew a deep breath, but remained silent, refusing to respond as she wheeled him back up the corridor. To argue with her would be futile in a situation he knew nothing about, and he would risk losing her support altogether. She may not have offered much, but he couldn't cope on his own just yet. Wren watched the linoleum floor go past in a haze. He returned to his room. His cell. There were only two things he needed to get free from that place – patience and eyesight.

Wren was running short on both.

23.CONT|RITION

The car door slammed so hard that the whole vehicle rocked sideways on its suspension. Wren got the message. He could almost see the anger in Lloyd's wife, bubbling beneath the surface. She wore pleasantries like a mask, as he wore the skin of her dead husband. Her true self was a ball of seething rage.

She didn't seem happy to escort him home, as though two weeks of living apart hadn't been long enough. As she walked around the vehicle and climbed in behind the wheel, he fixated on the creases of her face. Her eyes were sunken, with deep valleys beneath her eyelids. Her hair looked artificially dark and uniform. He placed her age somewhere in her mid-sixties, perhaps even older, not too far from his father's age before his untimely death.

It was reasonable to assume that Lloyd was also in his sixties. Ten days post-reawakening, Wren's eyesight had returned, to the point where he could have attempted to drive the car himself. But he still hadn't seen his reflection. He didn't even like looking at his borrowed hands, averting his gaze whenever he needed to use them. That part wasn't too difficult. Despite attempts to convince her otherwise, Sarah was treating him like an invalid. He had scarcely lifted a finger to help himself.

'I assume you have everything?' she asked, bluntly. He didn't answer, still hating his new voice. He wound his window down and relished the rush of cool air as they moved off, daring it to turn violent and end his suffering.

'Your sister was asking about you,' Sarah said, making a second attempt at conversation. 'Not worried enough to come and visit, of course, but she sent her best regards.'

He nodded, disinterested. The roads were familiar. Wren knew his way back to the village and could think of little else. It seemed that once again his mother had chosen the nearest host who met her dark criteria, someone freshly deceased. But with Lloyd, she had chosen poorly. There was an ache in Wren's chest that he couldn't explain. *Was it phantom pain, or part of the same ailment that had finished Lloyd off?*

Even sitting down, he was noticeably taller. Lloyd would have towered over Scott by more than a foot. He kept slouching in the passenger seat to compensate, which hadn't escaped Sarah's attention. He tried to listen to the rhythms of his body, guessing at natural behaviour. He grunted and muttered rather than speak in full sentences, hoping Lloyd was a man of few words.

His supposed wife had fought to keep him in the hospital for as long as possible. He got the impression that she didn't want to have to care for him until forced to. He had thwarted her efforts, refusing to react as he was poked and prodded, until there were no grounds to keep him on the ward. Now, all he had to do was avoid giving her cause to turn the car back around and he could embrace new freedom.

'Thank you for collecting me,' he said, involuntarily slurring his words.

'It's good you're feeling better,' she conceded. Some had called his recovery miraculous, but such words were meaningless to Wren. He had heard them all before. This was more like a punishment, having to assimilate a life he wanted no part of.

'What happens next?' he asked.

'I've been instructed to keep you housebound for the time being, and keep an eye on you, meaning watch your vices. The doctors think you could relapse if you try to pick up where you left off. This is the end of your drinking and the end of your smoking.'

'Understood.' Cigarettes explained the tightness in his lungs and the effort it took to breathe.

'It's serious this time,' she said, taking her eyes off the road.

'Yes,' he replied. 'I know that.'

'We can't act like this one didn't happen. Two strokes is enough. You won't survive a third. You need to stop doing whatever the hell you feel like.'

He shrugged, but she kept making eye contact. He got the impression there was a subtext to her words. 'No more hospitals,' he said, as though repeating her words.

'Even if your brain wasn't right, I can't forget some of what you said to me before you collapsed. You were horrible, Lloyd. I've moved myself into the back room. Once you're settled, we'll have to decide where we go from here.' She didn't get an emotional response, so she relented. 'Anyway, that's for tomorrow. Your things are in the glove box.'

Wren opened the compartment to find a mobile phone and a brown leather wallet. There was an open packet of cigarettes, but on sight of them, Sarah leaned over and snatched them away.

'You're not having those.'

The phone fell out onto the floor of the car and slid under his seat. He didn't bother to retrieve it. With mild interest, he rifled through the wallet. There were credit cards and appointment cards. Lloyd had a vaccination certificate with ragged edges. His surname appeared to be Bennett, which meant Sarah's would be, too. Regrettably, there was no cash, which rendered the contents worthless in his eyes. He traced the patterns of the cracked leather surface with his fingertips. The cool air on his face turned colder as they picked up speed.

A clouded sky reflected off a white bonnet. They were driving through the Valleys now. He stared at passing hilltops, unwilling to admit his relief at having his eyesight back. He couldn't accept positive emotions, as though he didn't deserve them. Pontrhyd-y-werddon wasn't signposted – long forgotten by the world – but he knew the twists and turns would bring them close. Were it not for the rough terrain, he could have been there in less than half an hour. The proximity raised his confidence, enough to push his luck.

'How old am I, exactly?' he asked.

Sarah flinched. 'Are you being serious, or is that a play for sympathy?'

'I just wondered. I don't feel as old as I suspect I am.'

'So your memory's gone? Is that what you're telling me? Why didn't you tell the doctors?'

'They still would have sent me home eventually, Sarah.'

'But they could have looked after you in the meantime.' A frosty silence was short-lived. 'You're sixty-five.'

He toyed with the wedding ring on his alien hand. It was tight enough to make him wonder if it would ever come off. 'How long have we been married for?'

The car slowed down as she eased off the pedal. 'What kind of a question is that? Nine years. The children belong to your ex, before you figure that one out.'

'And I fell over?' he asked.

'You had a turn. It didn't knock you out. It knocked you senseless. That's when I brought you to the hospital. See, even after you're cruel, I still do right by you.'

She accelerated again, this time in anger. The air began to tug on the wallet in his loose grasp. At that moment, he wanted more than anything to disconnect from his current circumstance and regain his independence. He lacked both the energy and the interest to smooth over whatever dispute the couple had been embroiled in. He didn't care. Lloyd was dead, and Wren had no intention of taking his place. Instead, he raised his arm and relaxed the pinch of his fingers. The wallet whipped out of his hand and through the open window.

'What was that?' Sarah leaned forwards to check her rear-view mirror.

'I dropped my wallet,' he replied. 'Sorry.'

She slammed on the brakes. The seatbelt bit into his shoulder as the car screeched to a halt. 'Did you do that on purpose?' she barked.

'Of course not,' he lied.

She turned and looked over the headrest. He adjusted the wing mirror until he could see the wallet lying at the side of the quiet road. An expectant silence ended when she groaned with frustration. 'I'll go, then,' she said. 'Wouldn't want you straining yourself.'

'It was an accident.'

'I'm sure it was.'

She reversed the car fifty feet, flung open the door, and pulled herself out. He waited for his opportunity, then unclipped his seatbelt and pitched himself over the gearstick. Her reaction was immediate. As he moved off, Sarah flailed her arms, doubtless realising she had been tricked. She screamed an obscenity, but he didn't care one iota. He would happily never lay eyes on her again. There were more important places to be, and he had waited long enough.

As she disappeared behind the rolling landscape, he put her out of his thoughts, something very easy to do. It was only a couple of miles to the unmarked track that led to Pontrhyd-y-werddon. Instead of turning up the hillside, he pulled into the undergrowth. He didn't want anyone to see him coming. He had made that mistake before. Long grasses and low hanging branches swallowed the vehicle whole, like the jaws of a hungry animal. Passing vehicles wouldn't see it there. The rest of the journey, he would attempt on foot.

The base of the hill hadn't changed since he had explored it as a child. Dense bushes obscured patches of exposed rock where the incline was too steep for vegetation. But a narrow path ran between it and the road. After a few hundred yards, the sound of trickling water spurred him down to a culvert on the edge of the forest. He met with the stream that ran all the way to his father's back garden and beyond.

No one would see his approach, not even from twenty feet away. He trudged through thick, untended woodland. It was difficult to keep from making any noise, but as he passed beneath the village, he stopped caring. The only windows looking down on him were either smashed or boarded up. It seemed unlikely that anyone still lived there. Wren finally saw that place for what it was – a poisoned community, decayed, with the scornful, jealous eyes of both the living and the dead aimed at every outsider.

From this new vantage point, he could clearly see the trail of carnage Eira Franklin had described. Time and again, he saw wooden panels nailed to walls, patching over wounds that were incapable of healing. Alwyn Speake had left his mark on every house. Wren saw the extent of his undertaking. *Alwyn must have realised they were under a sustained attack, so why didn't he say something?*

Down there on the valley floor, trees numbered in their hundreds, perhaps even in their thousands. They afforded good shelter. Wren was able to progress towards his father's house without drawing attention. There were never any cars on the road above him, nor people on the streets. He couldn't see or hear another living soul.

Not that it calmed his nerves. With a sharp breath, he broke from cover and rushed the short distance to the broken garden wall. He felt sluggish compared to his time in Scott's body. Even small manoeuvres required a great deal more effort. He thumped up the slope on rigid limbs, going straight towards the French doors. They were boarded over like the window beside them – more of Alwyn's handiwork. Nails were driven into mortar, and Wren managed to tease them back out with a few stiff tugs.

For the first time in days, daylight poured into the kitchen. Stale air poured back out. Wren was struck by the sickly odour of dried blood and cleaning fluid. He tasted bile in his mouth as he realised he could sense a strange energy, perhaps the same energy Eira Franklin had told him about. A tingling sensation rose beneath his temples – an electrical charge, akin to the resistance of repelling magnets. It was stronger now than he had felt in the house once before, as though accentuated by recent death.

The hairs on the back of his neck stood to attention. It was like sensing a presence, and one he recognised immediately. He closed his eyes. For a second, he felt as though he was back in the bungalow with the yellow door, in bed, in the small hours of the morning. He could almost hear Isabel breathing as she slept beside him. In his mind, there was no mistake. She was in that room.

He could picture Goodwin's eyes looking down into hers, as though the two were still embracing on the linoleum floor. He could picture her red-stained hair. Any smashed glass had been swept clear, apart from a few chunks embedded in the walls, but he could see immovable stains of sickly brown where he and his love had fallen.

A few seconds of the scene was more than he could bear. Wren fled into the hallway, passing beyond the kitchen door. The buzzing changed, a subtle shift. His thoughts moved to his father, who had died on the front doorstep. The gloom was more invasive than it had been when he first arrived. Perhaps, as Eira had supposed, the energy of the house had diminished until the sadness of death was all that remained. Perhaps Wren's own sensitivity had increased following his latest demise, as he distanced further from the living. Perhaps the ysbryd had been at work for the past fortnight, claiming the house for themselves. Perhaps all three notions were correct.

In any case, he found it difficult to remain in the property, and was filled with an urgency to leave. He likened himself to the sparks passing through the walls, to be yanked back out again, as though repelled by the inside. Maybe their reactions were more than involuntary. Maybe they couldn't stand being close to life.

His thoughts were interrupted when he realised the light switch had been taken from the wall, and the light fitting overhead. The washing machine had gone. He had dragged the appliance in front of the living room door to serve as a barricade after his first night back in the house. It had been an awful task. Now, someone had removed it, but they had been selective in their thievery. In its place, he found Isabel's suitcase, wide open, with its contents disturbed as though picked through in a hurry.

His heart leapt. There was physical evidence of her, something he immediately wanted to preserve. But someone else had got to it first. Unable to help himself, he knelt on the carpet, linking each item of clothing to poignant times of their distant past. The smell of her perfume filled his nostrils. Someone had taken anything of value, but beneath a washbag with a floral pattern, he came across a twice-folded sheet of notepaper. The handwriting was unmistakable, and it wasn't Isabel's. Instead, he scanned over a list of names produced by his father, a piece of research he had been told about, but hadn't been allowed to see.

He fought back tears. The sheet had been divided into three columns, recording details of people who had once lived in the village. A woman named Gwen Richards had moved to Suffolk, but had been kill by a train a year later. Another woman had overdosed in Loughborough. Wren Lawton had died of a heart attack. Three names had been underlined, all belonging to a family Wren had forgotten about – the Craddocks. He remembered the commotion when they had died in his youth.

Exactly where Isabel had found the list, he would never know, but she had seen fit to keep it from him, refusing to let him look over the detail. His hands quivered as he stared right through the page. *When did she lose her trust?*

Something stirred in the house. Wren froze at the sound of a heavy object being dragged along the hallway carpet towards him. There was nothing to see. He strained his ears against the silence, and as he did so, a floorboard creaked behind the sealed living room door. With a chill, he realised what was happening. His worst fears had been proven correct. Three deaths in a short space of time had lowered the strength of the property, breaking down its barriers. The sparks were no longer repelled and could pass freely through the walls.

They had taken the house. Wren, for his own many deaths, didn't seem to have the power to force them back out. Eira had suggested he belonged in their number, that he was ysbryd too, that they were brethren. Perhaps that was why they seemed different now. As his ears grew more sensitive, he heard noises everywhere. These weren't the telltale scratches he had become familiar with. Instead, he heard whispers, indistinct muttering from all around. With reckless abandon, he had blundered among the very same spirits that had ended his life. His aged knees cracked as he stood up. Terrified, he rushed back through the kitchen door towards the exit. The pile of research papers had gone, which was to be expected, but Andrew had left his father's annotated map of the village pinned to the noticeboard. Wren tore it down and brought it with him as he fled into the garden.

It didn't matter who could see him, not anymore. Isabel was gone. Her presence was now forever tied to the house where he grew up. And that house had been overrun, no longer safe for the living to enter. He wiped tears from his face, struggling to think straight. She didn't deserve an eternity of unrest. If there was even a chance that such a thing were possible, he needed to help her.

It couldn't end like this.

24.PATH|OSIS

Dilapidated buildings flanked the street on both sides. Patches of grasses and mosses hung from every shaded corner of brickwork. Wren knew almost every house belonged to the dead now, taken by force. Many of them would be watching him pass by while they sheltered from the late morning.

He reached the top of the village and, set amongst the trees, the white-painted façade of The Black Horse. The heat of its occupants resisted decay. It had become a bastion of the living. He peered up through the grimy windows, knowing they would all be in there – a dozen men of different ages, whiling away their pointless lives. Much like the ysbryd, they spent their days looking out at the world, and saw most things. But they had made no attempt to keep Isabel and Wren safe when the spirits had come for them. Instead, the cowards had waited until danger had passed, then ransacked the house for anything of value, perhaps even before the bodies had cooled.

He thought only of vicious reprisal. He wanted to burst inside the pub and beat a confession out of each one of them in turn, to find an outlet for his seething rage. But as his fingers wrapped around the door handle, the first seeds of doubt formed a voice beneath his anger.

'Don't go looking for a fight,' it said.

He had been aggressive with the village folk once before and got nowhere. Lloyd's body was no match for even one of the men inside, and he was hopelessly outnumbered. Logic prevailed. There was a much better way. No one around those parts would know Lloyd's face, nor what to expect from him. A nonthreatening approach could earn their trust, or at least a little information. They weren't going to volunteer what they knew about the ysbryd to anyone they thought could make trouble for them. He needed to keep that in mind.

The door put up no resistance as he swung it wide. Wren coughed to make his presence known, forcing a smile. A dozen glares were upon him in seconds. Everyone in the pub sat as he had found them twice before. An elderly man blew pipe smoke out through an open window. The youngest men – including Alwyn – sat farthest from the fumes. All wore guarded expressions, but Wren was a different kind of stranger this time, noticeably older. He could appeal to different members of the group.

'Prynhawn da,' he said, with the fragmented scraps of Welsh language he could remember from school. 'Ble mae Owen Craddock?'

Someone slammed their drink down. 'You're too far from anywhere to stumble upon us with a name like that, not so many years after he died.'

'I'm not looking to make a scene,' said Wren. 'My name is Lloyd Bennett. I haven't heard from Owen in a couple of years. I suppose now I know why.'

'He had no friends, not even us. What's your interest in him?'

'It won't matter now. We crossed paths once or twice. He must have been pushing seventy, the last time I saw him, so it doesn't come as a complete surprise to hear that he's passed.'

Wren could remember being told that Craddock and his family had died. They had been a mainstay of the village throughout his childhood, active within the community. He had known Owen's daughter from school. Pontrhyd-y-werddon had been a different place once, and news of Owen's exclusion from the clique came as a genuine surprise.

A man bared yellow teeth as he spoke. 'You've no business here, if you came for that man.'

Wren rocked his head from side to side, pretending to think. 'The truth is, he owed me money.'

To his relief, one of them smiled. 'Oh, right. That's different. A few of us, too.'

Someone snorted a laugh. There was a subtle shift in the villagers' behaviour. 'Most of us knew him for thirty years and more,' said the man with the yellow teeth. 'The strongest man I ever met, but nevertheless, good riddance to him.'

'What took him down?' asked Wren. 'His heart?'

'All we know is he collapsed.'

'Let me ask a question.' Alwyn Speake interrupted the conversation. He looked out through the front window of the building, his thick, red eyebrows sunken into a frown. 'How did you get here? I don't see a car.'

Wren tried to think fast. 'There's a bridge down at the bottom, by that wreck of a house with the sunken roof. If you follow the path, it cuts right through the valley to the far side. I've walked it a few times. It's scenic.'

He caught a couple of men glancing down at his shoes. They were flat-soled and unsuitable for long walks. He could see them processing his claims, deciding whether they had been too hasty engaging with his new guise.

Annoyed, he turned to Alwyn. 'Owen had a daughter. I remember meeting her. Would she know more about what happened?'

'She's also dead. And the mother is too, before you go knocking. I heard it was leaking gas. Look again on your way back. You'll find a lot of houses had a similar problem. None of them are fit to inhabit.'

'Beca,' said Wren. 'That was her name.' He remembered her well, and knew Alwyn would, too. There hadn't been many girls in the village growing up.

'It was.' Alwyn shrugged with a solemn expression, then took a deep swig of a dark beer and wiped the dregs from his beard. 'She's gone now.'

His tone reset the mood. Each man withdrew from the discussion. Wren could see it happening. 'Well, then. If I've no one to collect debts from, the other thing I need is use of the bathroom.' No one responded. The air was now dense with fervent disapproval. 'It's a long way back, is all. Either that, or I'll have to relieve myself down the side of one of these buildings, which from what you're saying, sounds unsafe.'

One of the men rolled his eyes then extended a finger, pointing towards a narrow doorway at the back of the room. They signalled Alwyn with another gesture, who visibly raised his guard. Wren made his way into a tight corridor, as directed.

Silence filled the air, the group listening to his every step. The walls seemed to close in around him.

Overgrown branches pressed against the unwashed windows to the rear of the building, creating an eerie dimness. He found two doors, facing one another. Checking that no one could see him, Wren turned both handles at the same time. The creaking of one set of hinges masked the creaking of the other, and he was able to open both without arousing suspicion. Behind the first, he found a toilet and sink. The second held a stockpile, not of food, but of stolen goods.

Three televisions stood in a row. An oven rested atop an old refrigerator. He saw coils of wire and a cardboard box of light fittings. He recognised his father's decrepit washing machine, standing in one corner, doubtless waiting to be stripped of metals and anything else of value. On top of it was a mobile phone and some jewellery.

Isabel's jewellery.

It confirmed what he had already thought. The men of The Black Horse had looted from the village, eking a survival from the possessions they stole. No wonder they were so secretive. There were many implications, and he knew what to do next. Leaving the door ajar, he slipped into the bathroom – squeezing into the narrow space – then loudly opened the window.

Alwyn was there in seconds.

'Close that right away.'

Wren played innocent. 'I was just letting some air into—'

Alwyn reached past him and grabbed the latch, hurriedly pulling it closed again. If further proof were needed, there it was. They would allow a window at the front of the building to be open, but not one that opened into the dimness of the forest. They knew about the ysbryd, and they were scared.

He allowed himself to be escorted back to the others, aware he wouldn't get the chance to explore any further. It seemed clear that the villagers could have warned him about the danger on any of his previous visits, but they had chosen not to. Their lack of honesty had condemned him to death, and for that crime, they deserved no mercy.

'Don't you think it's sad to see the decline in this community?' he said with venom as he re-entered the main room.

'Can't stop it now.' The man with the cigar – the oldest man there – climbed to his feet, holding the table for support. 'You can see there's nothing here for you. You'd do well to stay away in future. I say that for your own sake.'

'I'd be willing to help. You seem like you need it.'

'Honestly, just go.'

Wren nodded, happy to comply. They were too proud for charity, more willing to accept decay. They were beyond saving, which suited him fine. With a parting nod, he let himself back outdoors without having to be shown, emerging into a fleeting burst of sunshine. He looked down over their domain, across the rooftops. Since his teenage years – and especially in the last five – a community of two hundred had diminished to a dozen scavengers, as protective as they were ashamed. He couldn't see a single sign of life between him and Jon Lawton's bedroom window, where his father would have watched them back, and was hated for it.

Wren's former home looked peaceful from afar, but he knew differently. He shuddered at the thought of his mother's death in the bedroom, of his father's death in the hallway, and of Isabel's death on the kitchen floor. He shuddered at the thought of their lingering presences. Now that the building had been ransacked, the villagers would take nothing to do with it. It would belong to the dead until the day it collapsed. Isabel was in there, perhaps vague and unaware, or perhaps strengthened by the unrest he felt in the pit of his stomach. She could have been free to roam the village at night. He had no way of knowing.

Conscious of being watched through the front windows of The Black Horse, Wren started down the hill. As his confidence rose, he reached into his pocket and retrieved the hand-drawn map he had torn from the kitchen noticeboard. He turned the folds back on themselves so he could read one section of the map at a time without drawing more attention. Owen Craddock's house wasn't hard to locate – a well-tended semi-detached with a wide bay window. There looked to be nothing wrong with it, other than neglect. Any broken windows had long been replaced.

With his free hand, Wren retrieved the list he had taken from Isabel's suitcase. These were the villagers who had died outside of Pontrhyd-y-werddon. Matching names with the map, and applying some of his own knowledge, he quickly discovered that most were clustered around the bottom of the hill, which was to say that the people who had fled the village seemed mostly to have lived near the bottom. The pattern was clear. Eira Franklin still lived at the top end, as did Alwyn Speake. The Black Horse, where the survivors gathered, was the farthest point from the stream, or rather farthest from the threat. He turned his attention to the dense knot of trees reaching out across the valley floor. Along its outer edge, orange leaves continued to drip from every other branch, no different to the other forests around him. But from his elevated position, he realised that, a few rows deep, there were no leaves at all. In fact, the further back from the edge he looked, the more the forest seemed a season out of place, stripped completely bare.

As though dead.

Looking down from on high, it seemed obvious. Wren gasped. Something had to be in there, a hundred metres from his birthplace, beside the garden he had played in as a child. Eira was either lying or mistaken. The power in that region wasn't coming from the hills. It was more specific than that. It was coming from inside the forest.

25.INFI|LTRATION

Wren must have looked over that forest ten thousand times before and never once thought it worthy of attention. As a child, he would even have been allowed to explore its depths, and had no memory of finding anything unusual.

He stood on the grassy slope, thirty feet from the tree line, directly below the gaping hole in his father's garden wall. A quick glance backwards would have revealed the wooden panel over the lounge window. The panel he had removed from over the kitchen door would be lying on the lawn. He didn't have the courage to look. The pain of his loss was too great.

He doubted he would ever look again.

An intermittent breeze pressed into his back, as though trying to compel him into action. He was using the property as a shield from the prying eyes of The Black Horse, but had frozen in place, trying to understand why he hadn't suspected the forest before. The outermost branches formed a leafy barrier of sorts. Beyond them, he could already tell the trees were bare and the ground was barren. Brown bark faded to a dull shade of grey, its vitality sapped.

There was a distressing sense to the new logic. The ysbryd – the dead – emerged from the forest in the chill of the night when they could move most freely. They approached the windows of houses, as though stalking the living. Maybe they coveted the lives they had lost. Maybe they didn't understand what they were doing. Maybe Rees Franklin was giving them orders, and for some reason, they followed.

Whatever the truth, dozens had been attacked, and dozens had lost their lives. The only two people Wren had ever loved were among their victims. Wren, himself, appeared on the handwritten lists his father had made, bringing his own fate into question. Could spiritual intervention have played a part in his heart attack? Could the spirits be strong enough to have targeted him, so many miles from home, in the middle of a hot summer?

If Pontrhyd-y-werddon's last survivors knew the answers, they weren't sharing. They huddled together for safety instead, reduced to wretched scavengers. He would never forgive them for not putting up a fight years ago, before everything got out of hand. And he refused to be like them. Ignoring the sickness in his stomach, he allowed the breeze to push him towards the stream, clearing the trickling waters with an awkward leap. He was pleasantly surprised when Lloyd's knees didn't punish him for the hard landing.

Eira Franklin had warned him not to poke around, but he was happy to defy her. She had too much stake to be impartial. He had nothing left to lose. He stepped inside, quickly disappearing from the outside world. Smooth, dry dirt was covered in a criss-cross of shadows from the canopy above. There was little debris. An occasional crop of isolated bushes crowded under clearings, but they looked brittle and lifeless, as though ready to break apart with the slightest knock.

Lloyd's body was unfit, and the terrain worked against him. Protruding routes took care to navigate. Despite two layers of clothing, he felt colder with every step, holding tree trunks for support to discover they were bone dry. By fifty metres deep, the forest looked unrecognisable. The bark was white and unnatural. The ground was almost black.

He descended into some kind of shallow pit with sides that crumbled at the slightest disturbance. There were no tree trunks within it, but the canopy extended across what should have been a clearing, such that Autumn daylight still didn't reach the surface. He noted the absence of wildlife, and any natural sounds. Over the painful silence, he began to hear whispers, faint but unmistakable. A pair of voices circled around him, as though flanking. He could make out words he recognised, but didn't understand.

'... *tresmaswr* ...'

The hairs on his neck stood on end. A third voice behind him hissed in apparent anger. There were scuffles and murmurs, growing in confidence as he shrank from their presence.

'... *camgymeriad peryglus* ...'

He edged towards the far bank, seeking protection amongst the trees. He could make out a young-sounding woman uttering words he understood, close enough to his ear that he recoiled with the strongest feeling that someone was standing right beside him.

'You never should have come here,' it said.

'I want to help,' he replied. 'What happened to you all?'

Wren extended an arm, as though holding back the air. Someone laughed, or maybe it was a scream. His aggressors seemed to multiply until he was surrounded by restless chatter – detached, yet frighteningly close. His shoes had little grip on the smooth, barren slope. Trying not to panic, he grabbed hold of a low-lying branch, but it snapped off in his fingers, sending shockwaves through the forest. The voices fell silent, leaving him alone with faltering breath steaming from his mouth.

'Hello?' he called. The dimness swallowed his voice, with no trace of an echo. He reached for a thicker branch, one less likely to break. A strange force started to work on his insides, like gravity, only stronger. It pulled him downwards, dragging him towards the ground. To resist required the effort of every muscle in his body, quickly draining his strength. It wanted him to lie on the ground, distorting his perception of his surroundings in the attempt. The incline seemed to grow steeper, tilting as he fought back. The ground became a cliff face, stretching above and below him. The treetops felt as though he could have walked over to them.

Something stung his outstretched arm. He yelped, unable to defend himself, finding a scratch in the lowlight that had broken the skin. Footsteps pitter-pattered. In the corner of his eye, he saw sparks floating in the darkness. New voices rose. They were incomprehensible, but had a singular tone. There seemed to be dozens, even hundreds of spirits around him now. Something gripped him by the shin and tugged downwards. Wren sank to his knees, where he heard a man's voice draw an urgent breath.

'Get us out of here,' it said.

A sharp object dug into his leg. His T-shirt ripped, the skin beneath gouged by invisible claws. Then something shrieked through the undergrowth, parting the branches. Wren felt the pressure lift. He sprang to his feet, pelting back into the trees.

Eira Franklin's words continued to resonate, cementing his dread. *'You'll never escape. They can't outshine the sun, but they're watching from the shadows.'*

His instincts were right – the forest was crawling with the dead. The disorientation lifted as he fled from the clearing, never knowing who would strike out, nor from where. He vaulted over a fallen branch, but something softer clipped his heel. Wren slid in the dirt and landed on his elbows. For a second, it felt as though a weight landed on top of him, then was pulled off just as quickly, as though the ysbryd were fighting with one another.

Cold seeped through the ground. He glanced back to see what had tripped him up and his stomach lurched. Curled up on the black soil lay a body, clad in a winter coat. He could see lifeless skin, dried out, wrinkled and bright white. Raised arms had concealed the face and become petrified, frozen in time.

He scrambled to his feet, feeling a gash on his forehead bleed into his eyes. It was a haunting sight – ghostly, inhuman, and almost unrecognisable. He had no way of knowing for how long it had been there, but it was clear he wasn't the first to explore the forest. Now he understood: Together, the trees had borders and a roof, no different to the houses in the village. Death not only weakened the barriers that held the ysbryd out, but enough death lured them towards it, perhaps even trapped them there.

Whatever drove the process, it was out of control, and the forest was feeding the ysbryd unnatural power. He heard wind. He swore he felt it through the earth. The howling had been stirred up and was coming for him. Every branch in sight shivered. Some started to bend. He took flight as the environment erupted into chaos. Soil and twigs were swept off the ground and launched after him like a hail of bullets. Pinches of cold from invisible fingers threatened to make his muscles seize up and bring him back down.

The terrain was too uneven to amass any speed. He wove between the tree trunks, trying to baffle the wind into losing its strength, but the opposite came true. Funnelled to a point, it gained focus. With an almighty groan, an entire tree was heaved up at the roots and thrust aside. The bellowing made his ears whistle, so intense that he lost his bearings. He fled in a blind panic, trying not to scream, praying that he was getting close to the edge of the forest.

And then what?

Clouds of grit stung his arms. Protruding roots seemed to snatch at his ankles as though the trees themselves wanted him to stay. Despite the arid conditions, there was a sense of pure energy lingering somewhere he couldn't put his finger on. Wren rose onto the balls of his feet. He couldn't tell if it was his own urgency or the wind at his back. His heels barely touched the ground as he hurtled from trunk to trunk, glancing off each thick and heavy limb, unable to slow down.

He grabbed a passing branch, but it was yanked out of his hands. The ground dipped and his feet weren't ready for the change in gradient. He stumbled, losing control. But instead of falling to the ground, he gained momentum. A bitter cold enveloped him, forcing him downhill. Wren tumbled through the air, no idea which way was up. He slammed into a tree, feeling a hideous crunch down his spine. Then, to his horror, he felt icy fingers drag him onwards, purposefully trying to cause him harm. He tried to dig his nails into the dirt as the world whipped past. He smashed into another hard surface. Something cold and hard struck the back of his neck. His whole body seemed to pivot about that most delicate of points, and he was powerless to resist.

He stopped trying. The wind wasn't going to let him live. Lloyd Bennet had been nothing more than a brief diversion. Impact followed impact. He resigned himself to fate, cartwheeling like a ragdoll. No life flashed before his eyes. And with a crunch and cracking of bone, his whole world rushed to darkness.

26.ABYS|S

Wren found himself beyond pain and suffering. Once the horrors of his final moments had passed, death came as a relief. He was drifting, as ever, in a vast and empty space – the echoless void he had visited several times before. It had never truly left him. Even in his most lucid moments, he could always feel it willing him to return. He likened it to the ysbryd's experience of the haunted forest. Here was a force he couldn't define, which pulled him towards it like so much gravity. In its presence, nothing else seemed important. The energy was pure, the release absolute.

In those strange surroundings, all sensations were eclipsed. He knew nothing of the beating Lloyd's body had suffered only moments before. He knew no pain. He peered into an endless distance, as though far outside of the known universe, where no starlight could reach. He lacked a frame of reference to determine how long the expanse went on for, but he had the impression it was infinite.

He would have gladly remained there forever, but as with his previous visit, he had company. Floating beside him in the darkness was the body of a man with silvery hair, covered in lacerations. He recognised the torn and dirtied clothing more than the face: Lloyd Bennett. Lloyd was illuminated, with no obvious source of light. He was close enough to touch. Crusted blood hung from his nostrils. Dirt streaked his forehead. His eyes were closed, and he made no attempt to move.

Wren had no idea how much of Lloyd was in there. He regarded the floating figure as an empty vessel, and a poor one at that. Lloyd had only ever served as a means to an end, someone Wren had never intended to inhabit for long. Lloyd was disposable, and Wren acknowledged how little that bothered him. Instead, he welcomed the prospect of a new body – someone like Scott, or Andrew Goodwin, people of a comparable age, with all of their faculties, bodies he could put to good use instead of merely having to tolerate.

Wren looked down at his own hands. There, in the void, he had taken his original form. His skin looked pale, weak, and blotchy. His arms were short and stubby. His body seemed brighter than it had been with his previous deaths, as though he glowed with more energy. It made the void seemed blacker, if such a thing were possible. He wondered whether the light upon Lloyd was coming from himself, meaning Lloyd's back would be in shadow.

He realised how much he didn't miss being Wren Lawton. The body seemed like too much of a compromise, now he knew he could do better. Long minutes passed, longer than he was expecting. Three times now, his mother had intervened before the process of dying had run its course. Three times, she had swept in and carried him to a new host. His collapse on the seafront at the age of thirty-two … that had been the first, transported into Andrew Goodwin. After his fall from the bridge onto railway tracks, he had transferred into Scott. Then after Rees Franklin's assault, he had endured two weeks as Lloyd Bennett.

He waited for his fourth rebirth, but nothing came. The process of dying began. A raft of sensations bubbled to the surface – pain, caress, dryness, warmth, all mixed together and yet somehow separate. He saw bright flickers of light as memories were sucked out of him, watching each one pour into the darkness and be lost forever. They were supposed to be setting him free, but he caught glimpses of Isabel. He realised those memories were all he had left, and therefore how precious they were. Those moments could never be replaced now she had gone.

The sense of expanse turned oppressive instead of comforting. He realised how much he wanted to live, and yet the purge was speeding up. His mother wasn't coming to his rescue. He hadn't seen her for some time, certainly not since he had taken his new form, despite the kind of anguish that normally drew her out. Something must have happened to her. He started to panic, though it was swallowed up by a conflicting barrage of anger, hate, sorrow, and despair. He reached out with those pale hands and seized hold of Lloyd's dirty clothing, using his strength to pull him closer.

Wren didn't want to do it. He wanted a body who was fit and young, one that wasn't broken and spent. But he also saw no choice. It was either accept death or have another go with Lloyd. In the darkness, he made his choice, one that wasn't fair.

He chose life.

***

Wren awoke with a gasp for air, returning to the land of the living. One eye refused to open, but the other revealed that darkness had fallen. The sound of trickling water filled his ears. He felt cold. Then came the pain.

Every inch of Lloyd's body sought to reject his resurrection. His brain pounded inside his skull. His face throbbed, despite cool soil against it. There was a stabbing pain in his ribs as he drew breath. The corpse must have lain on the ground for hours after being pulverised by the wind. He remained that way for several minutes more, in a state of disbelief. It defied the laws of nature, more so than anything he had done before. Lloyd's body should have been left to decompose. No one, alive or dead, would have been able to explain how it had lain inanimate for so long and then somehow recovered.

He became aware of the moonlit sky above him. He appeared to be at the edge of the forest, close to the banks of the flowing brook. Its relentless babble provided a much-needed anchor as he mustered the strength to move. He lifted his head, his spine cracking as it bent. Blood vessels in his neck felt swollen and stiff. He transferred his weight onto his hands and knees, wincing as his torso punished him for overreaching, then he began to crawl.

Each passing moment beckoned danger from the forest, but he couldn't move any faster. His left leg remained numb. It resisted being straightened. He was lucky it hadn't been ripped apart. Once he reached the nearest tree trunk, he pulled himself up to a standing position, uncurling his fists to pat himself down. Every square inch of him had something wrong with it – a lump, a scrape, or a bruise. But against all odds, no bones appeared to be broken.

With some rapid lesson learning, he managed to stand unsupported, squinting with his good eye. The orange haze of street lamps ran throughout the village on the far side of the brook. A thin autumn mist hung low, obscuring the potholed tarmac. Every building looked empty, darkened, their owners dead or missing. Only the distant windows of The Black Horse showed any signs of life, keeping a lonely vigil from its high vantage point.

He wiped his palms on his trousers, unable to tell whether they were dirtied or bloodied. The most hostile of the ysbryd would be prowling through the village at that moment, seeking new victims. Rees Franklin would guide them wherever he chose. Although there were no movements in the air, Wren doubted it would remain so for long. He hobbled down the near bank, following the path of the water. It guided him towards the main road where he had hidden Sarah's car, his only hope of escaping before anyone realised he was there.

Staring at the black soil, he could make out stones and fallen twigs, enough to keep from tripping over. He suppressed moans of agony with each tentative step, scarcely able to raise his numb leg more than a few inches to clear any obstacles. The darkness played canvas to horrible images. He couldn't shake the memory of the corpse lying frozen in the heart of the forest. It seemed likely they were someone his father had written about, perhaps one of the Craddocks. He had probably known them.

Wren managed to tease open his swollen eye, but a pressure on his eyeball gave him double vision, so he closed it again. He struggled to move in a straight line, afraid of being unable to get back up if he fell. He couldn't run if he was attacked, nor even attempt to defend himself. Without his mother's protection, another death could have spelled the end.

There was a biting chill. A delicate mist rose from the waters, curling through the air like a twisting veil, as though reaching out in sightless exploration. He caught movement from within as the first sparks came to investigate. They emerged from the ground as though rising from the grave, weaving aimlessly left to right, until being captured in his orbit.

Out there in the open, they behaved differently. They seemed energetic, as though encouraged by the cold. Wren's fear rose. He extended an arm in front of his chest and tried to move faster, taking short strides into the unknown. As they increased in number, they banded together in twos, threes, and fours. And they became more inquisitive. A pair approached his outstretched fingers and passed right through his palm. He felt the slightest prick – not painful, more like a tingle of electricity – then they skimmed off the ground and circled away, all in near silence.

Others followed suit. Some chose to spiral around his outstretched limb, getting close without ever making contact. Others dared to penetrate his twice-deceased flesh, something he doubted would be possible with any other living creature. A handful of them dove into his chest. One whipped through his face, catching his swollen eye and burning his retina from within.

He felt scratches, like being stuck with something cold, until his entire body tingled with pins and needles. Try as he might, he still couldn't run. He heard the distant call of a lost girl over the trickling waters, but he wasn't fooled. Other voices followed. A tired man grunted, another screamed. These were the lost inhabitants of Pontrhyd-y-werddon, those cut down and slaughtered, many having died there years before. None of them tried to harm him, but they were drawing attention. Wren looked down at his hands and realised he could see them clearly in the surrounding light. He felt a mix of horror and wonder that such a thing was possible.

He gained distance from the village, counting each step. As the forest thinned out, the air grew warmer, returning to a natural state. The spirits' movement became noticeably more laboured. Once he reached the brilliant white streetlamps of the main road through the Valleys, he found the number of sparks had dwindled to a handful at most, relegated to the shadows and darkest nooks where they couldn't be outshone. He threw himself down the bank of the stream, giving his battered body no choice. His foot plunged ankle-deep into icy water. Much of his life had been spent watching the village being taken over, without even realising he was on the front line. The worst part was knowing his father had at least suspected, but not enough to act. Now, Jon Lawton's voice would forever be among the forlorn.

By the time Wren reached the turnoff where he had hidden Sarah's white car, he appeared to be alone again. He staggered back to the vehicle, using every last ounce of energy. He had no way of knowing whether the spirits were all around him, whether he was safe or in terrible danger. There was too much ambient light.

His leg caught on the long undergrowth, slowing his progress, like wading through quicksand. He fumbled in his pocket for his car keys as a hauntingly familiar sensation crept up his spine, an insufferable urge to stop moving and sleep. He didn't dare to resist. With a clunk, the doors unlocked. He grabbed the nearest handle, sliding onto the back seat. He prayed the vehicle, like the forest and the buildings, would have absorbed the energy of its owners and would provide some protection from invasion.

Even if not, he had no choice. Darkness welled up inside him as he drifted towards an uncontrollable, irrepressible slumber. He closed the door, and his eyelids closed too, sealing him in. As he lay down low and began to drift, he said a silent prayer that he would last until the daylight came.

Please don't let them get me.

27.SUFF|OCATION

Early morning light was anathema to every cell of Wren's borrowed body. It seemed to pierce his exposed skin, rousing him before he had a chance to begin recovering from his injuries.

He was sprawled across the back seat of the stolen car, more or less in the exact same position as where he had passed out. The cracked leather was bathed in a blue hue which suggested it wasn't long after sunrise. His tormented muscles hadn't healed. Instead, they had seized up and refused to be straightened. It was near-impossible to move. He thought of rigor mortis and wished his mother would come to his rescue now he had some distance from the forest, carrying him away to a less broken host.

No such salvation came. Instead, he became aware of a figure standing at the window. His heart sank as he recognised them – Sarah, Lloyd's wife. Her hands were cupped against the glass as she peered inside.

'Talk to me.' She kept trying to lift the door handle. 'Are you okay? What's happened?'

Her hair looked unwashed and her skin pale, as though she hadn't rested since he left her standing in the middle of the road a day before. He hadn't cared then and he didn't care now. If he had been in the front seat and able to move, he would have started the engine and driven away. But his chest felt flattened, his lungs squashed inside his ribcage. He had no choice but to interact with her.

'How did you find me?' he said.

'I came as soon as I could. I missed your call.'

Again, his heart sank. Wren flexed the fingers of his left hand to find he was clutching a phone, the same handset he had let slip from the glove box the previous afternoon. Only one person would have thought to contact her. No one else would want to. While he had been unconscious, Lloyd must have woken up with a measure of control. Maybe the violence had shocked him back into existence. Maybe he had been there all along. Either way, it could only spell trouble.

'I need to get away from—' Wren had to stop mid-sentence, struggling to breathe.

'Unlock the door,' said Sarah. 'We'll get you back to the hospital.'

He didn't have the strength to argue, loath to admit he was scared. If Sarah and Lloyd united against him, Wren would have nowhere to turn. And with so much uncertainty around his mother's protection, permanent death was a real possibility. He searched for the key and let Sarah enter the vehicle. A cool breeze drifted through the open front door and he recoiled in fright.

'Do you want to sit up?' There was no trace of the sour temperament she had displayed at the hospital. She offered a hand for comfort, but he didn't take it.

'Please get me away from here.'

She strapped on her seat belt and started the engine. 'Alright, I'll take you back to the doctors—'

'Not there,' he urged. 'We agreed no more hospitals.'

'But I can't leave you like—'

'Please.'

She looked startled by his tone of voice, but didn't argue. Instead, she changed gear and pulled out of the undergrowth. 'What are you doing here?' she asked. 'Are you in trouble?'

'Just drive.' He slipped across the seat as she turned onto the main highway. He forced himself to keep calm for fear of losing her cooperation. 'Get me somewhere I can rest and don't stop until you get there. Somewhere safe.'

All he wanted at that moment was to be far from the haunted forest, far from the violent wind, far away from the hostility of The Black Horse, and far from the house where he had lost everyone he ever loved. He gazed up through the window at tall branches and clouds whipping past. He didn't care where they went, so long as he could hide there and recover. Then he would take off and leave her again. Wren didn't want Sarah around him, nor anyone else. He only needed his mother, but had no idea how to get her back.

**

Hours passed, perhaps days, perhaps even a week. Wren was rarely conscious longer than it took to sip water, then he went straight back to sleep.

Back into the darkness.

Whenever he made his presence felt, he heard a door open, and Sarah appeared. She would try to convince him to eat, never able to serve him more than a few mouthfuls of something cold and unappetising before he stopped responding. It must have been a harrowing time for her, but she heeded his pleas not to return to the hospital, even as the days rolled on.

His surroundings never changed, other than the change in weather. Wren had almost grown accustomed to such disturbing passages of time. His mind fought with his body, as though the latter sought to eject him. Every slumber felt like death, and easily could have been. He had no guide, and no way of ever knowing.

Eventually, Lloyd's body relented, healing enough to permit Wren a more prolonged period of control. He awoke with his head half-buried in the pillow, free from discomfort, in a fresh morning light. A photograph in a picture frame had been placed on the bedside table. It looked like something from a catalogue – two people on the deck of a cruise ship, arm in arm. The man had silvery hair, receding midway up his scalp. Skin sagged beneath his sunken eyes.

Wren's mind was sluggish at first, his comfort too complete. He needed a full minute to connect the image to the hands that responded when he flexed them. After weeks spent avoiding thinking about his latest host, this was his first unavoidable impression. Lloyd was objectively past his prime, and indeed had already died, leaving Wren with chewed-up leftovers.

Everything came flooding back. Revulsion pushed him off the mattress. He was stiff and weak, from his wrists to his shoulders. Poorly dressed wounds on his back caught on his nightshirt, pulling at scabs. He was in a bedroom at the top of the house. A low ceiling sloped down to chest height before connecting with the walls, leaving little space for windows. But still, the room was light. He could feel the sun's energy permeate every cubic inch of his surroundings, like the energy of the living, holding the dead out.

He also felt every inch of his circumstance – beaten to death and resurrected. His body had been forced to continue living and didn't want him to forget. After gathering the courage to stand, he limped over to the window. Wren was in the countryside. A generous driveway was flanked by tall trees. Dead leaves smothered the ground in the colours of autumn. Two cars were parked outside. He felt unmoved, even on a subconscious level. No pleasure came from this latest chance at life – perhaps his fifth now. He refused to stay there a moment longer than was necessary.

On a hook by the door, he found a dressing gown and slid his arms into the sleeves. There was an odour to it, one he instantly disliked.

Cigarette smoke.

He resolved to dress fully instead. A neat pile of clothing had been arranged on a dressing table. He slipped on a T-shirt, a red cotton jumper, and a pair of jeans. His stiff legs were awkward from such a long time without being used. He had to sit down to put on his trousers. The bedroom door led onto a narrow landing, with a skylight in a sloping ceiling. He passed two other bedroom doors, both open, both with the same pristine white linen, without a single crease on either.

A family portrait hung on the wall at the top of the stairs. It was printed on canvas. Lloyd appeared to have three daughters and at least six grandchildren. Sarah didn't feature. With some difficulty, he descended to ground level, where the sense of space expanded. He shuffled down a wide hallway to a living room that stretched from the front of the house to the rear, opening out into a large conservatory.

A sunbeam entered through the front window, making the room bright. Sarah was sitting on a chair in the conservatory, surrounded by glass. He approached, compelled to make his presence felt. She closed a book and set it on her lap.

'I thought I heard you moving around,' she said. 'Why are you dressed?'

Wren smiled thinly. 'I thought maybe I'd slept enough.'

The conservatory offered a grand view of the garden, where untended grass stretched on for dozens of feet. He savoured the burn of daylight on his face. He didn't want conversation, nor to show gratitude for the care he had received. She wouldn't have done any of it, had she known he wasn't her husband.

'There's more colour in your face today,' she said. 'I take it you're feeling better?'

He locked his knees and tried to stand straight. 'Nothing hurts, though nothing works properly either, not yet.'

'Are you finally ready to tell me what happened?'

He shook his head several times while thinking of an answer. 'A long fall,' he said. 'There are some really steep drops hiding under the vegetation. You don't know until you're on top of them.'

Her jaw twitched as she tensed it. 'I didn't think you'd remember yesterday's excuse, but for the record, it was completely different.'

His heart sank. Wren couldn't remember ever leaving the bedroom before that morning, and he especially couldn't remember explaining himself to Sarah. It confirmed his worst fears – Lloyd had indeed regained a measure of consciousness, as though kickstarted back into existence by the trauma his body had experienced. He had enough control to roam around.

Wren had been dreading such an outcome. 'This has happened a lot, then, I take it? You might as well tell me what I said.'

He closed the gap between them, but she rose from her seat and withdrew. 'Something equally pathetic,' she said. 'The rudeness, the lies … none of it goes away. My assumption is that you owe someone money again and you're too embarrassed to admit they caught up with you.'

She shot him a loaded glance, but he didn't react. His thoughts were of Lloyd, and being pushed to the background, something he couldn't tolerate. 'I fell. What else did I say? Maybe yesterday, I was confused.'

'You knew what you were saying, every word of it.'

He couldn't meet her glare. It was uncomfortable. Sarah was incensed, whereas he felt nothing. Every statement carried subtext, hints of a stranger's issues. When he didn't give a response, she turned her back on him, staring out of the window. He joined her, albeit from a distance, willing the moment to pass.

'I don't want to argue,' he said, with sincerity.

'Being married to you is hard,' she said. 'I never know what you're thinking.'

'Thank you for keeping me away from the hospital.'

She didn't answer. The wilting flowers of creeping buttercups were scattered throughout the lawn. Their yellow petals stood out against the vibrant green. He looked beyond the wooden fence. A discoloured haze obscured the distance, but he could make out a familiar spread of buildings a few miles away – a high street and a low street. With a jolt, he realised where he was. Lloyd's house was on the north side of the valley, the same valley he had been born, had lived, and had died in.

He was looking at Pontrhyd-y-werddon.

The sound of creaking glass broke the silence. Wren came to focus on the conservatory door and his heart skipped a beat at the sight of tiny fractures. All that time – all those days and nights – he had been so close to the forest that the ysbryd hadn't needed to look very far to find him. They would have gathered outdoors each night, slowly increasing in number, until they had the power to come inside.

A thin crack appeared in the corner of a double-glazed window and began to spread, buckling under pressure from the outside. He took a step back. Cracks were forming on every pane in the conservatory, even the ones above him. A voice in his head screamed. *Get moving.* He grabbed Sarah by the hand and dragged her away, almost tripping over himself as he fled into the lounge. 'What are you doing?' she yelled, trying to resist his grip. Glass crunched and she stopped protesting.

Wren pulled her into the hallway as the first panel gave way. He pushed her head down and sought cover behind an open door. He tried to work out where to run next. *Think, Wren. Think.* The spirits would already be in the house, in huge numbers, and invisible. With every door hanging open, another broken pane would let them form a terrible wind and sweep through the building.

He needed to escape. Wren pulled Sarah into the hallway as the skylight collapsed above them in a chorus of cymbal crashes, raining glass down onto their heads. As he rushed to the front door, a torrent of sparks descended. Heavy footsteps thundered along the landing. Floorboards shook. He heard something tumble down the rooftop, as though tiles had come loose.

Sarah shrieked with fear. The ysbryd were overrunning the house while they were still in it, numerous and powerful enough for the presence of the living to prove no hindrance.

'Where are the car keys?' he cried. The bedroom doors slammed open and shut. She pointed to her handbag at the end of the hallway and Wren made a run for it, twisting the front door latch as he scrambled out.

'Come on,' he cried. 'Hurry.'

She was slow to follow, rooted by terror. Sparks poured over her shoulders, some of them making contact with her body. Wren gambled that the spirits were mostly at the back window and plunged into the open, heading up the driveway, struggling to run on his stiff legs. In the brightness of the daytime, he staggered and stumbled, afraid of being cut down any second.

'Let me drive,' Sarah said as she overtook him. 'You're in no state.'

'There isn't time. Come on.'

'You won't get two miles—'

He looked her in the eye. 'Sarah, please.'

Behind them, the wind bawled, angry and strong. She lost her nerve and bundled herself onto the back seat as he dove into the front and started the engine. Something struck them from behind with the force of a freight train. The white vehicle rocked up on its suspension. Wren was thrown off balance, jarred by the steering wheel as tyres scraped across the ground for a clear six inches. Sarah yelped and covered her face. The car was shunted – again and again – sliding forwards along the ground.

'Get moving,' she screamed.

He could hear metal fold in on itself. He slammed his foot on the pedal. The engine wailed, but nothing happened, as though the wheels had no traction.

'Put your seatbelt on.' Wren threw the car into reverse and drove at the invisible force, the only thing he could think to do. He heard hissing voices surround the vehicle and drowned them out with his hand on the horn. A blast of noise exploded through the air. He revved the engine as loudly as he could. And he screamed. Wren took a deep gulp of air and roared at the top of his voice, using all the energy he could produce. The cacophony seemed to buy him a vital split-second. As he lifted the clutch, wheels spun on the gravel and the car shot up the driveway, carrying them onto the road.

He only looked behind him once, in time to see the windows of the front room explode into tiny fragments, bursting from the inside out. Sarah's home had been taken right from under their noses, despite their presence inside it. Any resistance had lasted for less than a minute. From the confounded look on her pale face, she didn't understand what was happening.

He had half a mind to tell her.

28.BLOO|D

Wren drove. He took Sarah's car deep into the countryside, far from anywhere he recognised, driving so fast that nothing even vaguely human could have kept up. He went for miles, unable to tell what would be far enough. The ysbryd had tracked him from Pontrhyd-y-werddon to the far side of the valley, and without knowing how, he couldn't keep it from happening again.

He needed to gather his thoughts, but Sarah denied him the chance. She kept gasping with panic, keeping a close eye on the road behind them. No sooner were they out of danger than she lost herself completely.

'Stop the car,' she uttered. 'I said stop the car. I need air.'

'That's a bad idea.' Wren lowered the windows instead. The inrush of air helped to drown her out.

'What the hell did we just witness?' she asked. He shook his head, eyes steadfastly on the road. She leaned forwards until he couldn't pretend not to hear. 'Do you know what that thing was? Is it how you got injured?'

'Yes.' He had no desire to lie, nor did he care enough about her feelings to sugar-coat the truth. 'It's not one thing; it's hundreds, at least. I've seen them many times before, but never quite so powerful. You should sit straight in case they force us off the road.'

He meant every word. Eira Franklin had warned Wren that he glowed with negative energy, something he couldn't prevent. But her story had been spiritual, taking some things for granted. There were gaps in her understanding. As he gained distance from the valley and Sarah began to calm down, he found that driving helped him to think. He put together pieces of the puzzle that Eira had overlooked.

Dying wasn't an end. It was more like a change of state, one that affected its environment. The transition from life to death drew energy from its surroundings, converting heat into this dark alternative. More death drained more energy. Houses and forests were depleted, their energy changed into something else. Instead of the power to attract the living, they instead began to attract the dead.

Wren had absorbed this energy throughout his childhood, simply by being in its presence. But what made him unique was the fact he had died since then, and many times. Each death gave him more energy. As his body glowed heat, his spirit glowed unusually large amounts of whatever this was. It would have come as no surprise to learn that he had shone like a lighthouse from the far side of the valley.

And there was another problem, one more familiar. As Wren drove, he felt strong, compelling urges to slow down. He felt misplaced pangs of concern for Sarah's well-being. The implications terrified him more than being attacked. Lloyd was conscious again, and trying to exert a measure of control. Wren knew that if his heartrate slowed too much, he might be thrown out of consciousness so the other man could have a turn. He pushed the accelerator pedal closer to the floor, trying to sharpen his senses. He glanced at Sarah to see tears streaming down her cheeks.

'What do they want with us?' she cried.

'I don't know,' he said. 'I honestly don't. Maybe they still see me as a threat.'

'What are they?'

'People, or they used to be.'

He kept driving, twisting through the Valleys. There was nothing else to do. He drove for an hour with no destination in mind, gaining more and more distance from Pontrhyd-y-werddon. He drove until there was almost no fuel in the tank, at which point he set his sights on the nearest town, somewhere teeming with life. He wasn't disappointed. Grumbling traffic thickened as buildings increased both in size and number. They crossed a ring road and he searched for the nearest hotel where they could hide out and be safe.

Such a place wasn't hard to find. He pulled into a large car park, overlooked by a building with four dozen windows. It promised the combined power of countless guests and staff, surely enough to keep the spirits out. While Sarah remained quiet – drained and tearful – Wren couldn't stop moving, afraid of the fatigue slowly building in his aching limbs. He jumped out of the car and took her straight to the check-in desk, insisting on a room on the top floor.

He made her pay, taking note of the money in her purse. Once they were alone inside a sparsely furnished bedroom, he meticulously checked the window pane for cracks. Sarah perched on the edge of the mattress, her skin almost white.

'I can't believe this is happening,' she said.

He drew heavy curtains closed and turned on all the lights. 'I was like that the first time,' he said. 'If it's any consolation, I've been through worse.'

She turned her head to look at him sideways. 'Then why have you never mentioned it, Lloyd? We've been married for six years. When did this start?'

He walked over to the thermostat and pressed buttons. 'A few years ago now, when I had my heart attack.'

'They were strokes,' she said, 'not heart attacks.'

'Whatever.'

He kept a close watch on her handbag as she placed it on the floor. At the first opportunity, he planned to take that bag and leave. She would be safer for it.

'Those things in the house,' she said. 'The shower of little lights … were ice cold. I felt them passing through my body.'

She hugged herself. Wren leaned into the bathroom and took a large towel from a shelf above the radiator, tossing it onto her lap. 'It's not exactly a blanket, but it'll do well enough until the heating kicks in.'

'You said they used to be people. What kind of people?'

'It would take too long to explain,' he said. 'It's me they're after.'

'Will they still be there if we go back?'

'Almost definitely,' said Wren. 'Now they have the house, they may never let it go.' He thought of the wind forever racing through the broken ruin at the bottom of the village, curling out through the roof cavity and in through the hollow front doorway.

282

'The house might have absorbed something they need, from a couple of things that have happened there lately. They'll stay until it's all gone, or at least some of them will.'

She put a hand to her chest. 'And the rest?'

'… will be out looking for us.'

Sarah shuddered, delicately spreading the towel over her legs. 'This is real, isn't it? Are they ghosts? Is this death?'

'It's an afterlife,' said Wren, 'Whether it's the only afterlife, I can't tell you. It might even be a choice.'

He paced up and down impatiently, afraid to drop his guard for the risk of being supplanted. If his heart rate dipped too low, Lloyd could sweep in and take his place. That was more dangerous than ever. Lloyd wouldn't have a clue what to do. Inevitably, he would go to the police or return to the hospital.

Either result was bad.

'There's nothing else you can do for now,' he said. 'Why don't you have a shower or a bath? It might help you to calm down and maybe sleep for a while.'

'How could I sleep with those things out there?'

'We left them an hour away. And even if they catch up, they won't be able to come in. There are too many people around.'

'How does that make a difference?'

'Never you mind.'

The best thing for everyone, he reminded himself, was to get her settled and then abandon her. The ysbryd wouldn't care about her, once he had gone. 'If you can't sleep, let's order food. Take your mind off it.'

'I don't know if I'll be able to eat, either.'

'Well, I'm famished. This is the longest I've been conscious in days, so let's get something full of sugar, and quick.'

***

Wren took a cold shower, using the time to examine his many injuries. A tapestry of burst veins and healing bruises stained his pale skin in yellows, browns, and deep reds, the colours of autumn. He found the most tender areas and rubbed them hard, relishing the shooting pains for how awake they made him feel.

Sarah didn't move from the spot during his absence, evidently too shaken to attempt anything productive. Seeing her so anxious softened his resolve. The stray thoughts at the back of his mind invoked a measure of sympathy, and once he had dressed again, he sat beside her.

'Someone tried to explain it to me recently,' he said. 'Every spark is a person who died on the far side of the valley, where you found me. Something's keeping them alive.'

'And you said in their hundreds?'

'Yes, it's possible they've been drawn there from much further away than anyone realises. We should warn everyone who lives around us.'

'My friend Margaret's away, thank goodness.' She kept one eye on the heavy curtains as if expecting them to move. 'Whatever's going on, do you think there's a way of putting it back to normal?'

'I'm hoping so.'

His encouragement seemed to fix her mood. She straightened her back and inflated her chest. 'I wouldn't even attempt to reason with them,' she said, 'not after what they've done. I'd hose them down and snuff them out.'

'Me, too. I doubt water would do anything, though.' He chose not to reveal the full extent of his knowledge, that they crossed over the stream when they emerged from the forest at night and it never seemed to cause them any trouble. 'Besides, they're not actually sparks. Sometimes you can see them more distinctly.'

'When that happens, do they act differently or do they still float through the walls?'

'They don't move much. I suppose they act more human, but I wasn't willing to get close enough to find out more.'

Sarah nodded and turned to face him. The creases in her forehead deepened as she raised her eyebrows. 'Now is the time to stop, Lloyd. Take what you know to the authorities and let them figure out the rest.'

He stared through the floor. Wren wasn't sure whether he would have accepted any kind of assistance now. The need to avenge those he had lost consumed his every waking thought. No authority would share his thirst for blood.

'All the evidence we can point to is an empty village the world seems to have forgotten about,' he said, 'protected by a group of survivors who've lost their grip on reality and would deny everything.'

'Wouldn't the vacant houses be enough to raise suspicion?'

'Don't count on it, not for swift action. Any bodies will be in the forest, and no one setting foot in there gets out alive. Anyone you convince to try, you send to their death.'

She snarled, an expression that suited her. 'Well, our house can't stay occupied forever. I'd sooner burn it down than let them keep it.'

Something in her wording took a moment to register, then they struck Wren so hard that he slapped his forehead for not having thought of it sooner.

'You're a genius,' he said.

She had stumbled upon something, an extension to his logic. The warmth of the living repelled the dead. It pushed the sparks out when they tried to invade homes. Eira Franklin had explained that to him, the night Isabel had died. *'Alone, they're easily repelled by light and heat and sound,'* she had said. *'Their energy isn't infinite. Once spent, they cease to exist.'*

His head had been too full of her other revelations to realise the implications. Fire would give him energy in abundance – light and heat and sound. He could use it to reach the centre of the forest and discover what was lurking there, maybe even destroy it.

Sarah must have read his body language. 'I wasn't being serious,' she replied. 'I want my house back in one piece.'

'But they can't fight fire. You're absolutely right.'

'Don't get any big ideas,' she said. 'Neither of us are superheroes. We're too old for a fight.'

'There won't be a fight if we plan this correctly. They won't stand a chance.'

'We're not suicidal, either.'

'So you say.'

He could see her face drop, but he didn't care. She had given him the solution. Already, his mind was working overtime, trying to come up with the best way to get back home before anyone could intervene. Sarah couldn't come with him. She would hesitate. She would hold him back.

'Lloyd, please listen.'

He sat for a moment in silence, his eyes darting from one item of furniture to the next, wondering what would burn. His restless legs begged for action, and their prayers were answered when a telephone on the bedside table started to ring. He jumped to his feet. 'That'll be reception calling,' he said. 'The food must be here. I'll go down for it.'

Before she could speak a word of protest, he snatched her handbag from the floor and left the room. He was already down the corridor and in the stairwell by the time the door slammed shut behind him. Sarah had done more with an idle comment than Alwyn, Eira, and the men of The Black Horse combined. But he couldn't listen while she preached caution. All he needed was a source of heat and he could go wherever he wanted. The ysbryd wouldn't be able to touch him.

Beside the reception desk in the lobby stood a delivery woman in a grey sports jacket, carrying a bag of takeaway food. Wren didn't acknowledge her. Instead, he strode past her and out of the building, into the car park. He made straight for Sarah's car, moving as fast as his injuries would allow. As he walked, he unfastened the handbag's clasp and fumbled inside for the car keys.

They weren't there.

'Where do you think you're going?' said a voice. Wren spun around to find Sarah hot on his heels, as though she had been ready for him to try something.

'You know where,' he replied.

'Did you think I'd leave the keys lying around after you left me stranded in the middle of the road?'

His whole body tensed. 'I did you a favour. We both know you can't stand the sight of me.'

'You're bringing me along, and I'm sure as hell not going back to the house without calling the police. You may think I'm heartless, but I won't let you kill yourself.'

She clutched her keyring, letting the fob dangle from between her fingers. Wren stormed over until they stood face to face, using every inch of Lloyd's height. 'You wouldn't last five minutes out there. Give me the keys.'

'Now you sound like your usual self, all alpha male and assertive.'

He grabbed her clenched fist and prized the fingers apart, giving her no choice but to let the keyring go. She seemed startled by his sudden ferocity, but put up a fight, kicking him in the leg.

'You're an idiot,' she screamed. 'You'll die.'

'Go inside. It's not safe.'

He unlocked the car and climbed into the driver's seat. Frustrated, Sarah slammed her palms down on the bonnet with such violence that he stopped to glare at her. The woman was infuriating. Maybe Lloyd deserved every harsh word. It was irrelevant. But she needed to get out of his way. He had half a mind to tell her who he was, that her husband wouldn't die in any heroic gesture – he had already been dead for weeks. In a fleeting rage, he would have liked to see her face when she realised, and to let her know how little her objections mattered.

A long strand of hair lifted from her neck and coiled around her face as an unexpected breeze broke the stillness. She noticed it too, but before either of them could move, the inside of the car erupted in a hail of sparks. They entered through the roof, filling the air with flecks of light that rained down over him. Wren was punctured dozens of times, freezing him to the core. His muscles seized, including his heart. His vision turned white.

Despite being an hour from the village, the ysbryd had somehow found them. A sharp pain spread up his neck. His jaw tightened. He pushed the brake pedal down and punched the start button, bringing the engine to life, then he stabbed every button on the dashboard – the heated seats, the climate control – until a burst of warm air flooded his face.

It worked, counteracting the cold. The sparks grew sluggish before his eyes, like mosquitos struggling to fly against an upward gust of wind. One by one, they were driven out of the cabin until he was alone again, clutching his chest in shock. But it wasn't over. An invisible force slammed against the front windscreen and a chip in the glass quadrupled in size.

'Sarah,' he cried, 'get out of here.'

He twisted in his seat, trying to spot her. Sarah had backed away from the car, but she was clutching her arm, as though something had taken a bite out of it. Her hair tussled around her head until he couldn't see her face. The fabric of her clothing flattened down against her skin. Deep cuts appeared on her exposed flesh. Inch by inch, pale skin turned scarlet.

She flailed wildly, as though trying to defend herself from a swarm of insects. In response, the wind blew so hard that she stumbled. Wren watched in horror as her entire body rose until she appeared to be suspended off the ground, her feet kicking thin air. Everything happened at once. She was thrown at the windscreen with explosive force. On impact, her perforated skin split open like torn rubber. Innards spilled out, purple and scarlet. Her squeals were cut short by a crunch of bone, muscle, and sinew ripped apart.

The crack in the glass grew wider.

A voice inside Wren's mind screamed – the agony of a man forced to witness something horrible. It had to be Lloyd, paralysed and helpless. Sarah, herself, was beyond screaming.

Wren dropped the handbrake and backed out of the parking space. The body slid off the bonnet and tumbled onto concrete, leaving vile streaks of entrails in its wake. A pair of onlookers fled for their lives, but he doubted they were in danger. The spirits wanted Wren, and Wren alone. He put his foot to the floor, and this time, they didn't get the chance to intervene. He pulled out of the car park and back onto the road, blood lifting from the white paint and splattering all over the windscreen. He tried desperately to focus. *Just get out of there.*

Anywhere.

Keep running.

29.IMPR|ESSION

Wren made it less than three miles before his car ran out of fuel, but that forced him to think straight. Sarah's blood covered every visible inch of the vehicle, rich scarlet like his cotton jumper. It contrasted with the white metalwork, drying in long streaks that were impossible to miss. The rear end was crumpled from the ysbryd's assault on Lloyd and Sarah's house.

Only as the engine failed did he realise how the vehicle must have looked to other people. He pulled off the main road, using his last momentum to crawl under the yellow branches of a weeping willow. Once stationary, a sudden dread urged him to keep moving. He stumbled out onto the pavement. The remnants of painkillers in his system went some way to making him agile, but Lloyd's body wasn't fit for running at the best of times. His wounded knee refused to bend under his weight.

Sweat poured down his face as he hobbled along the street in the bright mid-afternoon. He clutched Sarah's handbag, haunted by the sound of her cracking bones. Even at her worst, she hadn't deserved to die. He had no idea how to keep anyone safe, not if distance made so little difference. They had driven many miles away from the forest and it had taken no more than an hour to find them.

How did it happen so fast?

How did the spirits know where to look?

He marched blindly through the afternoon, but fate was on his side. Wren spied a petrol station and used Sarah's money to purchase a metal canister, as much fuel as he could carry, and a bottle of water. He hauled them back to the car and washed off the stains, using a branch to wipe the bloody streaks into something less recognisable, at least enough to avoid attention.

He put two-thirds of the fuel into the tank and saved the rest. There wasn't a second of time to waste if he was going to put an end to the massacre, and there was someone he needed to see.

***

Sarah's own car was still parked beside the turnoff for Pontrhyd-y-werddon, close to a rectangular patch of flattened undergrowth where he had hidden the white car. She had come to his rescue on the strength of a missed phone call, her loyalty running deeper than her obvious resentment.

He didn't stop, nor even slow down. The steering wheel tried to pull itself out of his hands as he swung off the main road and tore up the hillside, bursting through the canopy towards the village. Determination strengthened his grip, the thirst for revenge. Thickening clouds cast a gloom across the valley. He prayed that the spirits were far enough behind him to grant several precious minutes before the next attack.

With reckless abandon, he raced towards The Black Horse then turned left into a corner of the village he hadn't been to in years. Alwyn Speake lived somewhere up there, and it didn't take more than a quick glance to figure out which property was his – a south-facing terrace with the windows boarded up, even the ones upstairs.

This was the home of a man with secrets. Alwyn had removed the glass from the front door and replaced it with a sheet of metal, creating a fortification. Nothing living or dead would get inside without permission. The garden was overgrown like everyone else's, despite him claiming to be a gardener. Incensed, Wren parked and approached the door on foot, rapping his fist against it. There were no peepholes, so when Alwyn finally emerged, he had no choice but to open it, to see who had come for him. And in any event, he couldn't have known Wren's true identity.

'I thought you were just passing through.' Alwyn made no attempt at pleasantries, nor attempted to hide his displeasure at being disturbed. He looked Wren up and down, paying particular attention to his many healing bruises. 'What happened to you?'

'I went into the forest, and now I'm going back.'

'Did you find something in there?'

'Don't humour me,' said Wren. 'You know what's going on. This doorstep isn't a safe place to stand, is it?'

'So leave.' Alwyn went to push the door closed.

'There's more than my own life at stake here,' said Wren. 'They've spread beyond your village. No one in this valley is safe. I'll go in alone if I have to, but without your help, I won't last long.'

'I don't care.' Alwyn slammed the door, loudly enough that the metal panel rattled.

Wren raised his voice to be heard through the barricade. 'How long do you think before they find me standing out here? A few minutes? Half an hour? How long is it usually?'

The door opened again, just a crack. 'Keep it down,' Alwyn snarled. 'You never know who's listening.'

'Then talk to me,' said Wren. 'I'll keep it brief, where I can. We can share information. Don't let me die without that much, at least.'

Alwyn chewed the inside of his mouth. His eyebrow twitched, then he reluctantly moved aside. Wren entered to a narrow hallway with a tiled floor and a low ceiling. Blunt instruments were propped up within easy reach, presumably for use as weapons. Alwyn bolted the door closed in three different places. Beyond that point, the only light in the building was artificial.

An oppressive warmth poured from a long radiator in a cramped lounge. He could smell the melting paint. Anglepoise lamps stood in every corner, pointed in different directions. They banished all trace of shadows. Wren immediately noticed a pile of papers on a low coffee table, covered in handwriting he recognised.

'What's this doing here?' he asked.

Alwyn shook his head. 'I don't get what you mean.'

Wren was looking at Jon Lawton's research. He hadn't seen it since the day that he and Isabel had died, spread out across the kitchen table where Andrew Goodwin had been working. He had assumed Goodwin had taken it back to the city, but it seemed not.

'These papers don't belong to you,' he said.

'What makes you say that?'

'Because I've read them. I know about the ysbryd. I know about Rees Franklin, the shadows, the sparks … I know about that stash of goods in The Black Horse and the people who hide there. But what I don't understand is why everyone puts up with it.'

'You think we're happy?' said Alwyn.

'You've done nothing to fight back, from what I can tell, which makes you complicit in countless murders. Ten years ago, no one was afraid to leave their houses. What changed?'

The bearded Welshman narrowed his eyes. 'Answer some questions for me, first. Why have you come here, claiming to know so much? Who beat you black and blue?'

'I wasn't beaten, Alwyn. I died. I'm Wren Lawton.'

Although it was hard to tell beneath the thick bristles of his heavy beard, he thought Alwyn's jaw fell open. 'You can't be.'

'It's true. This writing is my father's.'

Alwyn's whole demeanour changed. A visible shockwave ran from his head to his toes. He steadied himself on an armchair, then slumped down into it. 'When did this happen?'

'Two years ago.'

'And that man Scott?'

'That was me as well. I change bodies whenever I die. I can't control it.'

It felt good to speak his confession out loud, something Wren had only done once before. But unlike his predecessor, Alwyn seemed to accept what he was being told. Doubtless, that was because of the unnatural things he had already witnessed.

'You should have told me,' he said.

'Perhaps, with hindsight.'

'What about the man you're inside now? What happened to him?'

Wren shook his head. 'This one had a stroke, I think.'

'What's one more death, right?' Alwyn stood up again and walked behind the chair, apparently thinking hard. His words became laboured, slurred. 'Something out there has been killing for decades, since long before we were born. People started disappearing, then turning up again in the shadows.'

'Like my mother,' said Wren.

'So that's how you did it.'

'How long have you known? I grew up by that forest, for Christ's sake. I used to play in there.'

'It's changed,' said Alwyn. 'You have to understand it was nothing like this when we were young. I was twenty-three when I saw my first.'

'I still lived here when you were twenty-three. You could have warned me.'

'You wouldn't have listened. It would have sounded insane.'

'You still should have done *something*.' Wren's arms flew into the air, so fast that Alwyn jumped. That sudden flash of vulnerability spoke volumes. Realisation dawned. 'You're afraid, aren't you? I mean properly afraid.'

Alwyn muttered under his breath, then closed his eyes and sighed. 'We're trapped. We don't leave because we can't.'

It was Wren's turn to look for something to steady himself against. 'My father had a list of names … mothers and their children. You sent them away from here, didn't you? You thought it would keep them safe, but they died anyway.'

Alwyn squirmed. 'Anyone who moves away winds up dead within a year. The ysbryd plague this valley, but they're everywhere, the whole world over, and they're drawn to whatever it is we're carrying.'

Wren stepped back, conscious of the weakness in his sore leg. Every word made perfect, horrible sense. The ysbryd hadn't followed him and Sarah to the hotel, an hour's drive away. They wouldn't have been able to keep up. Instead, they were ubiquitous, already there. As soon as he had come to a halt, the spirits would have begun to congregate, drawn to the energy he exuded. It was the same energy that everyone who lived near the forest had glowing inside them. In his case, they had absorbed enough strength to lift a human being off the ground and throw them around like a ragdoll. They had done that in minutes. For the others, it may have taken days, weeks, or even months, but sooner or later, in one form or another, death had still come for them.

It wasn't suicide, depression, illness, or misfortune. It was the ysbryd, every time. They had stalked him at the bungalow with the yellow door. They had stalked Isabel because of the energy she had absorbed whilst sleeping by his side. Thinking he was living in newfound bliss, he had instead condemned her to death.

His voice quivered. 'Why is this happening to us?'

Alwyn shrugged his shoulders. The Black Horse seemed a more tragic place than ever – the shredded remains of a damned community, united by the losses they had suffered. They were unable to go out at night and took a risk going out on the warmest day. They were unable to flee, mourning the loss of mothers, sons, daughters, sisters …

'Did you have a child?' asked Wren.

'Not me.'

'But there's someone you care about, someone you lost. We have to stop this. Isabel—' Wren couldn't say her name without his voice breaking. Jon Lawton had worked all of this out for himself, and had been killed for his discoveries. 'I'm heading into that forest right now and doing what I can to end the slaughter. You either help me or I'll do this without you.'

'It's suicide, even for you. They'll never let you leave.'

Wren couldn't argue. If Lloyd's body was torn to pieces, he might very well face the end without his mother's protection. But his need to act was too strong, to put everything right. And the daylight outside wouldn't last. He couldn't let himself be dissuaded and become like the survivors in the village. He marched into the hallway and started undoing the bolts on the door, refusing to show his distress.

Alwyn came rushing after him. 'There has to be another way.'

'Tell Rees to make them back off.'

'He won't listen. He's got too much to lose.'

Wren turned. 'One thing I don't understand … You told me that you tended to my father's garden, but that's clearly a cover for something else. What were you really doing?'

Alwyn shrank. 'We didn't trust him enough to share what we knew. He was always an outsider.'

'So you were spying on him, as he spied on you?' Another piece fit into the puzzle – the mundane nature of Jon Lawton's research, hundreds of observations without a single hint of what was really going on. 'You covered up the deaths he recorded.'

Alwyn nodded. 'He saw what happened to the Craddocks, so when he left town, I took pages out of his notes and destroyed them.'

'Did he realise?'

'He must have done.' Alwyn fidgeted, scratching his face. 'But he never said anything. It seemed like the only way to keep him quiet. Just his word against ours.'

'Except that was still too much risk for some of you, wasn't it?' Wren's brain was working overtime, close to overloading. 'You couldn't shut him up forever. Only the ysbryd could do that, and they could never break down the stone wall in his garden.'

He closed his eyes and saw rubble all over the grass – collapsed stonework, as though struck by a hammer.

'That's a wild accusation,' said Alwyn.

'But I'm right,' said Wren. 'Rees Franklin wanted my father stopped for the same reason he tried to kill me, but the wall was part of his property, so they couldn't get close enough to the windows to flush him out. You helped him.'

Alwyn closed his eyes. 'Not by choice.'

'So why send me to Eira? To gloat?'

'I thought if you understood—'

Wren clenched his fists. 'The woman I love is dead because you took down that wall,' he yelled. 'You had at least three chances to warn me.'

'It wouldn't have made a difference, don't you see? They would have got to you. They would have got your father.

There's no escape, no matter how far you run, or where you try to hide.'

Wren felt a sudden swell of rage. There were hand tools by the door, lined up across the skirting board. He lifted a two-foot hatchet and gripped the handle. 'You could have helped me and you didn't,' he said.

'I'm not proud of it,' said Alwyn.

'Who else died because of you?' He felt the weight of the weapon begging to be swung, fuelled by a burning need for revenge, and yet a second voice inside him begged for mercy. He had no way of knowing whether it was his own reasoning or the compassion of a half-dead stranger.

Enough killing, it said.

'I'm taking this.' Wren flung the door open, bringing the hatchet, needing all of his willpower to walk away.

'They'll rip you apart. Come and talk things over with the rest of the villagers.'

Wren chose not to listen to any more of Alwyn's biased advice. There was no way he could become like those wretched residents, huddled together while they cowered from death. He tried to silence any further stray thoughts. Another back-seat passenger was the last thing he needed, especially if it meant having to relinquish control of that body whenever he slept.

He marched down the road with unshakable resolve. There was a force out there that no one understood, killing anyone it wanted to, turning the survivors against innocent men and women. It was indiscriminate. For everyone's sakes, but mostly for Isabel and his father, the time had come to end it.

30.ASHE|S

The days were growing shorter as the year aged. By late afternoon, the sun was already over the horizon, leaving minutes of remaining daylight.

Wren wasn't put off by the threat of darkness. He parked the bloodstained vehicle at the low end of the village, on the grass verge beyond the footpath. He strode down the embankment with the fuel canister in one hand and the hatchet he had taken from Alwyn Speake in the other. Already, there was movement in the air. He threw his trappings over the stream and leapt after. Lloyd's battered, aged frame made for a graceless manoeuvre, but he didn't care who could see him.

No one would dare to follow.

He searched for the greenest branches he could find and hacked two off, trimming them down until they were metre-long sticks. Next, he removed his cotton jumper and tore it in half, wrapping a piece tightly around the end of each, and securing them with wire. There was enough petrol in the canister to douse the rags thoroughly, and like that, he had two makeshift torches. They would burn for several minutes, but he didn't need to light them, not yet. He took them in hand, along with the bladed weapon, and marched into the forest.

The temperature plummeted with his very first step, raising goosebumps along his bare arms. It was more like entering a cave than stepping amongst trees. As he moved away from the trickling waters, the ailing daylight seemed to fade unnaturally fast. Silence descended, swallowing every noise he made. The air was charged with expectation, as though the forest welcomed his return with open arms that enveloped him, then blocked his escape.

The ground rose and fell, shallow roots from clusters of trees competing for room. He could understand why the ysbryd were drawn to such a place. They could move freely in the cold. They could shelter from the intensity of daytime. It offered nothing for the living, but still, a compulsion spurred him onwards. Perhaps, beneath all that borrowed flesh, he had even more in common with the dead than he cared to admit.

A swift, muffled chop of the hatchet cleared the way through tangled branches. The forest devoured him with each successive step. A haze appeared around his feet, a low-lying mist that distorted the air. It was cold, with an unnerving churn. There, at last, his doubts got the better of him. He worked his fingers into the tight pocket of his jeans and retrieved the cigarette lighter he had taken from the glove box in Lloyd's car. He pushed the trigger with his thumb, and with a grinding crunch, a flame burst to life that glowed blue like the flame of a jet engine. His host's lungs had been polluted by years of smoking, but a robust lighter was the by-product of his habit. No mere weather could have stopped it.

He lit the cotton rag. The effect was immediate. A bright flicker peeled back the darkness, as though the forest itself was recoiling from the heat. The mist parted, retreating towards the shadows. Within seconds, he could see clearly again, as though it was midday. Taking a torch in each hand, he felt uplifted and secure. The forest continued to permit his entry, offering not a hint of resistance. The earth beneath his feet became slippery – dried out, to the point where it scarcely resembled dirt at all.

His compulsion was like gravity now, tugging him along. It drew him past disturbances on the ground that he recognised from his previous visit, so many days before. He came to the south bank of the eerie slope, something he doubted was down to luck. Even with the torches, he refused to go back down there.

The atmosphere seemed to be restricted, as though a false darkness hung over the pit. He swept the flames from left to right, questioning his own eyes. He could see for several metres to his left and right, but no more than a few in front of him. It was like the night had become a tangible object with opaque edges. It resembled smoke, only static.

'Do you realise what you're looking at?'

Wren hadn't heard Rees Franklin's voice in years, but he recognised the thick Welsh accent immediately. He spun around to see his adversary standing amongst the trees, as though sheltering from the flames. Rees had form, more so than any ysbryd he had seen besides his mother. Wren could see the pockmarks on his pale skin and the buttons on his black shirt.

'You can speak now?' he asked.

Rees nodded. *'There's less need to conserve our strength in here. Blasu'r pŵer. You must be able to feel it, Wren Lawton, given you're one of us.'*

Wren didn't blink, afraid to. He positioned the torches so that one burned between the two men and the other warded off the darkness. 'I wondered if you would recognise me,' he said.

'Neither of your disguises fooled us for a second. We see more than your face. I'm surprised, but glad, to find you in here again.'

'Alwyn told me everything.'

'*Everything he knows. We don't trust him with the full picture and neither should you. His energy may be bright, but he'll never be like you and I.*'

'We are not the same.'

'*Too right. You left everyone behind, off to the city. I stayed and tried to help. I'm helping to this day.*'

Rees glared. He advanced as he talked, drifting with a smooth motion, despite jagged movements. The firelight made him shimmer, dispelling his illusion of palpability. Wren couldn't help backing away, even though it meant inching closer towards the edge of the slope. He became aware of other figures amongst the tree trunks, all without discernible features.

'Do you really think you're doing good?' said Wren. 'You've killed to keep your secrets.'

'*To protect the forest,*' Rees corrected. '*You should thank me. Your mother's in here somewhere. Being full of energy makes you a target. The others want it. This is the only place where she can take refuge, where there's energy for everyone.*'

Wren glanced at his outstretched hands. The torches felt heavier by the second. He could see the flames recoiling from the darkness, bending back towards him. He knew they wouldn't burn forever.

'Let her go,' he demanded.

'I'm not holding her. They'll leave her alone in here. Out there is a different matter. There's no law or consequence. The strong kill the weak. You need to give them a reason not to attack, and there's only one thing they're interested in. It's why I need your help.'

'My help?' Wren raised his voice as he scoffed. 'This darkness beside me … that's death, isn't it? That's what I'm looking at, the darkness we've all survived. Do you want me to draw people in here so it can feed, or would you rather I smashed down walls like Alwyn Speake?'

To his horror, Rees didn't flinch. 'Whatever buys us time.'

'Time for what? The dead you serve are lost. There's no way back for them.'

'Of course there is, you hypocrite. You're living proof. You're no less of a spirit than the rest of us, but you're alive at the same time. We need to figure out how others can do the same.'

Wren recoiled from the suggestion. His affliction had put him through hell. He had ruined the lives of everyone he knew, and anyone he had met along the way. He thought immediately of a thousand lost souls trying to copy him, those who had already proven they were beyond morality. What would they do if there weren't enough bodies to inhabit?

He shuddered at the thought of mass-resurrection, of abominations that would be hailed as miracles. 'Go to hell,' he said.

'What are you going to do, instead? You were cursed with this existence, the moment you absorbed this energy. You were stained by it, as we all were. There's no normal life waiting for you out there. Even if you escaped tonight, you're visible for miles. You can't hide. The truth is they'll tear you to pieces if you don't offer them something. You're already a slave. You just can't see the chains.'

He pointed to Wren's feet. In reaction, something grabbed Wren by the ankles – something invisible, rising up from underneath. Cold fingers yanked him downwards. So close to the edge of the pit, the ground couldn't hold itself together. A huge patch of dried-out soil collapsed and he tumbled with it down the slope, into the strange darkness. He accelerated as he went, as though carried at speed, colliding with an outcrop of smooth rocks near the bottom. All the momentum was driven through his shoulder, it seemed very much on purpose. Something crunched; he both heard and felt it. A bolt of pain shot up his arm.

One of the torches flew from his grasp and rolled out of reach. The darkness seemed to recoil from the heat, peeling back to reveal a stretch of barren ground. With his remaining torch and the hatchet in the same hand, he struggled to his knees. He could feel a stabbing pain in his bicep, as though splintered bone was digging into muscle, but something else stole his full attention.

A body lay beside him, close enough to touch. It was curled into a ball, its arms hugging its knees. Its skin was dried out and wrinkled, the flesh degenerated until it resembled leather. He couldn't guess at the age – he could hardly even guess at the gender – but the size of its frame suggested someone young, perhaps only a teenager. A persistent cloud of crumbled soil hung in the air, fine like volcanic dust. The pit had been exposed, in a way he hadn't seen before. He realised there were corpses everywhere, littering the ground. Dormant shapes lay atop one another, intertwined, drained until petrified. Limbs were broken and contorted. A woman had perished on more exposed rocks. Her neck appeared snapped.

This was the scene of a massacre, each kill preserved like a hideous trophy. Vomit rushed up his throat and he emptied the contents of his stomach onto the ground.

'All these people are part of the forest now,' said Rees, appearing at the top of the embankment. His unclean face flickered in the distant firelight. *'Their spirits will be somewhere in here, not that you could tell them apart.'*

'Is this your handiwork?' said Wren. 'Are you proud? How many did you lure inside so the ysbryd could beat them to death?'

'I didn't start this process. You'll find my body in that pile. Once they cut me down, I learned to guide the ysbryd, to keep them away from the people I care about. You can bargain with them, Wren. If you have something to offer, they'll listen.'

Wren clambered to his feet. His injured arm hung limply from his side, gnawing at him from within. He kept the torch raised, fully expecting to be ambushed at any second. He was under no illusion. Rees would either recruit him to protect the forest or else finish him off. He had no way out of the pit without relinquishing his only means of defence. If his mother couldn't carry him away to a new host then his prospects were bleak.

'What exactly do you want me for?' he asked.

'You need to listen, Wren. I thought the thing in these woods was unique, but you could be even better. You could provide all the energy we need, and you'll never have to die. We'll do whatever your mother does. We'll do anything. All we ask in return is that you help us to figure out how to be like you. Help us to find a way back.'

He shook his head, almost involuntarily. 'You killed the only two people I ever loved.'

'Try to understand that I had to.'

Somewhere deep inside his mind, Lloyd urged him to give in, as though begging for mercy. But the thought of compliance turned his stomach. Serving the ysbryd would be a fate comparable to the many deaths he had already suffered. There was only one alternative. He loosened his grip of the torch and let it slip from between his fingers. The burning rag landed on the nearest dead body. Within a few seconds, dried clothing caught alight. It put up no resistance. Everything in the pit had been sucked dry by the forest's thirst. Now, it was kindling.

Flames spread quickly from one garment to another, then from corpse to corpse. The smoke-like darkness receded, revealing decades of executions. The fire grew bright, the heat intense. The ground itself seemed to glow red. Inevitably, it found ways out of the pit, escaping via branches, fallen logs, and in places, the ground itself. The darkness roared in protest, as though frightened by the blaze.

The wind roused.

A cacophony of snapping branches was followed by waves of flying debris. They encircled the pit, filling the air with activity. But they couldn't get close, driven back by the energy. Wren's gamble had paid off. The ysbryd were powerless to reach him.

'*Stop this,*' Rees yelled, but his voice came out breathy, like a whisper. In truth, nothing could stop the fire now. The conditions were too perfect, the air devoid of moisture. Using the hatchet and his good arm, Wren worked his way up the crumbling slope before the heat consumed him. Nearby trees burst into flames. Something deep inside him recoiled – a parallel disbelief from another mind.

Monster, it said. *You're no better than the rest.*

That voice had the opposite of its intended effect. It steadied Wren's resolve. His hunger for revenge was stronger than ever. He thought of Isabel and his father, both stranded in the house on the far side of the brook. He thought of how they had died at the behest of that deceased madman. Wren's wounded arm pulsated. Anger spread beneath his skin like the flames across the trees. Rees Franklin deserved to be snuffed out, and any spirits that had ever helped him.

One final death for them all.

He could see Rees shouting, his jaw moving up and down as he scorned. But the crackling blaze stole his voice. The heat drove him back. Wren positioned himself as close to the fire as he dared. Steadily, almost casually, he stepped amongst the trees and began to work his way out of the forest. It couldn't have been more different to his last visit. The shadows of tree trunks danced in the firelight, creating ever-moving bands of darkness. Sparks piled out of tree knots, snaking through the forest like schools of minnows.

Something exploded high above him, sending more sparks raining down from the treetops. Black smoke blended with the darkness, creating a sickly smell. He heard distant shouts of panic, and scuffles, as though ysbryd were clawing past ysbryd. Flames licked against his bare skin, burning through the sweat, pushing him forwards as he continued to cradle his injured arm. The fire overtook him in places, the scene beginning to resemble hell.

Wren retraced his steps toward Pontrhyd-y-werddon. The spirits came with him. High above, the canopy became a web-like mesh of crackling branches, sending ash raining down in clouds of black speckles. His eyes dried out, so he narrowed them to slits. He gained speed as the ground hardened, moister near the outskirts. The sparks seemed to fan out and disperse in the open air.

He seized the chance to run and ploughed into the night, without a thought for where he was going. The terrain dipped. He fell into icy water, landing face down in the stream. The hatchet slipped from his hands. With a gasp, he righted himself, looking up the far embankment to see a clear night sky.

He heard splashes from along the treeline and turned to see ripples in the water. There were signs of movement flickering on the edge of the firelight. Wren scrabbled to his feet and carried on up the hillside. He couldn't stay. Wherever the street light didn't reach, he saw the makings of a stampede. He saw black shadows, figures rushing through the waters and away from the woodland. There was panic in every patch of darkness.

The exodus had begun.

31.PRES|ENCE

Wren's sodden trousers clung to his legs, making it difficult to run. He kept looking over his shoulder as the fire in the forest spread unchallenged, passing effortlessly between the intertwined branches of long-dead trees.

It seemed like the whole valley was ablaze, sending plumes of black smoke into the night sky. Even from a hundred yards away, he had to shield his face from the heat. No spirit would stand a chance of moving through it. Any whom the fire encircled – the ones who couldn't escape – let out horrible screams as their remaining strength was forced out of them. He had never heard a thing like it, nor wished to ever again.

A chorus of death wails.

It hammered home just how many spirits there must have been, and how widespread they were. The survivors fled, pushing past one another in a bid to escape a similar fate. He saw branches swept aside, energy wasted thoughtlessly. Firelight may have tricked him into believing he was alone, but in reality, he would be anything but.

He continued up the hillside, unable to even think about driving with his injured arm. Drenched clothes were as heavy as lead. He half expected to be wiped out at any second by creatures who didn't even realise he was in their way. As he gained distance, that risk increased. The atmosphere cooled, but the noises didn't diminish. If anything, they grew louder. Wren realised he wouldn't last for long in the open, so he abandoned the road altogether and made a break for the trees that flanked the High Street houses. The woodland there was a stark contrast to the one he had escaped from. It was alive – supple and moist. It wouldn't catch fire so readily.

He pushed blindly into the trees, unable to see more than a few feet in front of him. Leaves rustled underfoot. He had no bearings except the angle of the slope. He went deeper into a commanding silence. The ysbryd were already there. Wren heard them moving in a way he could barely describe – shifting, as though attracted to the cold.

A constant breeze wove between the tree trunks. He didn't make it far before his nerve collapsed. It wasn't safe. Nowhere was. It rapidly became too dark to navigate. The cold bit through his clothing and nipped at his flesh. He stowed himself behind a tree trunk and stuffed his good hand into his armpit, trying to keep warm while he gathered his thoughts. He fought with his pocket, trying to extract the cigarette lighter. Then there was a flash. White light filled the forest. Wren screwed his eyes shut just a split second too late, feeling his retina burn.

'I should have known this would be your doing.'

A figure appeared with an air of malign tolerance, betraying no fear. They carried a torch, angled towards the ground, illuminating clouds of steaming breath.

'Alwyn?' said Wren.

'Are you trying to burn the whole valley down?'

The beam of light rose again, strong enough to dull his other senses. 'I can't see. You're blinding me.'

'You're welcome,' said Alwyn. 'I discovered a while ago that the ysbryd don't like strong lights. They tend to go around them. Path of least resistance.'

Through the sound of his chattering teeth, Wren thought he could hear it – voices diverting. 'Have you come here to help, or were you sent to finish me off?'

'I came to stop you killing yourself, nothing more.'

'Trying to ease your conscience?'

'Maybe so.'

Alwyn peeled off his duffel coat and approached, presenting it as a peace offering. 'You can't stay out here,' said Alwyn. 'They'll outrun you in the dark, no problem.'

'We'll see about that.' Wren accepted the coat without giving thanks and marched past him up the hillside, to the limit of the beam. Padded sleeves rubbed against his sides.

'Where are you going?' Alwyn asked.

'Far enough away that Rees can't find me. With the forest burning, the ysbryd have bigger things to worry about.'

'And that makes you safe? Their fear will turn to anger. I've seen it before. They'll come for you, and anyone else they can find.'

Wren tried to keep moving. Maybe he couldn't run forever, but anywhere was safer than the village at that moment. He felt the torchlight drift off his back as the bearded Welshman pointed it behind them.

'If we're lucky, most will burn themselves out from running and vanish,' said Wren.

'It takes more than that. You'd much rather they had a common goal. At least they'd only come from one direction.'

'If your torch can drive them back then who cares?'

'Don't rely on it.'

The beam swung uphill to light the way for a few moments. Wren saw a blockage of undergrowth ahead, like a wall of foliage. But before he could make a proper assessment, he was thrust back into darkness. 'I'll need a better look than that,' he said. 'There's no clear path. Didn't you bring a—'

He turned to find Alwyn sweeping the torchlight back and forth across the canopy, rather than the ground. 'What are you doing?' he asked.

'Protecting us,' said Alwyn. 'What does it look like?'

'Stop.' Wren scrambled down the slope and gripped the lens in the palm of his hand. Light shone through his fingers, making his flesh glow a vibrant crimson. 'There's no danger in the bloody treetops. You're not holding the spirits at bay, are you? You're broadcasting our location.'

'It's not as sinister as it sounds …'

'I'm right though, aren't I? They've already been instructed to leave you alone. You're showing Rees where to find me.'

Wren pulled the flashlight from Alwyn's grip. Alwyn didn't resist, but he protested. 'The light does work as a deterrent. We're safer when we have it. You can't trust anyone, Wren, and you can hate me all you like, but I know what it takes to survive here. You weren't around to see us get picked off one by one.'

'Which makes me wonder what else you're guilty of.'

He spread his fingers apart until only enough light seeped through the gaps to guide them along, not enough to draw attention. He started up the hillside in disgust. Alwyn had no choice but to follow or be left in darkness. 'You would have done both if it meant your life,' he said. 'I've spent years following orders. You can't understand how that feels.'

'But why?'

'Because it's for the best. Because the dead can't speak for themselves, like Rees can. And for people like Beca.'

Wren paused in his ascent. The heat passing through his fingers contrasted the cold breeze he could feel on his neck. 'Beca Craddock?'

'Rees is looking for her. She's in the forest somewhere, or she was.'

'They were a couple?'

Alwyn nodded. 'She vanished on the night her parents were killed. Everyone thought she went into the forest, so Rees went looking. That's how he died.'

'Oh.' The cold seemed to encourage him to hesitate, as though turning him into a statue.

'You judge him too harshly, as you do all of us. We've only ever been trying to protect the ones we care about. You and Rees are not so different, not when you think about—'

Alwyn collapsed to the forest floor. He crumpled, as though his legs had given way. Wren saw ripples in the air, almost like being underwater. The ysbryd had suddenly grown in number, surging up the hillside like a tsunami. He pulled his hand away and unleashed the full beam, turning the forest as bright as day. To his eye, the spirits vanished, but he had no way of knowing whether they were being repelled or merely hidden.

'What happened?' With no free hands, he simply barked at his companion. 'Can you walk?'

Alwyn shuddered on the ground, then scrabbled back to his feet. His eyes were wide with terror. 'Something passed through me.'

'We need to get inside. Can you make it to your house?'

'I'll damn well try.'

Alwyn stumbled, a hand on his thigh. Wren took him under the shoulder and helped him back out onto the road. The bearded Welshman was heavy, but determined, and they both knew where they were going. Emerging from the forest, they found Pontrhyd-y-werddon had come alive. The forest blazed, spreading unhampered towards the far side of the valley. The air was thick with the stench of smoke.

Shadows danced over almost every surface. The noises were arresting – crackling wood mixed with harrowing death knells. Entire trees crashed to the ground, steadily laying waste to the prison of the ysbryd. Wherever the light grew weak, Wren saw spirits racing, stampeding, clawing past one another with a weightless fleetness of foot. They were faster than any living person. Wren and Alwyn could never outrun them.

Alwyn guided him to the front porch of an empty house for a brief shelter. Wren prayed there was enough energy in the building to deter the spirits. Disjointed hordes passed them blindly, fleeing up the hillside. Wren realised they were heading for the summit, and in their path lay The Black Horse. Lights were on in every window, unwittingly painting the building as a target. Such energy may have kept the occupants safe in normal times, but that was against spirits in their tens or in their hundreds. There were thousands now, and they were panic stricken.

Wren was too far away to raise the alarm. He watched open-mouthed as a wave of faint glimmers and halos smashed into the tavern with palpable force, in numbers too great to be challenged. Glass shattered. An explosion of sparks flickered like lightning as they poured through windows and walls alike. Several voices shouted, then were silenced a split second later. The last survivors of that cursed village were overwhelmed, snuffed out of existence. None of them stood a chance.

'Turn the torchlight off,' Alwyn hissed. 'Keep it off, whatever you do.'

'What now?'

'We can't get to my house. It's too far in the open. We've got one other chance, if we can reach it.'

Wren took a sharp breath. There was only one other place with a remote possibility of being protected from the rushing crowds, not for the energy it gave off, but for the immunity of the occupant.

Eira Franklin.

Rees would continue to do everything in his power to keep her from harm. Even the most reckless spirit must have understood that her home, off in the trees, was a place to avoid. With his injured arm held tightly to his chest, Wren took some of Alwyn's weight and made ready to run. But Alwyn shook him off, choosing to hobble by himself rather than rely on assistance. 'Keep behind me, not beside me,' he said. 'I know the best way, even in darkness, and I won't go slowly.'

Pontrhyd-y-werddon had been overrun. Everywhere Wren looked, the shards of broken windows seemed to glisten. He saw shimmering tarmac and heard screaming – the screaming of the dead.

The front door of The Black Horse collapsed inwards with a deafening thud, torn off its hinges. Alwyn led the way towards the hilltop and the darkened shelter of trees. As instructed, Wren left the torch switched off, scared of drawing numbers too great to be deterred. His own shadow flickered and danced as they ran up the footpath. He felt as though the ground was moving, as though one misstep would bring him crashing down. As they reached the treeline and hurried down a narrow driveway, a bitter cold created patches of ice. He slowed, afraid of falling on his injured arm. A gap opened up between the two men.

He became aware of ysbryd crossing their path, passing between them before continuing up the hill towards the wilderness. Every second he was out there resulted in another near miss. The white walls of Eira's house stood out against the black. Alwyn was almost within reach of the door when three spirits appeared together, running in a group. Their outlines were fuzzy, but distinct, aided by the darkness. They barrelled across the clearing and collided with Alwyn Speake. There was no impact; they passed right through him. Alwyn crossed his arms and yelped, as though struck by a hail of bullets.

Wren abandoned any pretence of stealth and turned the torch back on. Alwyn slid to the ground, collapsing in a cloud of leaves.

'Are you alright?' said Wren. There was no answer. 'Speak to me. Come on, we're so close.'

Through the reflections in the front window, he saw figures in the trees. They had paused, as though starting to take notice. There wasn't time to think. He grabbed Alwyn's arm and pulled him towards the door. The man was like a dead weight. Lloyd's full strength barely shifted him at all. He threw the torch through the open door and reached down with his injured arm, taking hold of Alwyn's collar. With a grip in two places now, he leaned backwards, exerting all the force he could muster. Broken bones dug into tensed muscles. A sharp, debilitating pain tore up the left side of his body. He could feel the warmth of blood spreading beneath his skin. But ever so slowly, Alwyn shifted. Inch by agonising inch, Wren reversed until his heel made contact with the short step. His stricken companion reached the threshold, and with an almighty heave, Wren brought him into the house.

The two of them crumpled to the carpet, fighting for breath. A moment's disbelief was all he could permit himself, then back into action. Wren pointed the torch outside to drive the spirits away then put his ear to Alwyn's mouth, checking for signs of life.

'Can you hear me?'

Alwyn was as white as a sheet. Wren peeled his eyelids back to find no pupils. He used his good hand to thump down on the bearded man's chest, trying to force life back into his body. 'Come on,' he groaned, but Wren was no expert. He didn't have the confidence for chest compressions, nor enough hands to do it with. All he could do was thump until Alwyn gasped, convulsed, and curled up in a ball.

'What happened?' Alwyn croaked through a dry mouth.

'You're at Eira's house,' said Wren. 'Try not to move.'

'I can't feel my arms.'

Wren felt them for him. They were ice cold. He climbed to his feet and stumbled down the hallway into Eira's bedroom. She was exactly where he had expected to find her – her legs beneath the covers of the little bed in the corner of the room, eternally waiting.

'What's going on?' she said. Eira didn't seem surprised to see him, not after the noise of his arrival.

'Alwyn's hurt,' said Wren. 'We have to—'

He stopped dead on sight of the window. In the dimness of the weak bedside lamp, he realised how many shadows had ceased their running and turned their interests towards the little house. They were gathering by the glass as he'd seen them do so many times before, and there were countless of them already. Eira hadn't been talking to him. At the head of the pack, glaring, stood the strongest and most clearly defined of all the spirits in the valley.

Rees had arrived.

32.JUST|ICE

Terror stole Wren's breath. He stared through the thin windowpane at his enemy, surrounded by an army of faceless followers. The last time Rees had cornered him like that, shattering glass had ripped him into pieces. Only his mother's intervention had saved his life, but Rees had the power to keep her from getting close.

Death now would mean death forever.

Wren had one card left to play. With a lurch in his stomach, he backed across the bedroom until he drew level with Eira Franklin's bed. He uncurled a finger to point at her. The message was clear. An exploding window would mow them both down. Rees seemed furious at the threat. He approached the window and put his face against the glass. With a noise like scratching nails, he passed through it. No cracks appeared, and neither was he forced back out. Wren's childhood home may have been strong enough to hold Rees at bay, but any strength in Eira's house had long since faded. She lived without heat and with next-to-no light. She left the door wide open.

Rees seemed to come inside with minimal resistance, and he wasn't alone. Sparks of light seeped through the plaster and began to swarm around the far side of the room. *'Do you see what you've done?'* Rees spoke loudly, despite no longer being supported by the energy of the forest.

'Alwyn's in the hallway,' said Wren. 'He needs our help.'

'So what?' Eira, by a contrast, spoke quietly. She sat upright with her back against the headboard. Her appearance was unthreatening, but her words were sharp as ever. 'We didn't ask you to drag him into this mess,' she said. 'If you want help, go ask your mother.'

The remaining shadows gathered at the window, watching without speaking. Wren let his broken arm hang under its own weight, so as not to reveal any weakness. The pain was distracting. 'Alwyn took care of you both. He kept your secrets. Are you just going to let him die?'

Rees nodded. *'He took your side. He should have understood what that would mean.'*

'But we've known him since we were children. Surely that counts for something? Everyone else is dead now.'

Eira's face fell. She looked to her son. 'Is that true? Are they gone?'

'Wren burned down the forest. The ysbryd are loose.'

She hissed like an alligator. 'Have you seen her? Why aren't you out there?'

'It's chaos. No one could tell them apart. She could be anywhere.'

Wren could feel the fury in the room. He raised his guard. A chill snaked in through the windowpane, hinting at how cold it must have become outside. 'Beca would want you to help Alwyn.'

'Don't you say her name.' Rees flushed red. Despite the dimness of the room, Wren thought he could see through him to the circling sparks, as though Rees's energy was already starting to fade.

'Calm down,' Eira instructed. 'Conserve your strength. Don't speak unless you need to.'

'But I want him to know. He thinks he's so righteous. He hasn't got a clue what he's done.'

'You started this, Rees, when you killed my father.'

'Rubbish.' Eira's voice became animated, but she barely moved. 'Your father brought it on himself. We've all read his notes. He sat back and watched the Craddocks die without lifting a finger to help.'

Wren glanced back and forth between them, afraid of being attacked at any moment. 'He was an elderly man. They would have sliced him apart.'

'He could have raised the alarm,' said Rees. *'You know as well as I do what his mere presence would have done. He wasn't clueless.'*

Rees shook with repressed anger. His voice trailed off – dimmed – until his mother spoke for him. 'Beca ran away when she lost her parents. None of those cowards wanted to look for her, too scared of the ysbryd's wrath. My child died alone in the search, so I say good riddance to all of them.'

She closed her eyes and a burst of effort flashed across her face. Rees seemed to grow more solid. 'This will give her peace,' said Wren. 'Death is nothing to be afraid of. It's a damn sight better than what I saw down there.'

'*Y lembo*,' Rees bawled at the top of his voice.

'Stop this, both of you.'

Wren froze mid-quarrel, as did his adversary. Standing by the door was the bearded form of Alwyn Speake. He had somehow managed to drag himself off the hallway floor and stood leaning against the door frame, one hand clutching at his chest. 'You're both murderers,' he said. 'I've seen you at your worst.'

'I'm protecting our loved ones. We can't afford to have limits.'

Alwyn fought for breath. 'Maybe Wren's right. We were too hung up on trying to bring them back that we didn't think about the existence they're reduced to. Maybe the fire is a blessing in disguise.'

'You're wrong.' Eira's voice couldn't compete with the others, but even under the immense pressure of keeping her son alive without the forest there to support her, she was able to speak her mind. 'You're wrong, and you're a dimwit. Rees and I would turn the heavens upside down to save the ones we love, whether they knew it or not. Until we find a way to bring them back, any existence is better than death. And if they can't have the forest then we're left with one alternative …'

She sucked air in through her teeth and closed her eyes, concentrating hard. Rees seemed to grow more solid, swelling with negative energy. The spirits at the window became agitated, shuffling on their feet. Rees raised his arm and pointed. As if on command, the sparks in the room surged towards Alwyn Speake. He was peppered from head to toe. He gasped, wide-eyed.

'Stop,' yelled Wren. 'Stop. You don't need to do that.'

We do, said Rees. *We need an empty vessel for you to inhabit next. You're going to die again, Wren Lawton. We're going to boost your strength, make you shine as bright as possible. We're going to kill you again, and again, and again, until you're strong enough to sustain every spirit you set loose for a hundred years and more. That's your sacrifice. You're going to become the new forest, like I wanted. You could have been a part of this with us, but since you won't comply, we'll take what we want anyway.'*

The dead began to pour into the room through every wall, even the internal ones. Wren had nowhere to turn. Once they were finished with Alwyn, the sparks would come for him. There was nothing he could do, or perhaps there was. He looked over at the frail form of Eira Franklin, her face contorted, donating her energy to her son.

He saw his way out.

Wren lurched across the room and descended upon the timeworn woman with outstretched arms. His weight fell on top of her. His fury channelled through the fist of his good arm. She didn't groan or recoil; she crumpled, unconscious in a heartbeat.

Rees stopped in his tracks. His colour returned to its former state as his power diminished. *'What was that?'* he demanded.

'Like you said, I have no choice.' Wren swiped one of the pillows from behind Eira's back and placed it over her face.

Rees took on a different tone, starting to plead. *'Think of your father. Think of all your loved ones.'*

'They're gone.'

'You don't know that. With your energy, we could bring them back to life. You'll never know if you won't try.'

The pillow smothered Eira's airways. She snapped back into consciousness and grabbed Wren's wrists, her cold fingers putting up a feeble resistance. Rees cried out and stormed towards the bed, plunging both hands through the fabric of Wren's clothing. Wren let out a constricted scream, but the muscles in his arms tensed as he ploughed more effort into his own actions.

Eira clawed with her nails. Rees pushed deeper, shivering with the effort it must have required. Wren sank towards the mattress, his innards seizing, but he kept the cushion tight against the old lady's nose and mouth. The three of them locked in their struggle for several seconds, until inevitably, the weakest member succumbed. Eira went limp. The tension faded from her fingers. Almost at the same moment, Rees's energy diminished to the point where he could no longer compete with Wren's warmth. He shimmered like a sunbeam on the surface of a lake. He became transparent. Details faded. Before long, he resembled a silhouette, no different to the other ysbryd. His demeanour changed completely. He began to float listlessly, as though deprived of conscious thought. His featureless head turned in confusion, from left to right.

To left, to right …

Wren's own energy was similarly spent. He collapsed onto the floor, propped up on the elbow of his good arm. He could sense Eira's death, her fading aura. The building's remaining strength was drained, removing the last obstacle to the ysbryd's entry. Shadowy arms reached through every wall, pushing their way into the property. They seemed to gravitate towards Alwyn Speake as he lay still beside the doorway. Wren couldn't tell whether he was alive or dead, but assumed that death wasn't far away. He picked himself up slowly and clutched his useless arm, stealing a moment to gather his breath.

'Leave that one alone.'

The figures paused, reacting to the tone of his command. He saw impressions of the short and the slender, the young and the old. He saw nodding heads and hunched shoulders. He felt an icy chill.

'It's me you came for, isn't it? Let him live and I'll stop resisting.'

There was no immediate response, nor did he expect one. They were likely to take what they wanted, regardless. If Rees had been correct then, everywhere he went, the ysbryd would gather. They had ceased running from the burning forest to be near him, drawn to his energy to give them strength. He couldn't shake them off and he couldn't outrun them, but at least if he bargained, the last surviving person from the village of his youth would have a chance at survival. He could do something good after all of his transgressions.

An eerie calm descended. The shadows stood motionless, as though in silent contemplation. A single step in any direction would have meant certain death. 'I mean it.' His insides were in knots. 'I'll give you what the forest did, but you have to leave him be. And there's someone else. I don't know what you've done to my mother, but wherever she is, bring her back. Set her free.'

He doubted the crowd were capable of answering. He didn't know whether he was trying to strike a deal with an organised group or a host of individuals. For a precarious moment, nothing happened, but then the mob began to withdraw. They didn't disperse, but they backed through the walls until he and Alwyn were alone. The temperature in the bedroom rose. He stepped cautiously to the window, finding an ocean of faceless figures on the other side. The role of overlord had been handed from Rees to him, something more terrifying than any fate he could imagine. They wanted his protection, his guidance, but most importantly, the energy he exuded. And they had listened to his requests. Distant fires continued to rage. Flickering beams of light penetrated the treeline. On the edge of the darkness stood a woman. There was one spirit with more presence than even

Rees Franklin, someone so focused that she only used her energy when he needed her.

Hope Lawton.

She had grown up near the forest, part of the generation before Wren's. She had energy in abundance, but she could also feed on his glimmer. She had given him life. He would feed her with death. He would do that for all the ysbryd.

In the intermittent dimness, he could make out her expression. This was a woman he had always feared, a woman he had never understood. For once, her own anguish seemed to have faded, replaced by something even worse. She looked troubled, wary, mirroring his own concerns. He was certain she knew the weight of his sacrifice. She was no longer alone in keeping Wren safe. It was out of her control. He was the new forest, glowing like a candle in the darkness. Any relief at seeing her returned to him was smothered by the circumstances. He was damned, condemned, enslaved.

Immortal.

He could sense it.

EPILOGUE

Emergency services were never summoned to the forest fire in Pontrhyd-y-werddon. It burned for two hours before anyone outside the valley even noticed. Everyone inside the valley was dead.

Police and firemen arrived to find a thick, smouldering pile of ashes spanning thousands of square feet, a huge black blot across the landscape. They saw a burned-out village full of empty houses and broken windows. They saw a tavern with a dozen corpses, each lying where they fell, brought to the ground as though their hearts had given in.

There was one survivor. In a dilapidated house, hidden amongst trees, the police found the frail form of Alwyn Speake. Though weak, he was conscious, and coherent enough to know how unlikely his story sounded. Wren was under no illusion about what would happen to him. Alwyn may have given his coat to keep Wren warm. Alwyn may have risked his life to get Wren to safety. Alwyn may have done a great deal to redeem himself, but none of it would atone for smashing the garden wall that kept the ysbryd from Jon Lawton's rear window. None of it would make up for Isabel's death. Wren had fought for months to bring her back into his life and now it was over, gone. He didn't want to be decent, kind, or merciful.

He wanted payback.

When the police stormed Eira Franklin's home, they found her in bed, suffocated in her sleep. Alwyn had no alibi, but he would have all the time in the world to think about his offences.

Wren, himself, was long gone by morning. He drove as fast as he could with his broken arm, trying to shake any ysbryd who may have followed him. He hoped they wouldn't have the strength to keep up, but he could never know for certain. He returned to the city and headed for the little bungalow where he had twice found happiness. In the redness of dawn, it looked peaceful. For a moment, it was like nothing had ever happened, as though he could knock on the door and his love would be waiting. But a subtle wind kept him grounded in reality. The life he knew had gone forever, properly this time. No part of his old world still existed. Even if his grief had the power to sustain, as Eira's had, his childhood home had gone, burned to the ground.

For better or for worse, Isabel and his father would have gone with it. They were never coming back.

The bungalow appeared to be locked up. Without Scott's body, he had no right to enter, nor any claim to its contents. Strangers would soon descend to clear it out, as he should have let Isabel do with his father's house. There seemed little point trying to salvage keepsakes when he had nowhere to take them. He had no home, no prospects, nor even any money.

Every sudden gust or fleeting cold was a reminder of the ysbryd, watching his every move. Wren's aura would sustain those who would otherwise be condemned to purgatory. He gave them consciousness, presence. To them, he was both literally and figuratively a beacon in the darkness – a shining light, adrift in an endless black. And if he denied them his energy, they would react. They had great strength in numbers. He wondered whether they could band together and create something else like the forest of Pontrhyd-y-werddon, somewhere they could kill repeatedly, to feed like vampires off the amplified energy. They would have something to protect, and as Rees had said, *'You'd much rather they had a common goal.'*

He couldn't argue with the fact that he and Rees were frighteningly similar. They had the same afflictions – life beyond physical form, and all-consuming love. Rees had done terrible things to protect Beca Craddock, picking the villagers off so that he could keep searching for her. Wren realised he would have been the same. He had no limits. He would have done anything to keep Isabel alive. Now, it was her memory he needed to preserve. Standing there on the pavement, before the little bungalow with the yellow door that they had called home for such a long time, all other objectives seemed secondary.

He saw his alien reflection in the kitchen window. He had few options left. Most of his future had now been determined. The challenge was accepting it. All he had left was the broken body of a man he had never known, whose voice grew stronger by the hour, like a whisper at the back of his mind that had turned into a murmur.

He didn't want another struggle for power, not for such a worthless frame. His broken arm hung limp and nagged him constantly. It could have taken months to heal. The glass warped his reflection, like a window to his twisted soul. Lloyd's face betrayed the horrors he had lived through in a few short weeks – twice killed, covered in scrapes and swellings. Beneath Wren's rising contempt, a fire was igniting that was becoming increasingly difficult to suppress. There were people who should be punished for his pains. He wanted to snuff that body out, to pretend he had never been forced into it. As the weather took a downturn, Wren put his good hand in his pocket and felt the cold pinch of his car keys. *There's no point hiding anymore,* he thought to the dawn, to the rousing gusts of bitter air. *No need for any secrets.*

Time for a reckoning.

END

PART THREE

CACOPHONY

On a bright winter morning, Ollie Giradenco's car is sideswiped as he drives to work. The culprit tries to drive away, but Ollie gives chase, to discover an elderly man behind the wheel, consumed by inexplicable rage. The man's actions belie his frailty as he purposefully veers off the road and dies, his face etched with a furious glare.

Haunted by the incident, Ollie is compelled to investigate. Who was this man, and what pushed him to such extremes? His search draws him into a covert war between a silent mob wielding extraordinary powers and a solitary figure caught in their crosshairs. In this conflict, anyone on the street could be a looming threat, no longer who they appear to be.

Faced with an adversary who cannot be reasoned with, restrained, or stopped— even by death — Ollie and those around him are left with only one option: run.

AVAILABLE NOW

ISBN: 978-0-9572414-6-6